# IN A STRANGE LAND

*Recent Titles by Margaret Thomson Davis*

A BABY MIGHT BE CRYING
THE BREADMAKERS
THE CLYDESIDERS
GALLACHERS
THE PRISONER
A SORT OF PEACE

# IN A STRANGE LAND

Margaret Thomson Davis

This first world edition published in Great Britain 2001 by
SEVERN HOUSE PUBLISHERS LTD of
9–15 High Street, Sutton, Surrey SM1 1DF.
This first world edition published in the USA 2001 by
SEVERN HOUSE PUBLISHERS INC., of
595 Madison Avenue, New York, NY 10022.



British Library Cataloguing in Publication Data

Davis, Margaret Thomson
In a strange land
1. Love Stories
I. Title
823.9'14 [F]

ISBN 0-7278-5693-6



Typeset by Hewer Text Ltd.,
Edinburgh, Scotland.
Printed and bound in Great Britain by
MPG Books Ltd, Bodmin, Cornwall.

# Acknowledgements

First and foremost, as always, my grateful thanks to my dear son, Kenneth Baillie Davis, who, having my best interests at heart, never fails to give me thoughtful and constructive criticism of each of my books.

A thank you also to my old friend and enthusiastic fan, Phyllis Goodheir, for her helpful suggestions.

For this particular book, I owe much to my Pakistani friends, especially Mirza, Raj, Shereen and Shoaïb Shafaatulla for their kindness and patience in helping me with my research.

Sincere appreciation also for my typist, Maggie Seaton, who helps me in more ways than one.

# One

*Glasgow, 1957*

The woman kept trying to catch his eye. She was purposely attempting to distract his attention from the serious business of examining the house. White women were very cheeky. He could never quite get used to how free they were. How they made eye contact. It still shocked him. It was most disconcerting. He prayed to Allah that she would go away.

The back of the building looked not too bad. He had already made sure the house was structurally sound but it seemed very sad and dilapidated. The last owner, an old grandmother, had lived in it alone and could not be expected to clean and paint. Her family had neglected their duties. Now she had gone to live in an institution.

That was another thing about the British he would never get used to and which shocked him most deeply. They did not care for their families.

Now, in 1957, in the whole of India and Pakistan, there would not be as many abandoned and lonely people as there were in this one Scottish city of Glasgow. In Britain, widowers, widows, grandfathers, grandmothers, unmarried uncles and aunties by the million lived separately from their relations and were lonely. They lived in dingy slum tenements like the one in the Gorbals that he had just left. They lived in nice places like this in Pollokshields. What did it matter where you were if you were lonely and abandoned and no one paid you any respect?

The lawyer had refused to tell him what nursing home the owner of the house had gone to. He had to telephone every nursing home in Glasgow before he found Mrs Ogilvie. Then he and his family had gone to introduce themselves and explain how much money they had and why they wanted a nice house in Pollokshields.

Anjum, the mother of his daughters, could not speak much English so she sat very quietly; but his oldest daughter and her husband, and his grandson and his two younger daughters spoke most politely.

Mrs Ogilvie agreed that they should have the house – it was a very happy arrangement – and they said they would move in right away. That made Mrs Ogilivie chuckle.

"I can just imagine the stir that'll cause in Pollokshields Square. The neighbours will have kittens."

His grandson, his youngest daughter and his son-in-law all laughed. But no one else understood what the old grandmother meant.

Her hair was very thin against her pillow and as white as his beard. He thought again how cruel her son must be to give her away instead of welcoming her into his own home.

The prophet Mohammed (may Allah's peace and blessings be on him) said, "The Lord hath decreed . . . that ye show kindness to your parents. If one of them or both of them attain old age with thee, say not 'fie' unto them or repulse them, but speak unto them a gracious word. And lower unto them the wing of submission through mercy and say: My Lord: Have mercy on them both as they did care for me when I was little."

The visit had been a business one. The grandmother had agreed to sell her house to them and accepted the fair price they had come to offer and it was later all made legal by the lawyers.

He wondered if she wanted them to visit again just to keep her company and pay their respects. He thought it too cheeky for him to say anything of such a personal nature and waited for her to invite them. They hung around the bed repeating polite goodbyes but no invitation came.

The house was one of the seven houses situated on three sides of Pollokshields Square. At the back of his side of the square there was a railway track. On another side of the square, there were no houses – just a lane called Pollokshields Lane with a line of trees and a high grassy bank. Pollokshields Lane led from the main road and ended at the railway line. At the back of the houses on the other two sides of the square were long gardens joined on to the back gardens of tenements. Not crowded and black like the Gorbals tenements, but very respectable red sandstone buildings with stained-glass windows on landings and closes lined with china tiles. The Glasgow people called them wally closes, which meant tiled closes. Very respectable people lived in the large flats there. But now he was even more respectable with a bungalow. He was very proud.

His bungalow consisted of four rooms and a big kitchen and bathroom on the ground floor, and four converted attic rooms with sloping ceilings and dormer windows, two facing the front of the house and looking down on to the front garden, and two looking out to a long back garden. At the foot of the back garden, bushes and trees muffled the sound of the occasional train.

At the moment, everything in the house was covered in filth and dark brown paint – the doors, the walls, even in the kitchen. The linoleum in the kitchen had once had a pattern but it was worn away into dark brown and into holes that showed the floorboards underneath. The carpets in the sitting room and hall were dark and dusty and frayed. The whole place had an oppressive and gloomy atmosphere. Entering the house was like being sucked into a fusty-smelling tunnel. Bashir, his son-in-law, would have to paint and decorate and the women would be kept busy scrubbing and cleaning.

They would make it a beautiful home in keeping with its beautiful surroundings.

The woman in the next garden had not gone away. She was a very large woman and she was leaning over the fence. Her unusually thick hair was heaped up on top of her head but tendrils and wisps strayed untidily down over her face and neck. A bridge of freckles stretched over her nose and cheeks and brown blotches covered her hands and arms.

Now she was calling out, "Have you actually bought the place? Or are you just looking?"

He fingered his beard and gazed worriedly down at some weeds. She was most cheeky. He squeezed words reluctantly through a sieve of reserve.

"It is true. I am Sharif Ali, the new owner of this house. I am now awaiting my family with a furniture van."

"Gosh!" Different expressions wandered over her face. "Anyway," she added, "as far as I'm concerned, you're welcome."

He thought he heard the van at the front and was going to move away but her voice detained him.

"It's funny when you think of it, though."

He waited with clasped hands and raised brows.

"A couple of the neighbours are English. Another one originates from the Highlands. I'm Glasgow born and bred. You're Pakistani. And your neighbour on the other side is Irish."

He gazed at the Irish house and marvelled. It was built in solid red sandstone and was much bigger and more imposing than any other in the square. It boasted of much wealth.

"It is good. They are immigrants too. I have read in the library about them . . . That's the van," he cried out. "I must open doors. Excuse me, please."

He hurried in the back door and through the empty house, shouting and brandishing keys. Already the van had pulled up, the removal men had the back open and were punching and jerking at his furniture. In his excitement he spoke quickly and loudly in Urdu.

"Aye, aw right, dad" one of the men said without looking round, "keep yer whiskers on!"

Another man said, "Christ, the posh yins round about here are goin' tae go a bundle on this!"

Sharif flicked a worried gaze down Pollokshields Lane. It led on to Pollokshields Road and the nearby Queen's Park – a very nice place with a pond and trees and flowers. No sign of his family yet. He felt naked without them. It was most strange to be on his own. And in such a strange place. It was almost as different from the Gorbals as the Gorbals had been different from his homeland. But at least the Gorbals had been noisy and had many children. Here, back from the main road and the clanging of tram cars, it was still and quiet. Nowhere had he ever been used to quietness.

He had told his family that the old house in the Gorbals must be left clean. After the furniture was taken away, they must sweep and scrub the floors. Then Bashir could drive everyone to Pollokshields in his car.

The removal men were staggering up the path, chins glued to a large old-fashioned sideboard.

Sharif squeezed back against the wall to allow them through the front door and called to them telling them where to put the sideboard while at the same time keeping an anxious watch on his other possessions in case any thief came by.

Next from the van appeared the sofa covered in green cloth by his wife Anjum who was very clever with the sewing machine. It was sunken in the middle but still very useful. There was a lot of good wear in that sofa yet and it would be a long time before he would be able to afford to buy another.

Chairs were balanced on the pavement, and rolled-up striped mattresses tied tightly with string. A cardboard box rattled and clanged with pots and pans when he tried to lift it.

"Look, will ye jist leave it to us, dad. Yer like a wee bird hoppin' about there!"

He was not insulted. Everyone Scottish was all right to him and his family. They were quite happy with the Scottish people.

"Excuse me. I give you much trouble."

"Aye, yer right, auld yin. Away ye go in and make yersel a nice wee cup o' Pakistani tea."

Sharif laughed. Yet at the same time it occurred to him that these men would not see anything funny or out of place about a man doing women's work.

He had seen his son-in-law, Bashir, succumb to this Western outlook. Bashir had also acquired a broad Glasgow accent. He remembered when his eldest daughter, Noor Jahan, had been pregnant. She had felt very sick. One day everyone had been out except her and when her husband Bashir came home from work there was no curry ready, no chapatis made, no pickles or chutney on the table.

Instead of being angry, Bashir had prepared the curry and cooked the chapatis and set the table. Then he had said to Noor Jahan, "Come on. Sit at the table and eat wi' me. Everything's ready."

Noor Jahan replied, "No, I can't. I don't feel hungry."

"Och, well, if you don't eat, I won't eat," Bashir insisted. So Noor Jahan came to the table and ate with him and felt better.

She had done wrong.

"Your husband has worked all day and is tired," Sharif had chastised his daughter severely. "You have no respect."

Bashir Tanwir was like a son to him. "Noor Jahan," he kept reminding his daughter, "forever praise Allah that such a husband was found for you."

Bashir was the son of his friend Mahmood Tanwir who had a large supermarket in Maryhill. Bashir worked hard in the shop and was a good son to his father. It was a worry though that Bashir was turning so Glaswegian. He laughed and joked with customers in his father's shop and did not mind when they called him Jimmy. He only shrugged and said, "They don't mean any harm. They're just trying to be friendly." Sharif reminded himself that despite Bashir's Glasgow ways, he was proud of his Muslim culture and said his prayers regularly.

Bashir's brothers were at university. It had been Sharif's dream that the sons of his own flesh would have a good education. One of his sons, however, had died of amoebic dysentery and another had been killed at the time of Partition. There had been much danger and looting and burning of Muslim property, and killing of Muslim people, and they had been forced to leave and join the huge wave of refugees on the long walk from India to the newly formed land of Islam – Pakistan. There had been much lamenting for his sons. Now he had only daughters. Yet he loved them dearly and wanted them to have a good life, good health and a good education. That was why he had brought his family from Pakistan to Britain.

He had hoped to start a chemist's shop in Glasgow and continue his profession of dispenser but it was not yet to be. In India he had reached his tenth class at school and then trained as a dispenser before opening his own chemist's shop.

Partition had been a terrible time. He had salvaged as much as possible before coming to Britain. But to think he had once had his own business! He had been a man of substance, well thought of and respected. The people had regarded him as their doctor.

His family had grown and flourished. His children were driven to school and brought home again in a tonga.

But then, as well as the upheaval and dangers of Partition, personal tragedy had struck. He had lost his sons. To lose a daughter would have been a sadness but to lose a son was a grievous tragedy indeed. He felt he had to start afresh if he were to survive the terrible blow of losing not just one son, but two.

"We will go to Britain," he told his wife, Anjum. "My brother Mirza is there and he tells me it is a good country. He will help us. And he tells me the government looks after people there. People in Britain are healthy and wealthy. The government even pays for people to have a good education."

Anjum had continued to weep and wail for her sons and did not want to leave them. "The bodies of our sons are buried in the earth," he told her. "Their spirits are with Allah. We must think of our daughters."

So they had come; first to the Gorbals district of Glasgow, as had the Jews, the Poles, the Lithuanians, the Italians and the Irish before them. Now Sharif Ali and his family had come to this very different district of Pollokshields.

It was good here. There were no high black buildings like in the Gorbals although, in the Gorbals and in the whole of Glasgow, he had been amazed at the width of the streets. They were so unlike the narrow streets he'd come from. They had been crowded and noisy. He remembered the long sad steps and dignified heads of camels and the rattle of the rickety carts they pulled. There were prancing horses too, and carriages called tongas, and victorias lurching behind them.

He remembered his home country and all of these things with fondness, including the food traders. Oh, the alluring aromas filling the streets – aromas of goats' brains and bulls' testicles! Oh, the satisfaction of being able to choose a live chicken from a cage at his feet, to see that it was healthy and suitable for eating! Then to see it halal slaughtered, plucked, tandooried and dished up to him with a delicious sauce . . . He thought it terrible to see all the dead chickens in Glasgow shops: no one knew what they had been like when alive. He even remembered with nostalgia the cripples crawling and hauling their grotesquely deformed bodies along the streets, each one more pathetic and hideous than the next.

But it was good for his family's education to be in Glasgow. He must think of that. He must concentrate on how good it was in this square with its bright and beautiful houses. Here there were flowers. His heart warmed at the sight of the colour. The grass in the square had beds of roses.

Again he was reminded of his homeland and his narrow chest swelled out with a sigh.

It was the custom there to garland guests with flowers. He remembered many happy colourful occasions and the sweet perfume of many garlands. In his homeland, flowers were much loved.

One day the garden in Pollokshields Square belonging to Sharif Ali would contain many most lovely blooms.

He waved to the removal men as they drove away. He called out, "I thank you. Cheerio."

"Cheerio, dad," they shouted back, "and the best of British luck to you."

He felt lonely and strange again. He remained standing at the gate, small and frail, his skin black against the whiteness of his beard. He adjusted his glasses.

Soon the mother of his children would come, and with her his daughters, Zaida and Rasheeda. His eldest daughter, Noor Jahan, would arrive too with her husband, Bashir, and their baby son, Shah Jahan as well as their teenage son Maq. There would be much noise and happiness and warmth and rejoicing in Pollokshields. He assured himself of that.

# Two

"I'm telling you . . ." Alice Whitelaw fixed her short-sighted stare on her husband and repeated earnestly, "He's a Pakistani. He and his family have moved in next door."

Simon put his fork and knife down on to the table and pushed his plate away.

"That's all I needed!"

Alice gazed at him in surprise. He was a good-looking man in a gaunt kind of way. He was six feet two inches tall, which had been a great attraction to her from the first because she didn't dwarf him with her height, as she did most people. They could even dance very happily together. They still enjoyed the bowling club dance every week. Although she was normally heavy-footed and clumsy, when she was dancing with Simon she was as light as a feather. He'd often told her so.

She carefully cut a piece of steak, then balanced it on her fork along with some mashed potato. She savoured the food for a minute.

"How do you mean?"

"I work hard. I pay my taxes. I do no one any harm. Yet this has to happen to me!"

"They're very excitable, aren't they?" she murmured, in between enjoyable mastications. "You should have seen the state he got into when the furniture van came. I had to laugh."

"Oh Alice!" He shook his head in despair

"At first he completely ignored me," she went on. "I thought it was very boorish and bad-mannered of him but I eventually got him to speak and he was polite enough." Simon gave a deep sigh. "You've no idea, have you?"

"You've never known a Pakistani. Mr Ali could be quite a

decent neighbour for all you know. He looked . . ." she hesitated and thoughtfully picked her teeth ". . . interesting. I've never seen anyone with white hair and a black face before – well, not actually black but very dark. His head is shaved to the bone and he has quite a nice beard."

"And how many other interesting black faces were there?"

"Quite a crowd actually. But some of them were much lighter in colour. One was the double of Omar Sharif."

"The value of all the houses will take a nose dive. As if I'm not worried enough about money as it is."

Alice was used to her husband's talk of money worries. It failed to put her off her meal.

"Eat your dinner."

"Alice, I honestly can't understand how you can just there happily enjoying your food."

It was true she did enjoy her food and she continued to eat as he went on, "They'll have this square like a slum in no time. The value of this property will drop to zero. Who would have thought it? Pollokshields of all places!"

"Maybe they want to better themselves."

Her calm voice acted as an injection to quicken his.

"It's all very well for you. *You* don't worry about money. Well, if I know anything about Pakistanis, you'll have something to worry you all right. You'll soon see what I mean."

"You don't know any more about Pakistanis than I do."

"Alice, I've heard about them. They've no idea about sanitation for a start. Apparently they'd never heard of it before they came here."

"Nonsense! People used to talk like that about Glaswegians having a bathroom for the first time and keeping coal in the bath. It's just a lot of nonsense, if you ask me."

The back door banged and their son, Russell, burst into the kitchen like an invigorating wind.

"Hello," he greeted them cheerily. "There's a crowd of Pakistanis milling about in the garden next door."

Simon rose and went across the room to look out of the window.

"Sit down, Simon, and calm yourself," Alice said. "You know

getting upset gives you a headache. It's steak for dinner, Russell. In the hot drawer. Just help yourself."

The telephone rang and Simon strode past her.

"I bet that'll be Joe. He'll have seen them as well."

Russell lifted his dinner plate from the hot drawer.

"What's Dad all steamed up about?" Enthusiastically he shovelled up mashed potato and Brussels sprouts. He had inherited her height – was taller, even – and her voluptuous mouth but his father's lantern jaw and straight, blue-black hair. Of course Simon's hair was shorter than Russell's and more grey than black now.

"Oh . . ." She shrugged. "The Pakistanis, I suppose. Mr Sharif Ali and his family."

"The young girl goes to the Academy. Her name's Rasheeda."

"The tall one, you mean? Is she about the same age as you, do you think?"

"I suppose so."

"I wonder what they're like."

"Rasheeda's gorgeous. Is there a pudding, Mum? I'm starving."

"I wish you wouldn't gulp your food like that, Russell. You'll swallow air and give yourself wind."

"Oh Mum, I'm sixteen, not six."

"There's ice-cream in the fridge." Alice returned to the subject of pudding.

"Smashing! But you shouldn't take any."

"I am cutting out puddings, son, but not ice-cream. I could never resist ice-cream."

He waved his fork at her.

"Fatty! Fatty! I've got a big fat mum!"

Laughing, she got up to fetch the dessert. Her walk was careful, plodding, self-conscious. She could imagine every bulge rolling about in her slacks as if she were gazing at her tall figure with eyes hanging from the back of her head.

"You can't expect a woman in her forties to have the same sylphlike shape as your sixteen and seventeen-year-olds," she told him.

At the same time she determined for his sake to be ruthless. After today, no more ice-cream.

"Why not?"

She dished up a large portion for him, a medium one for Simon and tormented herself by taking only a couple of spoonfuls.

"All sorts of queer things happen to a woman's glands and metabolism at my age."

"That's a lot of nonsense, Mum. You'd look younger if you were thinner, and had something done with your hair."

He attacked his mountain of ice-cream with gusto. She felt in a bit of a huff. She was proud of her abundance of hair. Apart from being unusually thick and long, it was still the same brown colour as it had always been. She hadn't one grey hair.

Simon came striding back into the room.

"Joe's going to try and organise a meeting. We're all going to meet at his place once he finds a suitable time for everybody."

Russell had switched on the radio. In between spoonfuls of ice-cream, he jerked his head, stamped a foot and drummed his fingers in time to the pistol-cracking beat. A lock of his black hair flopped over his face.

Simon's voice struggled to sound patient.

"Switch that thing off, Russell. It's giving me a headache."

Alice said, "He's just young and full of the joys of life."

"When I was young I could enjoy myself without making such a racket. I used to collect stamps and cigarette cards. I used to sit quietly for hours sorting them all out and afterwards I always stored them neatly away."

Russell stretched up with a big sigh.

"You were so perfect, Dad, it's a wonder you've never sprouted wings."

Simon unexpectedly flashed up, "I was never impertinent like you to my father."

Russell gaped incredulously.

"What have I said?"

"Darling, go away through and switch on the television," Alice pleaded. "Dad's just upset about the Pakistanis."

"What about the Pakistanis?"

"Make up your mind, Russell," Simon said quietly. "Either go through to the sitting room or come back into the kitchen. There's a terrible draught from that door."

With a groan, Russell left, slamming the door behind him. The kitchen shuddered.

"When I was his age, Alice, I was helping my father in the shop."

Alice didn't pay any attention to this. She knew Simon would never allow Russell to work in his shop. He was actually proud of Russell doing well in his exams at school and planning to go on to university one day soon. Simon had left school at fifteen. He was continuously anxious that Russell had all the books he needed and every expensive item of school uniform. It had been Simon who had chosen the fee-paying, very select Academy for Russell. She would have been happy for him to attend the nearest mixed-sex secondary school. The Academy had two sections – one for the girl pupils and another for the boys. They had their own classrooms and were taught separately.

"You were a long time on the phone," she said.

"Pour me a cup of tea, will you? I really do have a headache."

"What's the meeting to be about?"

"The Pakistanis, of course."

A pleasant picture flickered across her mind. Joe Malloy and his wife, and Simon, and all the other established residents of the square, meeting to chat about how best to welcome and get to know their new neighbours. The vision faded after only a moment. She studied Simon closely, worriedly.

"They're not going to do anything rotten, are they? They haven't done us any harm. And it's a free country." She didn't *think* that Simon would do anything to hurt Pakistanis, or anybody else. His bark was always worse than his bite.

"Alice, for once will you please try not to stir things up. You're an absolute menace. You can cause more chaos than anything or anyone else I know. This situation is difficult enough as it is."

"It's not me who's going to stir things up. It's you and Joe Malloy, by the sound of it."

"We're going to meet together in Joe's house to discuss the situation like sensible, reasonable people."

"You didn't see any need for a meeting when the McFarlanes moved in."

"There wasn't any need."

"The first night they arrived, I went to their door and asked if there was anything they needed or anything I could do to help."

"Please, Alice, *please* keep clear of the Pakistanis."

Suddenly it was obvious to her that she ought to go straight next door to the Pakistanis and behave in exactly the same way as she had done when the McFarlanes had arrived.

Her heart began to thump. She could hardly hear herself think. She tried to be objective, to reason with herself.

*Alice Whitelaw, what on earth are you afraid of? From which childhood experience or influence does this irrational emotion stem*?

She was a great believer in psychology and spent a lot of time psychoanalysing herself and her friends. She had never known an Asian person. Asian families had only just started to come to Glasgow. Not one had ever come into her line of vision during her childhood. Never at any time had one touched the perimeter of her life. Yet as she concentrated she saw a dark face.

Her mother had gone to answer the door. There was an old man with an open case at his feet. Out of the case spilled ladies' blouses. The man wore a dirty turban over a face like a prune. His eyes were superficially bland as if only acting the part of liking the woman who opened the door and the child peeping out from behind her skirts.

He held a small object like a bead in his hand.

"Missy buy something and I give her lucky charm. Bring very good fortune."

"No thanks," her mother said and started to shut the door.

He jammed his case against it.

"Nice blouse, very cheap."

"If you're not away from my doorstep in one minute, I'll send the child to fetch the police."

The unexpected reference to herself startled and frightened Alice. At the same time the veil of blandness ripped from the man's expression revealing hatred.

She remembered it now.

"A curse on you. A curse on your sons and daughters," he

mumbled as he gathered up his case. "May curses heap upon their heads."

She had forgotten all about that. There was no reason to remember a bad-tempered old man selling tawdry blouses. Now that she came to think about it, though, it occurred to her that bad luck had come to her mother and father.

But she didn't believe in superstitious nonsense. What happened to her family had nothing whatsoever to do with that old man.

She pushed back her chair and announced firmly to Simon, "I'm going next door to say hello."

# Three

Rasheeda had to change from her school uniform and put on a qamiz, or top, the moment she arrived home. She was already wearing the salwar, or trousers, under her navy school skirt which she thought was ridiculous. She hated to look so different from everyone else at school. If she went out after school, she was also supposed to drape a doputta, or broad scarf, over her chest, head and shoulders. Everything was designed to hide any sign of a feminine shape. Her sisters, Zaida and Noor Jahan, enjoyed wearing the traditional dress. They said their qamiz, salwar and doputtas were in pretty colours and delicate materials.

Rasheeda gazed moodily at the wardrobe mirror and hated her reflection. Oh, how her heart longed for a fashionable dress fitted at the bust and waist and then flaring out and flouncing and swaying with lots of frilly nylon petticoats! She longed too for a marvellous pointed bra, and court shoes, and nylon or lace gloves.

If she had her way, she'd go to coffee bars and dances, the same as all the other girls at school. She'd sit with them and giggle with them as they enjoyed the juke box playing great records like Bill Haley and the Comets' "Rock Around the Clock" and Elvis Presley's "Hound Dog."

Once, when she had still lived in the Gorbals, she had actually gone into a café in Victoria Road with some of the girls from her class. There had been a crowd of boys sitting at another table. One of them kept staring at her. She held her head high and stared back instead of lowering her eyes as Zaida or Noor Jahan would have done. The boy was tall and slim, but with broad shoulders, and his hair was as black as hers.

One of the other boys called over to Doris Smith, "Hi, blondie! Did anyone ever tell you you're the double of Marilyn Monroe?"

Doris always got a lot of attention from boys. Rasheeda envied her her blonde hair, fair skin and pale blue eyes. She hated her own long black hair, dusky features and dark eyes. She wished she could have her hair cut into a more fashionable style.

Zaida had seen her in the café and told their parents, who had been shocked and angry.

"I just want to be like other Glasgow girls," she'd protested.

Her father had said, "You cannot be like Glasgow girls. You are not from Glasgow. You do not belong here. Your homeland is Pakistan. You are a Pakistani girl."

Soon, thank goodness, Zaida would be leaving school. Meantime, she had important exams to concentrate on. Sometimes she went straight from school to the Mitchell Library to study and do research, and so she could not watch Rasheeda so much and get her into trouble at home. Zaida was hoping to go to university and eventually get a Pharmacy degree. Their father was depending on her. He planned to get a chemist's shop, and have not only Zaida working in it.

"Rasheeda," he had commanded, "you must study hard too and go to university and get a Pharmacy degree. You'll also work in the chemist's shop."

Rasheeda kept experiencing surges of irritation. She felt continually hemmed in and inhibited. Her life was always being mapped out for her. It was confusing too. She was finding it more and more difficult to find her own identity. Over and over again, her father and mother kept reminding her that she didn't belong here. She was a Pakistani and a Muslim, a follower of the Islamic way of life. Islam was an Arabic word that meant voluntary surrender and submission. It also meant peace. But she did not want to surrender to anything. And what peace did it mean to her? She felt continually torn. She didn't feel she belonged to Pakistan. She remembered very little about the place and didn't want to. As far as she was concerned, she belonged to Glasgow. When she was at home with her family, she felt different from them. But at school she felt different from all the others as well.

That day when she'd been in the café, the boys had suggested a walk through the park and so they had all started walking together towards the main gate of Queen's Park in Victoria Road. All of them, except Rasheeda, lived on the other side of the park in Pollokshields, and it was nicer going through the park than walking the streets.

On her father's day off – usually on a Sunday – the whole family, including her brother-in-law, Bashir, his mother and father and her Aunty Shafiga and Uncle Mirza and their family, would all come to Queen's Park for a walk and to enjoy the green grass and trees and flowers. Her father had always said he must one day get a house in this area – near the Academy and Queen's Park.

The men of the family always walked in front, and the women trailed behind. Even this annoyed Rasheeda and sometimes she'd stride out in front, just for the hell of it. Of course, her father and her uncle were always very angry with her. Her uncle said she deserved a good beating. Her father agreed and threatened that if she didn't learn to behave with proper respect and be a good Muslim girl, she would get one. Her father never frightened her, however. He wasn't a violent man and anyway, she didn't think he'd be able to beat her even if he wanted to.

Her father was ancient. He was far older than the fathers of any of the other girls in her class at school. She was secretly afraid of her Uncle Mirza, though, and even more so of her Aunty Shafiga. They were big and strong and fierce-eyed and proud. There was no telling what they might do.

They had arranged a marriage for their daughter, Anver, who was only the same age as Rasheeda. Anver had told Rasheeda in confidence that she didn't want to get married. She didn't even like the look of her prospective husband who was much older than her.

Everyone would go to the house in the Gorbals for the wedding. Uncle Mirza's house was bigger than most in the tenements there. His house had once belonged to a doctor.

Anver had already left school. There had been a bitter twist to her mouth when she'd said to Rasheeda, "So much for my dreams of eventually going to university and becoming a doctor!"

That day after going to the café, when the crowd from school had walked through the park, Rasheeda had found herself beside the tall, dark-haired boy. The others were all laughing and fooling about in front. However, Russell – she discovered his name was Russell Whitelaw – didn't kid her on or fool about. He hardly spoke to her at all. Nor did she say very much to him. Yet, as they walked along together, there was an excitement between them that could hardly be contained.

When they reached the other gate of the park and came out on to Pollokshields Road, Rasheeda said, "I get a tram-car here. I live in the Gorbals."

"Oh, right. I'll see you tomorrow after school then?"

"Yes, sure," she replied with a toss of her head. "Why not?"

The next day they'd walked on their own and they'd spoken a bit more. He told her he lived in Pollokshields Square and his father owned a paper shop and tobacconist's in town. She told him her father was a lamplighter for the Glasgow Corporation. They spoke about their favourite music. They even sang "See You Later Alligator" together and then laughed at themselves.

The next day, they felt even more comfortable with each other. And closer. They began to tell each other how they felt about their lives and what they wanted to do with them. Russell wanted to be an artist but knew his father would have a fit if he found out. He'd told his father that after university he'd train as an architect. His father had found this more acceptable because he believed that architects could make a lot of money. His father was neurotic about money. He was always going on about electricity bills and phone bills and gas bills. It was a real bore.

Rasheeda sympathised although, as she explained, it wasn't money that her father bored her rigid with. It was all his talk about Pakistan. Her father and mother and her aunty and uncle knew more about what was going on in Pakistan and were more interested in that than in what was going on in Glasgow. She told him about her cousin Anver's coming marriage. Russell was shocked.

"That's terrible, isn't it? A couple should love each other and really want to marry each other."

"Yes, I know. The only thing that saves me is that my father wants to have a chemist's shop and have my sister Zaida and me work in it. He was a chemist back in India before Pakistan came into being. His dream is to have his own chemist's shop again and to work in it with us."

"Is that what you want to do?" Russell asked.

Rasheeda shrugged. "I don't know really. As long as it gives me some sort of freedom. But I doubt if it will. I feel so hemmed in at times. I wish I could fly away like a bird."

He didn't laugh at her. He understood. He took her hand and they walked along like that. She had never felt so happy.

But then something had happened to raise her spirits even more. For some time her father and Bashir had been looking for a house in a better district to buy together. Preferably nearer to the Academy. They had looked at several properties in Pollokshields Road and in Shawlands, all in tenements. Then they discovered a bungalow for sale. Up until then, Rasheeda had shown no interest in the house-hunting project. But immediately she heard the words "Pollokshields Square" her heart raced with eagerness and delight. With almost superhuman difficulty, she kept her mouth shut. If she suddenly showed interest in the place, her father would be suspicious. He was always suspicious of her. Always critical. If she said one word in favour of the bungalow in Pollokshields Square, it would be sure to put him off.

She had kept silent and, joy of joys, the house was bought. She would be living in the same place as Russell. They would be able to walk home together from school every day and go to school together every morning. Her heart sang with happiness. It was meant to be. Fate was throwing them ever closer together.

She had felt she couldn't wait to tell Russell.

The family milled about the house admiring it. Everyone chattered at once but Sharif's sing-song nasal voice had a resonance that demanded to be heard above the rest.

"I will have this room at the front as my bedroom. This room at the back will be for our prayers. One of the bedrooms in the attic will be for Zaida and Rasheeda. Another will be for Bashir and Noor Jahan and little Shah Jahan. The last will be for Maq."

They all clambered up and down the stairs behind Sharif bumping into one another, laughing, talking and giggling.

He led them proudly. Never before in his life had he been such a proud man.

"You are pleased now, Noor Jahan? You are glad that you took your father's advice?"

Noor Jahan's face split into a huge smile that showed both rows of perfect white teeth.

"Yes, Daddy."

Bashir also seemed happy, judging by the grin flashing white under his black moustache.

Bashir's father and mother and brothers lived in a well-furnished flat near the shop. Inside there were fitted carpets and golden curtains. The building and the close, however, were not much better than the one in the Gorbals. Here in Pollokshields, Sharif Ali and Bashir had a good solid house and a garden back and front.

For a time Bashir had taken Noor Jahan to live with his parents and Sharif Ali had missed her terribly. Noor Jahan had said, "The street in the Gorbals is not a nice street. There is darkness and dirt in closes and painted writing on the walls."

"Tell Bashir to come. I will talk with him," Sharif had commanded. "Together Bashir and I will buy a better place. We must be family together again and happy."

Now they had achieved their heart's desire and his grandsons, Shah Jahan and Maq, would grow up in a very nice district and near to the Academy, where they would have a most excellent education.

Already Maq had been settled in the school and was most happy, as were Zaida and Rasheeda and their cousin Parveen, Anver's sister. Anver had gone there too, but she had left because she was about to be married. They also went to school Saturday and Sunday mornings to learn Urdu and Arabic, so that they could be good Muslims and read the Qur'an.

These classes had to be organised for children like Shah Jahan and Maq and Rasheeda. Rasheeda spoke exactly like Scottish people. Many Pakistani children knew no words of their mother tongue and had never been to Pakistan. Sometimes it was very difficult to understand them because they had such a broad Glasgow accent.

Of course little Shah Jahan was not yet two years old and spoke few words. Maq and Rasheeda and Parveen spoke every Glasgow word and tried to say they had many studies to do and had no time for Urdu. But Bashir supported his father-in-law and said at least one morning must be dedicated to learning Urdu.

Noor Jahan found it easier to talk to little Shah Jahan in Urdu so he picked up Urdu words from her. From Rasheeda, who was as disconcertingly Scottish as Maq, he had learned the Glasgow. He would point at the fire and say "guramhee" and "burny" or "umwee" and "mummy" and "abujee" and "daddy". Shah Jahan was truly clever. One day perhaps he would be a hafiz, a man who could recite the whole Qur'an by heart. The Qur'an was an Arabic name meaning "The Recital".

The Qur'an was the Muslim Bible, the infallible word of God, a transcript of a tablet preserved in heaven and revealed to the prophet Mohammed by the Angel Gabriel.

Sharif believed that the Muslim community in the Gorbals were liked and well treated because their religion and that of the local people was so similar. Did they not all believe in one supreme being? Muslims called this being Allah and Scottish people said God.

Allah had sent down books for the guidance of mankind through his prophets. These books told all people to act in a way pleasing to God. Like all muslims, Sharif believed in all the Revealed Books of Allah: the Torah, which was the Book revealed to the prophet Moses; the Zaboor, the Book revealed to the prophet David; the Injeel, the Book revealed to the prophet Jesus, and the Holy Qur'an, the Book revealed to the prophet Mohammed. He also believed in the Epistles, revealed to the prophet Abraham. Prophets came from all nations and were all true prophets. Among them were Adam, Noah, Abraham, Moses, Ishmael, Isaac, Jacob, David, Solomon, John, Jesus and Mohammed. (Peace and the blessing of Allah be upon them all.)

The way Sharif observed the Christians to be different in their beliefs from their Muslim neighbours was in the fact that they said Jesus was more than just a prophet. The Christians maintained that Jesus was the son of God.

This was wrong.

It was written – Allah is one. He is the possessor of all good attributes and perfection. He has no associates. *He begets not, nor is he begotten . . .*

The prayer room was to be kept plainly furnished so that they could all use that room for their prayers. In such a room there must be no photographs or statues or ornaments or pictures or carvings of animals. Sharif was glad that the bathroom was next to the prayer room and it had a shower, because they must wash before entering the prayer room. Hands needed to be washed to the elbows, and face and feet had to be washed too. Prayers must be said five times a day – at dawn or before sunrise, at midday, in late afternoon, at sunset and before retiring. These prayers were called the *fajar*, the *zohar*, the *asar*, the *maghrib* and the *isah*.

In Britain this could be very difficult. His brother Mirza told him of a photograph in a newspaper of a Muslim bus driver who had stopped his bus and got out and knelt on his prayer mat on the pavement to say his prayers. The busload of passengers watched and waited with typical Glasgow patience and good humour, but he had never heard of the Muslim bus driver doing that again. Probably he had lost his job as a result, or at least been told that Glasgow was different from a village in Pakistan and he must not interfere with the bus time schedules again.

Anjum was very devout indeed. He too was devout but it was more tiring for him. He had to climb many, many stairs because he was a lamplighter. The situation filled him with much shame. He could not bear to tell his friends in Pakistan of the lowly job to which he was reduced.

He would have preferred to start as a "Johnnie Pedlar" and go around with a case until he was able to purchase a shop. Many Pakistani men before him had done such a thing. But his brother Mirza had an important job with the Glasgow Corporation as an inspector on the buses and Mirza had insisted on using his influence with the Glasgow Corporation to get him the job as a lamplighter. Mirza had helped him come to Glasgow. He was an excellent brother and so he had to be shown respect.

"I am helping the Glasgow Corporation in a temporary capacity," Sharif Ali told his friends in Pakistan. "Only until my daughters have finished their studies. Zaida has sat her Highers. Soon she goes to university to take a degree course in Pharmacy. Then we will have a fine chemist's shop of our own and I and Zaida and Noor Jahan and Rasheeda will all work in it."

A great deal depended on first Zaida, and then Rasheeda, securing a place at a university. The whole family were most anxious about the examinations. They had discussed the matter in family conference and decided that Zaida might very well have passed in Chemistry, Physics and Mathematics, but that the English was a cause for grave concern.

English was most difficult. They all had listened to people speak and studied the language very earnestly. All of them, that is, except the mother of his daughters. She had been very frightened indeed when she came to Britain and did not want to go out on the streets and mix with people.

He thought this very fitting. Anjum was a modest woman and an excellent wife. For many, many years, since she was a child in India, she had worn the burkah, a tentlike garment with only a slit for the eyes from which to peer out. No stranger had ever seen a hair on her head or looked on her face or any part of it. Nor did she ever look into a man's eyes.

He had not wished British strangers to look upon her either, and for a long time, he had kept her strictly inside the house. He had done most of the shopping himself, from his friend Mahmood Tanwir's shop, occasionally allowing one of his daughters to fetch groceries from one of the Pakistani shops in the Gorbals. Anjum's father had been strict with her like this but after he had given her in marriage, she needed to ask her husband and he would allow her to go out if he thought it was fitting or necessary.

In India and Pakistan, Sharif had not been as strict as some husbands who only allowed their wives out in a group to the fields to relieve themselves in the morning, then once again in the evening after their husbands returned from work. If the wives wished to use the toilet during the day, they did not dare cross the threshold. Instead they had to go up and use the flat roofs of their houses. Soon, of course, the sun dried everything up and the "shit buzzards" came down and ate what was left.

At his house on the outskirts of the town, there had been a walled garden. At one end of the garden had been his fine house with a verandah and three pillars. At the other end of the garden was the toilet and it was emptied regularly by the latrine cleaner.

In Britain they had found it most shocking at first when they discovered that toilets were built *inside* houses. They thought it very dirty of the British. But even his brother Mirza had a toilet inside his Gorbals house.

Mirza had bought the Gorbals house, as he had bought his. It was foolish to pay rent. Rent money was lost money. Far better to borrow money to buy a house and establish a business. British people seemed to think that borrowing money was somehow shameful or suspect. But borrowing money from another Muslim was only sensible and right. Under Islam law, no interest must be charged and the money borrowed need not be paid back. But if the money was not paid back, then the borrower was in the lender's favour. He must help the lender when asked because of the help he'd received from the lender. There was also *Zakah*, the annual two and a half per cent of everyone's net savings which was their welfare contribution for helping the poor and needy, the sick and disabled, and the lonely. It also had to be used to free fellow Muslims from the bondage of debt.

Some British people had a bad smell. Mirza explained that this was caused by drinks of the country called whisky and beer. British food had an even worse smell. Mirza had told him the names of two of these foods. They were cabbage and Brussels sprouts. They were truly most revolting, as was the animal fat they used for frying and cooking.

Once a British neighbour asked him what he thought of the Scottish, and he said truthfully, "The Scottish people are very nice indeed but their food has a bad smell."

He would never forget his surprise and distress when the white neighbour then cried out, "What a bloody cheek! Have you never smelled your curry? The close is stinking with it."

He had been ashamed.

Recently he had heard of some sort of hood that could be fitted over a cooker to take away smells. One day he hoped to have one over the cooker in his new house in Pollokshields.

"We will eat in the kitchen," he told his family. "There is plenty of room for us. We will put our big table in that other room at the front. Then when we have guests, we can entertain them there. It is a good house, is it not?"

Loudly and enthusiastically, they voiced their agreement.

"What part do you like best?" he then asked them.

Everyone cried out at once, "The garden."

And they all laughed joyously and hurried out to admire it again. It did not matter that it was neglected and weeds were tangling and strangling the flowers. To pluck the weeds out and tend the flowers would be a most pleasant duty.

While they were outside, two young white men passed. They both smiled, and jerked their heads in the custom of Glasgow and greeted them with, "Hey there!" One young man entered the next garden.

Sharif replied with a polite, "Good evening," but his family lowered their heads and said nothing as was modest and fitting. All of them, that is, except Rasheeda who had picked up bad and cheeky habits from Glasgow schools.

She tossed her long hair, looked straight at the young man in the next garden and smiled at him. The young man's eyes lingered on her.

Later, inside the house, Sharif chastised Rasheeda. "You will behave as a good Muslim girl should."

Rasheeda had groaned. "Yes, Daddy."

"Come," he announced. "We will say our prayers."

It was while they were saying their prayers that the doorbell startled them. Then he remembered that Mahmood, the father of Bashir, had expressed eagerness to come and see Pollokshields and the new house. So had his brother Mirza. Yet he was perplexed. It was not like Mahmood or Mirza to come so soon, and especially in the middle of prayers. As he continued to recite the Qur'an, he peered over the top of his glasses at Anjum. The bell rang again before she finished and rose to go and open the door.

# Four

Alice stared at the door. The bottom half was made of dark brown wood, lumpy with many coats of varnish. The top was of grey clouded glass. She could not see into the hall. No light warmed the inside of the house.

The porch enclosed her big, gawky frame in shadows. For a minute the wild idea possessed her that she had slipped back to another night in another time. Simon, Russell, her friends and contemporaries, the whole familiar world that she knew had vanished, leaving her standing alone in the dark.

Very faintly, through the brown door, came a strange chanting. Shrinking away from the strange and the unknown, her mind fastened on angry memory to protect herself.

Once before she had stood in the darkness waiting for a door to open. She had been twelve. Could it really be so long ago? Time was swooping away with her life like a bird disappearing over the horizon never to return.

The house had been a railway bothy beside a deserted stretch of weedy rail outside of town. Her parents had done a "moonlight" from their tenement flat because they could not pay the rent. There were no lights. Someone had given them a paraffin lamp but it was not yet lit.

She thought she heard a noise inside. Her mother's voice perhaps, faint and quivering with illness.

Then a long tunnel of silence again.

It was cold. A wind made drunken men of tufts of tall grass, swaying them sideways and forwards and backwards against the moon.

She battered at the door. It opened unexpectedly under her clenched fist and revealed her mother. A grey tent of flannel nightgown billowed huge in the moonlight. Framed by the bothy door her mother froze like a painting in her mind.

Death stared out from sad eyes and was recognised for the first time. Before that she had taken it for granted that mothers went on for ever.

"I couldn't find him."

"It's all right, hen," her mother said. "He's here."

Then she smelled him and saw the sprawled figure. Somebody else, one of his drinking pals probably, had helped him home. If this dump could be called home.

"That dirty drunken pig. I hate him! It's his fault we've landed in this dump. And look at you. He's made you ill."

Her mother sank back onto the bed in the corner.

"It isn't your dad's fault. You dad's been a good man to me. I remember when he had a job and pride in himself and everything was different."

She was always saying that. Times without number she said it to the stupid drunk as he careered between violence and maudlin tears.

Even now it made Alice feel sick and bitter to think of him.

She plunged her finger once more on to the recess of the bell. She felt shaken and distressed at such pain escaping to the surface.

Shadows were moving in the hall, were darkening and approaching. Alice's pulse foundered. She arranged her features in to a smile.

The door opened cautiously to show a woman's dark face. The cheekbones were high and broad, the nose large and hooked with nostrils flaring wide from its point. The face bulged beneath tightly pinned black hair and a flimsy scarf that she was clutching over the lower part of her face.

Alice smiled and raised her brows in what she hoped was a light, bright expression.

"Hello there. I'm your neighbour on that side." She flopped a coy finger in the direction of her own house. "Mrs Alice Whitelaw. Welcome to Pollokshields Square. I expect you're Mrs Ali."

Before she had finished speaking, the woman had retreated

back into the hall and was yattering in a sing-song foreign tongue.

It seemed a very bad-mannered and inconsiderate way to behave. For all she knew the woman might be calling out, "There's a big stupid-looking bastard standing on the doorstep."

The yattering stopped. The woman scowled, shifty-eyed, then, lowering her head, she disappeared into one of the rooms.

Alice thought that there was surely no need to leave her standing on the doorstep without one polite word, especially after all the effort she had needed to muster enough courage to come here in the first place. She swung away thinking, To hell with them, but she felt confused and hurt.

"Good evening." A clipped voice arrested her. Smiling automatically, she turned back.

A young woman had replaced the older one. The girl wore the same kind of steel-rimmed spectacles as her father.

"I am Zaida. Will you please come into our house."

A thick black plait hung down her back and her hair was smoothed back from her face.

"Well . . . just for a minute."

Alice did not feel at all happy about the idea but suffered from an insatiable curiosity. She could never resist any opportunity to indulge it. Peering apprehensively around, she plodded after Zaida. She felt huge and awkward and out of place. Zaida looked tiny and very exotic in a long-sleeved turquoise top and satin trousers fitted tightly over her ankles.

"This is our sitting room. But excuse, please. We have it still to paint."

A long table sat in the middle of the floor and lining the walls, stuck close together, were innumerable chairs. It was the way chairs were placed in a hall ready for a dance, not in a private house. In a private house, who would need so much seating accommodation anyway? An answer floated across Alice's mind. She visualised dozens of Pakistanis around the walls, all glowering and scowling and yattering like mad.

She subsided into one of the chairs and Zaida settled primly in the one next to her.

"My father said you would be the lady from the next house."

"Yes, that's right. I'm Mrs Alice Whitelaw."

"It is very kind of you to visit with us."

"It's very interesting to meet you."

Another girl had entered carrying a tray. The tray sparkled with delicate china tea-cups and saucers. The new girl burst out in a broad Glasgow accent, "Och, I've went and put the sugar in it. Sorry, I should have asked."

"We are in the habit of boiling up with sugar," Zaida explained.

"Oh, yes?" Alice clung to her expression of sympathetic interest. She loathed sugar in tea but decided not to risk causing offence. She accepted the cup. "That's all right, dear. Thank you."

"Mrs Whitelaw, this is my youngest sister. She is Rasheeda and the tallest of all our family."

Alice concentrated intently on every word.

"Fancy." She peered round at Rasheeda. "A lovely big girl. What gorgeous hair."

Rasheeda's long black hair hung loose round her shoulders and she flipped it back with a jerk of head and hand. There was an aloof dignity about her, a straight-backed perfect poise as if she had been strolling along effortlessly balancing water-jars on her head for generations. Yet she was loose-limbed and every now and again, Alice got the impression of a skittish young jungle cat with tawny watchful eyes.

"Have a biscuit." The eyes took stock of her.

"Thanks, I will." Alice's hand hovered over the plate. She was already feeling slightly bilious from drinking the sweet tea but she did not like to refuse the biscuits either. "Where do you girls come from?"

"The Gorbals."

"No, before that, I mean. Did you live in a village or a town in Pakistan?"

Zaida answered, "We came from a small town. It is very nice place with shops and many nice modern buildings."

"Really? Shops and buses and cars and everything just like here?"

"Not a big place like here. Some shops are modern and have glass windows. But most are like the bazaar and customers they argue for good price. Some Pakistani people at first do not know and try to argue here. Some say it is very dull to shop in this country." She laughed but lowered her eyes apologetically. "I am too cheeky."

"No, no," Alice assured her. "I am fascinated. Tell me honestly, what did you think when you came over here? To this country, I mean."

Zaida took a dainty sip of tea. "I felt I should go back. No black buildings at home, all whitewashed and cleaned and painted different colours after the monsoon. Some are cream, some white, some maroon. Inside, the rooms are all different with matching doors."

Alice helped herself to another biscuit in the desperate hope that it would hide the taste of the tea. It had always been a quirk with her. She liked sweet food but sweet drinks made her immediately feel ill.

"Sounds lovely."

"We had never seen tenement buildings before. I was shocked. What kind of people are these – they cannot whitewash? This kind of thing I thought."

"Fancy!"

"We arrived first at our uncle Mirza's house in the Gorbals. Uncle Mirza let us stay with him until our father found a place for us. Oh, I didn't like that house."

Alice peered closer, fighting to ignore the bilious spots swimming before her eyes.

"Why not?"

"Oh, I did not like the toilet."

"Didn't you?"

"Our toilet is much better. Oh, that very small, no' nice toilet. I didn't like to go to the toilet but I needed to go. So I went. But I was fed up. I was thinking, I should go back to Pakistan. I should not stay in this place."

"You had a nice house there?"

"Our house had electric ceiling fans and table fans too."

"Really? Have you any photos of it you could show me?"

"Sorry. No photos." Zaida quickly brushed aside the question and continued with her enthusiastic description. "And a lawn outside and eucalyptus trees and mango trees and very many orange trees also." Her prim bespectacled face softened. "In summer we sleep out on the lawn. Oh, I remember it. The orange trees were covered in white blossom. I remember it now. It had such a nice smell."

"Gosh, I can just see that." Alice twisted round on the edge of her seat with interest and immediately regretted it because the sudden movement made her feel violently sick. Her enthusiasm petered out. "It sounds lovely."

Zaida laughed with happiness and pride.

"We were wakened in the morning by small birds. Every morning they say, 'Chang, chang, chang!' We do not need alarm."

"Why did you come to this country if it was so nice over there? It seems a daft thing to do." To Alice's horror the words strayed from her mouth before she could control them. Hastily she tried to make amends. "I don't mean you shouldn't have come. I mean why shouldn't you come? I mean you were quite right to come if you wanted to."

Zaida's small dusky face became serious.

"I must continue my studies," she said earnestly. "It is most important."

Alice nodded. A lock of her hair slithered down and hung over one ear. "Scottish people have a very high regard for education too."

"Very good education here," Zaida agreed. "That is why we come."

A silence settled on them as they sucked in dainty mouthfuls of syrupy liquid. Alice's energy drained away with every sip as wave after wave of nausea threatened to engulf her. She longed to be spirited home to collapse into bed for the rest of the night.

A half-smile of politeness set like a pain on her face. She glanced round at Rasheeda who had not taken tea. Rasheeda did not smile in return. Slanting eyes stared unblinkingly. Alice felt like saying, "You'll know me the next time you see me!"

Had they been white people, she would have said it. She believed that she had quite a penchant for being honest and speaking her mind. It had to be admitted, however, that situations of stress did tend to prove exceptions. Like the time, for instance, when she had been pregnant and had gone to book a nurse to attend to her home confinement. The mere idea of pregnancy frightened her. It seemed a journey into the unknown. It meant being helpless and at someone else's mercy. The nurse at the interview had been brusque and efficient.

"Name and address?"

She had smiled in reply and tried very hard to look intelligent but had taken a ridiculously long time to find the answer to even that basic question.

"Well," she managed now, "I'd better be going."

"You've got a big son called Russell, haven't you?" Rasheeda asked unexpectedly.

"Yes. Russell's sixteen. He's only another year to go at the Academy."

"I go to the Academy."

"Do you like it?"

"Aye, it's fine."

Just as Alice rose and thankfully got rid of her cup, putting it down on the table, the door opened and Sharif Ali came in. At first he did not let his eyes light on her but spoke in his own tongue to Zaida.

Alice felt discomfited and even when he did turn to her with a polite good evening, she still felt estranged and cut off. He left the room after another burst of Urdu to his daughter and without looking at Alice again.

"My father says," Zaida informed her, "that you are most welcome in our house."

"Oh, thank you," Alice murmured, though she was far from convinced.

Outside in the dark square, she sighed and her face muscles slid down with relief. She had not relished the idea of gathering with the other neighbours for the meeting in Joe Malloy's house but now she quite looked forward to it. At least with people of your own kind you could relax. You knew where you stood with them.

You could say what you wanted and have a laugh without worrying about misunderstandings.

But right now what she needed was a long drink of liver salts and a good burp.

# Five

At first, Jenny Saunders had been frightened. Leaving her husband and family and starting a new life at her age was a big step to take. She was fifty-one after all.

It didn't make anything any easier to have suffered years of being told how stupid and hopeless she was and how she couldn't do anything right. His voice had become like the slow, never-ending drip of water in some Chinese torture. All right, he'd had a terrible time as a Japanese prisoner of war. He'd worked on what was called "Death Railway". Apparently big strong men had dropped dead like flies every day while working on that railway. But comparatively small, lean men like Percy Saunders survived.

She tried to make allowances. Poor man, she used to think. After all he suffered, is it any wonder he's become so negative and twisted? Not that he was like that with everyone. He could be all sweetness and light with their daughter, Fiona. It was only to his wife that he showed his dark side. It was as if he was intent on getting his revenge on her for all that the Japanese had made him suffer during the war. Poor man, she used to think. And she'd feel a protective rush of love and pity and sympathy for him. But all that got worn down over the years with his constant furtive negative talk. Never in front of Fiona or anyone else. In fact he became such a Jekyll and Hyde character that she sometimes felt she must be imagining it. She was going mad. He had certainly told her often enough that she was mad. She feared it had begun to look that way to Fiona. She'd listen to him doing his gentle, long-suffering act for Fiona's benefit and all her unhappiness and resentment against him would build up until it became unbearable and she'd let fly at him. Mostly it would be a verbal outburst but once she'd thrown a plate of stew at him. She'd been carrying it to the table and instead of placing the meal in front of him, she'd flung it across the table. She'd immediately felt awful about it.

Fiona had been shocked and had rushed to her dad's assistance.

"It's all right, Fiona," Percy had said quietly, gently – little, balding, reasonable, harmless man that he appeared. "Your mum didn't mean it."

That's what he always said. Then he'd go on about her erratic, abnormal behaviour. After Fiona had gone, of course. It got that she felt like killing him. Fiona was sorry for her dad and was always furious at her mother. Jenny told herself, If I don't get away from here, she's going to end up hating me as much as I've grown to hate him. She thought that for years but could never pluck up the courage to make the move. Where could she go? She had no money. How could she get a divorce? Percy was the local hero. He'd never raised a finger against her. He was a decent provider. Indeed, he denied her nothing in a material sense. They had a well-furnished house. She was always well dressed. Fiona lacked for nothing either. For years he'd had a good position in the Social Work Department. That was the really ironic bit. Before he'd retired, he'd been in charge of helping and advising problem families. Who would ever believe her? She could hardly believe it herself. Even up to the last minute – even now – she occasionally thought – poor sod. What he must have suffered. She wished things could have been different between them. She'd see photos of him before his capture in which he looked cheerful and happy, with ruddy cheeks and a good head of hair. Photos of his childhood too where he looked perfectly normal. No doubt he was.

The war had a lot to answer for.

She might have gone on living with Percy until he'd completely destroyed her. He was going to be the death of her. She became convinced of it. She might never have mustered enough confidence or belief in herself to enable her to leave. Until one day something happened, something trivial and silly, but it proved the proverbial last straw.

They had been in the kitchen sitting in silence having lunch. Fiona had finished hers because she was going out to meet Nigel, her boyfriend. She was through in her room fetching her coat. Jenny was thinking, He's trying to find something to needle me about.

Eventually he said in a very quiet voice, "Jenny, do you see how many bananas there are in that bowl?" He indicated the bowl of fruit in the centre of the table.

She counted the bananas. "Eight. Why?"

"There were four this morning. You've gone out and bought another four. You're always doing things like that. You don't seem able to think of what you're doing or why. You need to see about that failing memory of yours. It can be a symptom of . . ."

Suddenly, and certainly not thinking what she was doing or why, she leapt to her feet, sending her chair crashing back just as Fiona popped her head round the door to call cheerio.

"See you and your fucking bananas," Jenny howled, "you know where you can stick them!"

Shock! Horror!

"Mum!" Fiona gasped.

Percy said very quietly, "I will not have filthy language like that in my home. Especially not in front of our daughter."

"You know where you can stick your fucking home as well. I'm off," she flung at him over her retreating shoulder.

"Off where?"

"Anywhere."

She'd gone straight into town to see a lawyer. She'd asked about a mortgage. But he didn't hold out much – if any – hope. Apparently her age, her sex and the fact that she hadn't a penny to her name were against her. She took in typing work and made a decent amount at that but, fool that she was, she'd ploughed it all into the house.

She felt depressed. She was dreading returning to the house. She was – she had to admit – becoming really afraid of Percy. She stopped at a café. There were newspapers lying on a shelf and she'd settled at a table to drink a cup of coffee and leaf through an early edition of the *Evening Times*. Anything to put off the evil hour. Then, unexpectedly, her eye was caught by an advert in the Properties to Let column.

"Furnished bungalow to let in quiet square on the south side. Exceptionally low rent. Apply in first instance to Bell & Drew, House Factors. References essential."

Well, she could get impressive references. Quite a few of her satisfied customers had become famous, like Patricia Ashley, the novelist. Patricia was practically crippled with rheumatoid arthritis. She spoke her stories into a tape recorder. Jenny collected the tapes and, using her audio equipment, typed them into manuscript form. Then she delivered the manuscript back to Patricia who was always delighted with her work. Then there was old Mr Menzies who wrote his autobiography in such a spidery scrawl he often couldn't make it out himself. She had become really adept at translating it. He could oblige with a reference, she was sure.

She gulped down the rest of her coffee, then practically ran all the way to the factor's office. People turned to stare at her, a slim figure in a neat black suit, black hat, pristine white blouse and smart court shoes. She didn't look the type to be haring along Sauchiehall Street. She prayed that she'd be lucky and get there before anyone else. Most people could be at work and probably hadn't seen the paper yet. For once in her life, luck might be on her side. And it was.

The owner of the bungalow had won the pools. He was now worth a fortune and didn't need any rent money at all. He was charging a nominal sum that even she could afford. The reason was, apparently, that he couldn't bear to let go of the bungalow altogether. He'd bought a house in Majorca and was going to live there but the bungalow had sentimental value. He and his late wife had started their marriage and spent their few happy years together in the bungalow before she'd been tragically killed at a young age in a car accident.

Jenny was sorry to hear about the poor girl's death. At the same time she couldn't help feeling elated. It was as if somebody up there was looking after her and cared about her after all. What a bit of luck! Furnished and all. She could have danced in the street outside the factor's office. Already they'd promised it to her. She supposed it was a matter of first come, first served. They wouldn't want to waste a whole lot of time unnecessarily and get involved in a terrible hassle.

Both Percy and Fiona had been unbelieving at first. Even Fiona was convinced she'd gone completely mad. They both hung around her as she packed her case.

"Get out of my way," she told them. "I'm leaving."

To Percy she said, "Our marriage is finished."

Then to Fiona, "Here is my address. You're welcome to visit me as often as you like. I'd like you to come and live with me in the bungalow but . . ." She couldn't help a tinge of bitterness entering her voice. "No doubt you'll prefer to remain here with your father."

She had, of course. And she'd never forgiven her mother for leaving Percy, her poor, precious, hard-done-by, long-suffering father. She paid the occasional visit to the bungalow, but whether out of curiosity or duty, or in the hope that her mother wasn't managing and would be forced to give up and return to her father, Jenny was never sure.

She didn't think it was because of love. At least not for her. She believed, sadly, that Percy and Fiona wanted her to fail. They were furious when they'd seen the bungalow set like a sparkling jewel in the lovely quiet square. They couldn't believe that nothing had gone wrong and nothing was going to go wrong.

They had expected her to make a fool of herself, land up in some slum or become involved in some con or scandal. They thought she must have made the whole thing up. Percy had gone behind her back and checked with the factor. She had become afraid that Percy was trying to ruin her life in the square as he'd ruined it in their family home. Or find out some awful secret or scandal about the place so that he could gloat and point the finger and say, "I told you so." She'd had to warn him that she would go to the police and report him for pestering and harassing her if he didn't keep well away. She'd involve *him* in scandal. She promised it and he could see that she meant it.

"I don't want to see you again. We're finished, Percy," she told him. "I have made a good life for myself here."

It was a pity about the neighbours. Not that she saw much of them; she spent most of her time at her typewriter on the kitchen table at the back of the house. Some of them were out working all day. They had their own lives to live. The McFarlanes for instance. Mrs McFarlane was a teacher at a tough school at the other end of town, and had quite a bit of commuting to do. Her husband travelled even more because he was some sort of salesman whose job took him all over the country. She'd seen Mrs McFarlane occasionally to say hello to in passing and a couple of times they'd had a brief chat when they'd met at the shops. She seemed a nice woman, but a bit like mutton dressed as lamb at times. Always very busy, though. She had two teenage children – a boy and a girl, Will and Emma. Talk about Percy being Jekyll and Hyde! Mrs McFarlane was a bit like that too. In her appearance at least. On her own, going to and from work, she looked every bit the serious schoolmarm, her hair pinned back with kirby grips and wearing skirts and cardigans and flat comfortable shoes. When she was with her husband, however, her hair was back-combed into a beehive style. She also sported low-cut dresses and ridiculously high heels.

Then there were the Whitelaws. They had a son of about sixteen, Jenny reckoned. Mrs Whitelaw looked a bit eccentric. (A disaster, actually. That freckly face and awful hair!) She seemed to float about in a dream, a half-smile forever hovering about her mouth. Her husband was a tall slim man, rather attractive and distinguished looking.

In one of the other bungalows there was an elderly lady who was always peeping out from behind her lace curtains. Once Jenny had gone to knock at her door to introduce herself but although Mrs Bell was in, she had not opened the door. So that was that.

As far as the Malloys were concerned, she had no desire whatsoever to cultivate a friendship with them. They were obviously the *nouveaux riches* of the square. Hilda Malloy was the most awful snob, and always referred to Pollokshields as "The Shields". Joe Malloy was a loud-mouthed idiot. Their daughter, Kate, as far as she could see, was a right spoiled little madam.

Then there was the dreadful Mr Bierce and his poor, frightened shadow of a wife, Sissy. Mr Bierce was quite a small man, exactly the same size as his wife and much the same square shape. Jenny sometimes thought they looked like a pair of bookends. It was the loudness of Mr Bierce's voice and the strength and blackness of his emotions that gave the impression that he was of monstrous proportions. He was all for the return of birching and hanging. Birching and hanging were his answer to everything, it seemed. He was disgustingly prejudiced as well. According to him, "papes", "darkies" and "chinkies" should go back to their own countries, and the quicker the better.

She avoided the Malloys and the Bierces at every opportunity.

Now the "For Sale" board in the remaining bungalow had disappeared. Because she sat so much at the back of the house, she hadn't seen anyone looking round the place. She hoped the new owner would be a retired unmarried lady, somebody decent, who would welcome a bit of company. Or perhaps a lively widow?

The thought cheered Jenny enormously.

# Six

Although they had to use separate entrances to the Academy, and separate stairways up to the classrooms, it was possible for students to mix quite freely outside of the school. White boys and white girls walked together and talked and laughed together. Muslim boys and girls, however, did not mix in this way outside.

For Rasheeda it was different because she walked home with Maq and Maq had become friendly with the two white boys in the square, Will and Russell. She walked home along with them. Soon it became the habit that Will and Maq talked and laughed together and kicked a ball along the street. Rasheeda and Russell walked a little apart and spoke only to each other.

Right from the start, she'd felt a closeness to him. It was as if fate had meant them to be together. Each had not been complete before. To Rasheeda it was a wonderful, magical feeling for which she was truly grateful.

After a time, just walking to and from school together wasn't enough. They discussed the difficulties she would have with her family if they tried to meet more often. Eventually she spoke to her cousin Parveen. She pleaded with her and eventually persuaded her to become her ally. Parveen agreed to say that she was with Rasheeda so that she could get out in the evenings and at weekends and meet Russell.

"It must never be more than friendship, remember," Parveen kept warning. "Nothing more can ever come of it."

"I know, I know," Rasheeda eagerly agreed. Anything to be with Russell.

She lived for the moment, appreciating every minute, every second, she was with him. With him she enjoyed such freedom of spirit, such an awakening of her true self. Each time she was with him she seemed to grow in stature, to develop in self-confidence and self-worth. He thought she was brilliant, and beautiful, and no one had ever thought that about her before.

She had never done as well in exams as her older sister, Zaida. She was not even considered as clever as Noor Jahan. Even the fact that she spoke English better than anyone else in the family – except perhaps Maq – did not raise anyone's opinion of her. Quite the reverse. All she got was criticism. Nothing, it seemed, was right with her. She never looked right. She never dressed right. She didn't study enough. She was cheeky. She had no respect, especially for her daddy.

This was untrue. Although she often argued with him and accused him of being old-fashioned, among other things, she did respect him and love him. She loved him even more than her mammy. She understood their ways but unfortunately they did not understand hers. It was no use trying to explain to her daddy or her mammy how different it was to live in Glasgow, to be one of the Glasgow crowd, to have Glasgow pals at school and yet know she was not really one of the crowd because of her background, her family and the colour of her skin. She had always wanted to be the same as her pals, to go with them to the pictures, to join them in experiencing school trips abroad, to have boyfriends. But she never could because of her mammy and daddy, and even more so because of her uncle and aunt and her cousins. Her uncle had a bushy beard and moustache and was very religious. When he wasn't on duty on the buses, he wore the long loose shirt and trousers of his homeland and her aunty always had a vividly coloured sari covering her ample frame. Her uncle said Rasheeda didn't only sound cheeky, she looked cheeky as well.

She didn't want to be different. She wanted to do well at school and receive praise from her daddy and mammy and her uncle and aunty, but until she'd met Russell, she never received praise from anybody for anything. The only time she got any attention was when somebody was criticising her. Although she supposed it was better than no attention at all. But so many things fuelled resentment inside her. Why didn't her mammy and daddy let her go with everyone else on school trips to exciting places like Italy and France? Often she had felt in a kind of no man's land. Not belonging anywhere.

The only close friend she had was her cousin Parveen, the youngest daughter of her uncle. Parveen was a good friend. She understood Rasheeda's difficulties and her dreams. She had difficulties and dreams too. But she was resigned to the fact that her difficulties would never be resolved and her dreams would never come true. She would end up in an arranged marriage like her sister, Anver.

Rasheeda was not so accepting. Her uncle Mirza had called her a rebel and warned her mammy and daddy to "watch her". Sometimes Rasheeda wondered even if Parveen was her friend or if she was just being a dutiful daughter and chaperoning her everywhere so that she could keep an eye on her. Her mammy and daddy respected her Uncle Mirza who had an important job as an inspector on the buses. And they trusted Parveen. Of course they did not trust her.

But at least Parveen was covering for her when she was with Russell. Although she never tired of telling her, "Never forget, Rasheeda, nothing can come of your friendship with this white boy. Friendship and nothing more, remember."

Oh, how she treasured her walks with Russell and her talks with him! He was the first and only person who had ever given her respect and admiration. Out of all the pretty girls in the school, even all the pretty white girls, he had singled her out for his attention. He had chosen her. He had told her often that she was beautiful, and she knew now by the expression of wonderment in his eyes that he really believed it. He told her she had everything – beauty, brains, poise. Even the way she moved was wonderful, he said. She had such grace.

"I can't take my eyes off you," he told her.

Nor could she take her eyes off him: his tall, broad-shouldered figure, his straight, blue-black hair, his sensitive face with its slightly gaunt, haunted look.

She blossomed under his admiring eyes. She thrived on his attention. She felt so happy, so grateful. She longed to boast about Russell and what he thought of her, how he treated her.

She wanted to tell her mammy and daddy how wonderful he was and how she felt so at one with him. It didn't matter that he was a white Christian Glasgow boy. She didn't feel in any way different from him. Nothing separated them. He made her feel so safe, so special.

The only thing that spoiled her newfound euphoria was the fear of her family finding out. If they did find out, there would be one awful fuss. There would be a family conference at which Uncle Mirza would preside. He bullied her daddy and lorded over everyone because although he and her daddy were both employed by the Glasgow Corporation, Uncle Mirza was an inspector on the buses whereas her daddy was a lamplighter.

She couldn't see why that was a more humble job than an inspector on the buses but Uncle Mirza did. His big-bosomed wife was equally fierce and was always telling her mammy what to do and what not to do. Aunty Shafiga insisted not only on teaching Mammy English but taking her to shops and making her ask for things and do things and walk outside on her own. Mammy was terribly cowed and frightened of Aunty Shafiga. It made Rasheeda angry and she was very cheeky to her.

Aunty Shafiga said, "She's got to learn to go out on her own and not be so timid. It's ridiculous when she can't even go out to the post office. I'll have her walking there and back on her own yet."

Poor Mammy. How wide-eyed and terrified she'd looked. Aunty Shafiga didn't walk much herself. She drove her car everywhere. And very proud she looked sitting at the wheel.

Rasheeda wished that she had a car and could drive. One day she'd learn, she promised herself. Then she'd drive Russell away out to the country and they'd have a picnic and it would be like they were alone in the world. It was one of her dreams. She'd told Russell and he'd said that he was learning to drive. His father was teaching him. His father, he said, wasn't really a bad sort. He had even promised that one day soon he'd give Russell a car of his own. Russell said when that happened, he'd make her dream come true. He'd like to make all her dreams come true, he'd said. They'd been hiding in one of the back closes in Nithsdale Road at the time. A back close was one of the few places where they could find any privacy. He'd take her in his arms and kiss her and she'd strain to make out his face in the shadows. She'd lovingly trace his features with her fingers – his broad forehead, his slightly protruding eyes, his straight nose, the hollow of his cheeks, his strong chin. He was tall and well made. Nevertheless, his lean face gave him a somewhat anxious, even delicate look.

She felt keenly protective as well as loving towards him. She thought about him lovingly, longingly, worriedly, every moment they were apart. He said that he felt exactly the same way about her. They were completely honest and open with each other about everything. They even spoke about sex, though they called it love-making. He said he wanted her desperately – just as she wanted him – but he respected her and didn't want to do anything that would betray that respect.

She dreamed of marrying him. They would have to wait until he'd been to university and got his degree. That way he'd be able to get a good job and support her. She would get her degree and a job too, and help with living costs. They'd both make a lot of money and they'd buy a nice house and live together happily ever after.

It was such a beautiful dream.

She knew the reality would not be so easy to accomplish. Everyone would be against them. She would be completely cut off from her family. Not one of them would ever have anything to do with her again. She would be ostracised by the whole Pakistani community. The prospect of the absolute rejection, the total isolation, secretly frightened her. With a defiant toss of her head, however, she told herself that she could face all that and more as long as she had him. As long as they could be together.

She even daydreamed in great detail about the home they'd one day share. She planned where it would be and what kind of house it would be. Perhaps they could find a cottage in the country? That was one of the great things about Glasgow. In only about half an hour, you were into beautiful countryside. Yes, a cottage. That would be wonderful.

In her dreams she even planned what size it would be. She visualised the size of the rooms and how modern and convenient the kitchen would be. At the same time it could be built in a farmhouse style with wooden beams and herbs hanging from them. She visualised pretty chintz-covered chairs with cushions to match. There could be purple clematis growing round the front door.

Beautiful! Beautiful! She could see it all.

As well as Scottish porridge and broth and fish and chips and potato scones and pancakes, she'd cook Pakistani food. Russell liked Pakistani and Indian food.

They'd eat in the kitchen at a scrubbed wood table. Then later they'd enjoy their coffee in front of the sitting room fire. Later still they'd lie in each other's arms in the cosy pretty bedroom.

Oh, what a beautiful dream it was.

# Seven

"You're joking!" Emma McFarlane said, half amused, half incredulous.

"No, honestly." Her young brother, Will, was rooting about in the fridge, his head hidden by the fridge door. "Maq's in my class. His grandad's bought it. Or his grandad and his dad, or something. Anyway, they've all moved in together. His grandad, his grannie, his mum and dad, his two aunties. I think there's a baby as well."

Emma couldn't help laughing.

"At last. Something to liven up the place."

"How do you mean?" Will straightened, mumbling through a mouthful of cheesecake.

"Well, they're such a dull bunch here. It's like a wee world of its own, this square. Dad's the only bright spark among the lot of them."

"I wish he could be here more often."

"It's just his job."

"I know that."

He strolled through to the green-carpeted hall where there was an oak hat stand bulging with coats and jackets and a small oak table on which stood the phone and the phone book. In a few seconds she could hear him speaking on the phone to one of his friends. She wondered what she could do for the rest of her day off. Day and evening. She had a live-in job as a nanny in a big sandstone villa in Bearsden on the outskirts of Glasgow. She was even more appreciative of her dad than Will. She now knew how ghastly another dad could be. She worked for the Cunninghams and Mrs Cunningham was nice, far too nice for the monster she was married to.

Oh, Mr Cunningham was the charmer to outsiders, a pillar of Bearsden society, elder of the church, member of the golf club, the bridge club and God knows what else. He was also a director of several companies.

Inside his own home, though, he had no time for his son unless to chastise him. Sammy was afraid of him. So was his mother. Emma had soon found out why. Even from the nursery quarters at the top of the house, she could hear the poor woman's screams, and the crashes and thumps issuing from downstairs. On one occasion she'd rushed to Mrs Cunningham's rescue. Mr Cunningham had stopped as soon as he'd heard her coming, of course. He'd made some excuse about his wife having an accident. He'd been very uppity and cool and ordered her to get back upstairs. The inference was that that was where she belonged and she should mind her own business.

If it hadn't been for poor Mrs Cunningham and little Samuel, she would have left right there and then. She was sorry for the woman and fond of the child, but it wasn't a happy situation. It was lonely too. She had to eat on her own in the nursery after Sammy went to bed. She was sure that Mrs Cunningham wouldn't have minded her eating in the dining room with them; it was her husband who was the snob. Or maybe it was just because he didn't want anyone to witness how dreadfully he treated his wife.

Despite her fondness for Mrs Cunningham and Sammy, Emma had begun to look at the Situations Vacant column. She hoped she could find something nearer home, something daily. There were plenty of families in big villas in Pollokshields or in the even more prosperous Newton Mearns who could afford, and perhaps would even prefer, a daily nanny.

Being off duty every evening would give her so much more freedom. She wanted to get out and around, have a social life, and meet people of her own age. She was nineteen, and apart from a silly crush at school she'd never had a boyfriend. That was only because of her job, she was sure. She wasn't bad looking. Quite pretty, in fact. She had her mother's clear skin and slim figure, and her father's curly brown hair and brown eyes. Once she was able to have some social life, she'd surely find a boyfriend.

Will had also inherited his father's curls but he plastered them down with Brylcreem and smoothed his hair back and into a side parting like Bill Hayley – although recently he'd been trying to grow sideburns and look more like Elvis Presley. Especially since he'd acquired a guitar.

"Can you imagine what the Malloys will make of it?" Emma said to Will as he joined her in the bright, chintzy sitting room.

"What?"

"What you were saying about the Pakistani family moving in next door to them."

Will flopped into a chair. "How about Bierce, the hangman's friend?" Emma rolled her eyes. "What a shower, eh?"

"I'm sorry for Maq," Will said. "He thinks it's going to be great here. He's been living in a stinking old tenement in the Gorbals."

"Well, it is a lovely wee square. I don't think he'll bother about the neighbours. I don't, do you?"

Will made a face.

"Silly old farts. They're not worth bothering about."

"That's Mum." They could hear her key in the door. "I wonder if she knows."

Will shrugged.

As soon as Constance McFarlane came into the room, she made straight for the sofa and collapsed on to it. She plumped her feet up on a cushion, took off her gold-rimmed spectacles and rubbed at her eyes.

"Pour me a sherry, one of you. It's been one hell of a day. Most of the little so-and-sos aren't in the least interested in art. They're not interested in anything."

Emma filled a crystal glass and handed it to Constance.

"Will's got a new friend. A Pakistani boy. The family have bought old Mrs Ogilvie's place."

"Oh?" Constance thankfully took a sip of sherry. "That's nice, son. What's his name?"

"Maq Tanwir. It's spelled M-A-Q."

"I've some Pakistanis in a couple of my classes. The girls are very serious. Ambitious too. But the boys have as much of a carry-on in class as the Scots boys. Every day the first thing I have to do is quell a riot and try to make all the boys sit down and be quiet."

"Why on earth do you stick it at that awful school, Mum?" Emma said. "You're wasting your time. You know perfectly well that half of them are just going to end up in jail like their fathers. Why don't you try to get into the Academy?"

"No, please, Mum," Will cried out in alarm. "I'd die of embarrassment."

Constance laughed.

"Don't worry, son. I've no intention of embarrassing you." She took a few thoughtful sips of her drink before saying, "No, I believe I get more satisfaction where I am. I sometimes do succeed in interesting them and awakening their enthusiasm. And when I do, it feels so worthwhile. They're not such a bad bunch of kids. They just need somebody to give them a chance."

Will looked relieved. "Can I bring Maq in to see my posters and listen to some music?"

"Of course, dear." Constance enjoyed the rest of her drink before replacing her spectacles and reluctantly struggling up from the sofa. "Do you mind if we have our meal a bit early? I've a pile of marking to do tonight."

"I'll help you, Mum," Emma said.

"Thanks, love."

"Is Daddy coming home this weekend?"

Constance's pale face brightened. (She only rouged her cheeks and wore lipstick when her husband was at home.)

"Not this weekend, dear, but even better, he's driving down from Pitlochry next Wednesday and staying over next weekend."

"Super!" Then Emma's mouth drooped. "I hate my job. I never manage to see Dad now even when he's home."

Their father was a travelling salesman – dealing in ladies' underwear, of all things. Constance wasn't in the least surprised that he did well and made plenty of commission. He had everything going for him – boyish good looks, charm, a sense of humour and a real talent for mimicry. All his women customers would adore him. She felt real fear at the thought. At forty-eight, Ronnie was ten years younger than Constance and looked even younger with his thick curly hair and boyish expression. This fact never ceased to torment her. In two years she'd be sixty. SIXTY! She felt terrified at the prospect. She'd be an old woman and Ronnie would still be in his prime, as good looking, as charming and as youthful as ever. He could get any woman, any young woman. Maybe he did. How did she know what he got up to on his travels? At times she felt consumed with jealousy.

She would have employed a private detective to shadow him but so far couldn't afford the cost. Already, practically every penny she earned was spent on trying to hold age at bay and keep as attractive as possible. Twice, sometimes three times a week, she visited the gym and that wasn't cheap. She had also bought an exercise bike and installed it in her bedroom. No matter how tired she felt, she pedalled furiously on it every night. She spent a fortune on beauty products and treatments. She bought books on diet and exercise. She even religiously performed grotesque facial exercises. She had her hair regularly tinted blonde and styled by the best hairdresser in Glasgow – which reminded her, she must make an appointment for tomorrow so that she'd be looking her best for Ronnie's arrival. She'd lay out her smartest outfit as well. She was like two separate people – the glamorous wife and the comfortably dressed respectable school teacher.

All the trouble she took was worth it as long as it meant she kept Ronnie. But no matter what she did, she could never feel sure of him. She was in secret agony every night he was away from home. She loved him far too desperately. She knew that. What she had never known was what Ronnie saw in her. All right, she worked hard and spent every penny making the most of her looks. Even so, she was still no raving beauty. Her spectacles didn't help. Nor did her job. There was nothing glamorous about being a school teacher – especially in one of the toughest schools in Glasgow.

"What?" She became aware of Emma speaking.

"I hate that man."

"What man?"

"Mr Cunningham. He makes me sick. I'm sorry for his wife but I can't stick living there any more. I've decided to leave and try for a day job. You don't mind me moving back in here, do you, Mum?"

"Of course not, darling! What a daft question. This is your home."

"Good. And the square sounds as if it's going to be more interesting."

Constance smiled. "Does it? Why's that?"

"The Pakistanis."

"Oh yes."

Constance's mind wandered back to Ronnie again. It was getting worse every time he left. Somehow, some way, sometime, she'd be forced to get the help of a private detective.

"Will and I were just saying we were sorry for them being stuck next door to the Malloys."

"It could have been worse," Constance said.

"How?" Emma and Will cried out in unison. "What could be worse than being next door to the Malloys?" Emma continued.

"Living next door to Mr Bierce."

They all laughed until Constance forced herself to be serious. "We shouldn't laugh. Poor things." Then she went to prepare the meal and concentrate on her more personal and important worries. Before Ronnie had even arrived she was tormenting herself with thoughts of him leaving again. Something would definitely have to be done.

# Eight

They were a good crowd in the Art Department. Constance was grateful to Mr Brownlee for giving up his free period to take over her class so that she could get away early. It meant she could have her hair done. Her dark roots were beginning to show. That was the worst of having her hair dyed such a bright shade of blonde. She had to be so careful about her roots.

She'd still managed to get home in time to change out of her sensible flat shoes, her dark skirt and comfy cardigan into a floral print dress with one of the pointed sweater bras underneath. She had to look just right to welcome Ronnie home. He had only been away ten days but even ten days felt like a lifetime without him. Every time he returned she felt like a young girl in love again. The excitement he aroused in her had never diminished. Sometimes the way her pulse raced and her cheeks flushed at the sight of him embarrassed her. Emma and Will often teased her about it.

"Will you never realise, Mum," Emma would say with mock sternness, "that you're an old married woman."

Constance knew that Emma was joking and was happy and delighted to see how much in love her parents still were. But the mere mention of the word "old" worried her. Sometimes she couldn't resist asking Emma, "What age do you think I look?"

And Emma would obligingly, comfortingly, answer, "At *least* ten years younger than you are, Mum." Then she would feel better. Yet always, at the back of her mind, was that frisson of fear and suspicion. In a way it intensified the excitement of seeing Ronnie again, being united with him. They couldn't get to bed quick enough. She didn't care if the children heard the wild sounds of their love-making. Ronnie said she was shameless. He whispered this in a teasing way and she was sure – or as sure as she could be about anything with Ronnie – that he enjoyed her being so wild and abandoned, so desperately in need of him.

Afterwards, in bed, she would lie cuddled in his arms, the smell of his sweat close to her nostrils, the heat of his body enveloping her, and she would secretly fight with herself, will herself to keep silent and not to question him, not to sound jealous or possessive, not to reveal how much she hated his job and desperately wanted and needed him to give it up.

She had tried to persuade him to change his job many times before. All it did was convince her that he would never settle in a job in Glasgow that meant regular working hours and living at home all the time. He had made that perfectly clear.

Normally he was an easy-going, happy-natured, good-tempered man. That was one subject, however, about which he'd begun to show irritation and the more she broached it, the more irritated he'd become. On one terrible occasion, he'd actually rounded on her and snarled at her, "Will you never shut up about me changing my job! I enjoy my job, can't you get that into your stupid head? My job is *me*. You're so bloody jealous, it makes me sick. You're getting more like a bloody jailer than a wife."

She had been shaken to her roots. Absolutely devastated. For a few seconds he'd actually looked as if he hated her.

Afterwards he'd apologised. He'd turned the whole thing into a joke. He'd laughed and she'd managed – she didn't know how – to laugh along with him. For a long time she hadn't made any reference whatsoever to his job. But gradually, she couldn't resist sly but apparently innocent and light-hearted little questions creeping in.

"How are things going these days? Selling lots of knickers, are you?"

Recently they had begun to be more personal, although still delivered in a lighthearted joking tone.

"You look happy. Been giving customers fitting sessions, have you? A new service, is it?"

She knew she was inviting trouble and was in danger of letting things get out of hand again. She could detect the warning signals in the hard glint in Ronnie's eyes. So far he'd kept his temper and not said anything. She must do the same. She must keep her mouth shut. Ronnie never mentioned his work now. He used to chat about it a lot. He used to make her and the children laugh at the way he could mimic some of his customers. Now he had clammed up. If she was out of the room and the children asked about his job, he'd chat away quite normally. As soon as she came on the scene, however, he changed the subject. Sometimes she hovered behind the door, her ear held close to it, listening.

If it had been any other job – even any other travelling job – if he'd travelled about visiting all the ironmonger's shops or DIY shops in the country selling locks or pots of paint, she would have felt all right. Or so she tried to tell herself. But *ladies' underwear*! That meant talking to women. That meant sharing intimate talk about intimate things. What sort of sales talk did he persuade them with?

"Look at this silky crotch. Feel it. Imagine how wonderful it would feel moving against the most intimate and private part of your body." She imagined in vivid detail whole scenarios in which one word, one action, led to another and ended with Ronnie having sex sessions with innumerable women. It drove her mad just to think of them.

If she couldn't afford a detective, she'd follow Ronnie herself, she decided. Then she imagined Ronnie spotting her hanging about in one of the lingerie departments and being furious with her, hating her. No, it would have to be somebody he didn't know and would not suspect. Somehow she'd have to find the money for a detective. But then, would it not look suspicious – a man hanging around a lingerie department? It suddenly occurred to her that maybe the detective agency would insist on putting a woman on the job. Then she worried about a woman detective coming under Ronnie's spell. Women loved him and he loved women. If she went to a detective agency and if they suggested a woman, she'd have to insist that it was an older and very unattractive-looking woman. A woman who if necessary would be made up to look as ugly as possible. Even that, though, didn't completely soothe away her doubts and fears.

Sometimes she felt quite ill. She didn't need to diet, although she was careful about what she ate. Her growing worries and anxieties about Ronnie kept her thin. What with that and all the hassle she had to cope with at her work, there was never any danger of her becoming fat and placid. Indeed, she was glad of her stiffly pointed bra to make the most of her small breasts.

Often she'd been told she was a good teacher. Even with the most difficult children, she usually managed in the end to form a good relationship with them. She believed she was a good mother too. Both Emma and Will were decent, well-behaved young people. She knew they loved her. Why couldn't she feel as secure about her husband's love for her?

She'd once said to Emma, in as light-hearted a tone as she could manage, "Dear knows what your dad gets up to with all the women he meets on his travels."

Emma had laughed. "Mum, don't be daft. Dad has no eyes for anyone else but you."

She longed so desperately to believe that. She wanted to keep him all to herself, even when he was at home. But he was so gregarious he always wanted either to go out with her to a dance, or a restaurant or a club, or any place where there would be company. Or he'd say, "Why don't we invite a few people round?"

On this occasion, he'd said, "I see we've new neighbours."

"Oh yes, the Pakistani family. I haven't met them yet but Will has made friends with the boy. He's called Maq of all things. M-A-Q."

"Why don't you invite them round? It would be a nice gesture. I bet they'd appreciate it."

She shrugged. "All right."

Just then Will came in. "Did you see all the Pakistanis out there, Dad? They're our new neighbours."

"Yes, I was just telling your mum she should invite them in for a meal or something. Get to know them."

"Super!" Will was enthusiastic. "Did you see the daughters? That youngest one – Rasheeda – goes to the Academy. She's absolutely *gorgeous,* isn't she?"

Ronnie laughed but Constance was sure he looked embarrassed, and guilty. So *that* was why he was so keen to get to know the Pakistanis. It was the beautiful Pakistani girl he wanted to get to know. Now her insecurity, her suspicion and her fears spread like an evil finger over her own home ground. She trembled with the depth and force of her emotions. She hated the Pakistani girl even before she'd set eyes on her.

# Nine

Jenny's daughter, Fiona, and her boyfriend, Nigel, were going to get married. They'd set the date. It was to be a church affair with a reception afterwards in the best hotel in the area. They'd even found a house near Nigel's parents in posh Newton Mearns. Nigel's parents were nice people but Jenny suspected they would be embarrassed at meeting her again now that she'd "deserted" Percy. That was the word Percy and Fiona used. He said he was thinking of divorcing her for desertion.

"Don't just think about it," she'd urged him. "Go ahead. And the quicker the better."

She didn't think he would. Unfortunately. Not yet. He was still hoping that something would happen to make her run back to him with her tail between her legs. She'd divorce him if she could. But what would be the grounds? He'd never looked at another woman. He hadn't been physically cruel to her. Who would believe emotional and mental cruelty? How could she say, "He's going to be the death of me. I know it"? They'd want proof. She had no proof. She had no witnesses. If Fiona was called she would deny that her father had been anything but patient, saintly in fact. That was how Fiona saw Percy. Or so it seemed to Jenny.

Anyway, she didn't feel able to face the hassle of going through the courts. She just didn't want anything to do with Percy. She'd never taken as much as a teaspoon from the house and she didn't want a penny from him in maintenance. All she wanted was to feel safe and relaxed and happy in this quiet little backwater. It was wonderful to feel her self-confidence gradually building up. She had plenty of typing work to provide her with a decent income. It wasn't the money *per se* that gave her such a kick. It was the fact that she could keep herself, that she was capable of doing it.

Sometimes, she'd break off from her typing to enjoy a coffee and she'd catch a glimpse of herself in the kitchen mirror. She saw a neat woman with small, even features and hair pinned back in a chignon. She wore a smart blouse and skirt. It always surprised her how relaxed and capable she looked. And content.

One day, no doubt, she'd get a divorce but right now she had freedom enough. Sometimes she'd be typing away for hours in her little back kitchen and beginning to feel tired. She'd long for a drink to give her a little boost but automatically tell herself she couldn't have one because Percy would accuse her of becoming an alcoholic. Then suddenly she'd realise that Percy wasn't there any more. *She was free*. She'd dance through to the sitting room, take a bottle of sherry or martini from the drinks cupboard and pour herself a drink. Lolling back in the easy chair she'd savour it like nectar. Oh, what joy, what bliss! She only wanted one drink. That's all she'd ever wanted.

There were times when she'd be in town doing a bit of shopping or perhaps delivering another chapter or two of Mr Menzies' life history. She'd suddenly notice the time and think, panic stricken, My God! I'll be late with Percy's lunch. I'll never hear the end of it. He'd accuse her either of being insanely extravagant. Or just insane. Then, joy of joys, she'd remember that Percy wasn't there any more and she didn't need to rush home, heart palpitating with fear and distress. *She was free.*

She could face the fact now that if anyone was insane, it was Percy. She could still think – poor soul! The war, and especially the Japanese who tortured and tormented Percy, were to blame for how he was now. But then she'd think incredulously, joyously, that she could do what she liked. She could decide right there and then to take a trip through to Edinburgh instead of going straight home. She could wander round the park. She could do anything, *anything* she fancied. What a wonderful life! She felt blessed.

It wasn't that she wanted to dash off to Edinburgh or anywhere else. All she'd ever wanted was to feel safe and have peace and quiet. Now she enjoyed all of these things.

She didn't expect to enjoy Fiona's wedding, though. The invitation surprised her. She hadn't expected to be asked to attend. In a way she was touched and grateful. Perhaps it meant that Fiona did love her. After all, she was the only mother Fiona had.

She treated herself to a new wide-brimmed straw hat decorated with a tiny posy of flowers. She bought a new floral dress and a navy coat.

At the wedding her heart sank a little when she heard Fiona calling her mother-in-law "Mother". But of course that was quite a normal thing to do, she assured herself. She didn't feel jealous. Jealousy had never been one of her weaknesses. But she did feel sad and somewhat deprived.

On the surface of course everything appeared perfectly normal and happy. There was plenty of laughter and congratulations. The service was lovely and she didn't just weep but had to stifle broken-hearted sobs in her hanky and struggle desperately for self-control.

There were lots of photos taken outside the church and then they all happily streamed away to the hotel for the reception. The food was wonderful, the speeches hilarious. Everything went well. In a way it was like a dream. There she was at Percy's side at the top table, chatting and laughing with the rest as if everything was perfectly normal. As if – God forbid – after the festivities she could return home with Percy in the same happy normal way Nigel's mother would return home with Nigel's father.

The only subtle giveaway signs that the Elliots knew that everything was not happy and normal was the way that they looked at Jenny with embarrassed eyes. Or avoided meeting her eyes. Jenny realised that they were trying very hard to make sure nothing spoiled their son and daughter-in-law's happy day. Jenny appreciated this. She was trying hard too.

At the end of the evening, after the bride and groom had been cheered on their way, she had gone to the hotel reception to ask them to ring for a taxi. Percy was still glued to her elbow. He said, "What do you think you're doing?"

"Ordering a taxi."

"Don't be stupid. I've got the car outside."

"Thank you," she said in as polite and cool and normal a voice as she could muster, "but there's no need for you to drive all the way to Pollokshields."

"Don't be stupid," he repeated, almost in a whisper. "You're coming home with me."

It was just one sign of many that proved he had never accepted, had continually refused to accept, that she had left him, did not realise that their marriage was over. She felt a shiver of fear as if for a second she too believed it. But the taxi came and she walked out of the hotel. Percy still stuck close to her side.

"Don't be stupid," he kept saying in that quiet undertone she'd been listening to for years. "You're just being stupid." Then as she opened the door of the taxi and climbed inside, "You're mad. You should be locked up."

The fear quickened in her stomach and she asked herself, as she had asked herself so often in the past when he said things like that, Is this the way he'll finally destroy me?

It was only once she was back in the peaceful square, inside her lovely bungalow where love had once flourished, that she began to feel safe again. Gradually she calmed down.

I'm all right, she kept telling herself. Nothing can happen to me here.

# Ten

Alice's freckled face was perched on top of a bright purple jersey and a long yellow waistcoat. She was also wearing tartan slacks that showed her ankles. She never could get trousers that were long enough.

Everyone else was dressed soberly for the occasion. The men wore lounge suits and the other women each had on a dress, smart but discreet. They always bought their clothes in a shop with an approved reputation. They invested in designer items as often as they could afford them. And of course they were never seen outside without wearing gloves.

"Nothing but the best, and in good taste," was the motto of Hilda Malloy and her friends, regarding clothes and most other things. Most of her friends lived outside the perimeter of the square but in equally good areas, all of which had a set of conventions or rules to help with proper behaviour. These were stamps or yardsticks with which one judged or "placed" a person.

Class had become an unpopular word and was now seldom used. But only a working-class person, for instance, would go to answer a front door – or even risk going near a window – and be seen wearing an apron or hair rollers or slippers. No one knew how to categorise Constance McFarlane, though. Being a teacher was respectable enough, but why did she teach in such a dreadful school, which everyone knew was a breeding ground for gangsters? She was odd in her dress too. Sometimes she dressed very properly. At other times she looked like a tart. Hilda always greeted her with a polite good morning or good afternoon in passing, however, no matter how Constance happened to be dressed.

There was something not quite right about Jenny Saunders as well. She had left a husband who was a war hero and had been a selfless social worker. But she always looked very nice with her tiny pearl stud earrings, and brown hair neatly back in a chignon. She favoured well-cut tailored suits in discreet navy or black or clerical grey, and neat little matching hats. Often she was seen carrying a good leather briefcase and dressed in a smart belted Burberry with the collar turned up. She was always included in the invitations to cocktail parties, supper parties, coffee mornings or afternoon teas but she didn't always come. Her refusals were always very charming and polite, however. She'd smile and say, "I'd love to come but I work at home, you see, and it's been piling up so much recently."

There was a fair amount of socialising between the people in the square, mostly among the women who didn't go out to work and so could indulge in coffee mornings. The men exchanged friendly words over the fence while gardening or washing their cars. There were bridge evenings, of course, and there was the bowling club, not forgetting the occasional cocktail party and dinner party. However, the families mostly met on other ground. There were dressmaking classes and keep fit classes and classes for floral arranging in the town. Hilda also took a first aid class and had become most proficient. She often boasted that she had taken charge at a road accident and saved a man's life. On another occasion, she had kept calm and saved youngsters at a fireworks display when some fireworks had exploded too near to the children. The result had sent everyone, except Hilda, into hysterics and panic. She had actually received an award for her efforts on that occasion.

Apart from the first aid classes, there were various church activities and the golf club and the bowling club. The bowling club dances especially were always well supported.

The McFarlanes hadn't turned up at the meeting. Every one had been very busy, so it had taken a while to organise a time that fitted with most diaries. In the end it was inveritable that someone wouldn't be able to make it, and this time it was the McFarlanes – they'd had another engagement. But Alice Whitelaw was there. They would rather she had not come. She had a habit of appearing unexpectedly at doors, her huge mass of hair tumbling untidily down. That broad freckled face with its sympathetic concentration and smiling determination to be helpful had made many a strong heart cringe.

Much sympathy was felt for Simon Whitelaw. He was a real gentleman who had been an RAF pilot during the war. What he had ever seen in Alice and how he had got entangled with her they could never fathom. Or so they said. In fact they understood only too well how easy it was to get entangled with Alice. She would have done all the running – or plodding, more like – and Simon would have been too polite to refuse her.

Hilda was always trying to organise Alice but without success, which was most frustrating. Hilda enjoyed anything that made her feel useful and important.

She would never in a million years have admitted it but she missed the slums of her youth in Ireland where there was such a close-knit community and everyone needed to help one another. Her late mother had acted as the local midwife in the overcrowded lanes and back streets among which they lived. She had brought every baby into the world. All of them had been born at home, usually in a gas- or oil-lit kitchen. Often, even as a young child, Hilda had gone with her mother and helped by boiling the water, making up the bed with clean sheets, running errands, doing whatever she could. She'd always enjoyed helping out, organising things, being needed. It gave a purpose to her life. But in the wealthy district of Pollokshields, no one ever needed anything.

Hilda didn't know what to make of the Pakistanis. Everything about them was so different, even their dress. She didn't know what standards to apply or how they would fit into the social strata. She felt threatened by their appearance in the square.

Of course Alice didn't feel anything. Alice just blindly plodded on. She was always poking her nose and planting her big feet in somewhere, like the famous incident that happened when she was pregnant.

"All I did," Alice later explained to everyone, "was 'quoo-hoo' across the back gardens to this woman who was shaking a duster at Hilda Malloy's back door. I didn't have a home help and I wondered if I could borrow Hilda's for a couple of hours, that was all. I didn't think she'd mind when I was so tired and so pregnant."

The woman had either ignored her or not heard the "quoo-hoo" call so Alice went round to the front door to rivet her with a desperate stare.

"I'm having a crowd of visitors and I'm in a terrible muddle. I can't do a thing because of this ghastly sore back." Clutching at her back she swelled out her elephantine belly. "You look such a kind person. I thought if I asked you, you'd understand and be only too pleased to come and help me. I'll have a word with Hilda and I'm sure she'll tell you to come."

The woman did not look at all pleased, Alice recalled in that naive perplexed way she had, and Hilda wasn't in.

"But she came," Alice said. "I told her to dust the dining room and hoover the sitting room and mop the kitchen floor. Afterwards I offered what I thought was fair payment but she stamped off in a terrible huff."

Alice went along later to ask Hilda's advice and her outraged neighbour immediately pounced on her.

"How dare you?" Hilda seethed. "How dare you come to my door and bully a guest of mine to come and char for you. I invite a friend from Ireland for a holiday and she's not five minutes in the square when you have the impudence, the downright ignorance, to badger the poor woman to do your housework. Can you imagine how upset you made her feel? Or how embarrassed you've made me feel?"

That evening Alice penned a letter of profuse apology. The next day she sent fruit and flowers. For the rest of the week, she pleaded by telephone to be allowed to entertain the whole Malloy family with a special dinner. She pushed notes through the Malloy door when it refused to open to her agitated knocking.

Eventually, for the sake of peace, they gave in. Hilda's friends could not help laughing but never in front of Hilda because Hilda had no sense of humour.

There were other things that Alice was guilty of that amused no one, of course. Like the way she encouraged gypsies, hawkers, religious maniacs and all sorts of people to come knocking at doors and to pester the residents. It wasn't that anyone wanted to be unkind, especially Hilda. For all her many faults, she was not a cruel woman. Or at least she never meant to be. But this was too much.

"I never ask them to come," Alice complained. "How is it always my fault?"

"Do you do as we do, Alice? Do you just shut the door in their faces?"

"Well . . . no . . ."

"There you are, then!"

She had once even allowed one gypsy into her house and had served her a cup of tea in the kitchen. Later she'd discovered the gypsy had stolen her purse.

"Maybe that'll teach you," everyone said, but no one had much faith in Alice learning a lesson about anything.

At fifty-six, Simon was sixteen years older than Alice but he was far from being the oldest resident in the square. He had been there longer than anyone else, however. Apart from the period when he'd served as an RAF officer, he had lived in his bungalow since he was a young unmarried man.

Mrs Bell, a widow from the bungalow called Rose View, was the oldest – well into her eighties – and had known Simon's father and mother before they died.

"Quiet, hard-working people," she told everyone.

Now she quavered, "I don't know what the square is coming to. I just don't know any more."

"Don't you worry," Joe Malloy said. "We'll look after the square. That's what we're here for." He was swaggering around with a bottle of whisky in a hand like a hairy shovel. "Everybody got a drink now?"

He had an aggressive voice that his Irish accent did nothing to soften. At one time his body had been a square box of hard muscle; now it was melting into fat. Fat bulged out of his collar. Fat wobbled inside his shirt and over the top of his trousers. But he had a spring to his step despite his fat and his fifty-nine years and, although his hair was steely grey, it was still thick and curly.

His wife's hair was her best feature too – a white crown that sparkled with a professional blue rinse. Hilda was big-bosomed but firmly corseted and she sailed behind her husband with a box of chocolates on a little gold tray.

"Would anyone care for an after-dinner mint? They're Ferguson's own make. Frightfully expensive of course, but I always think it's worth spending money to get the best, don't you? It always pays in the end. I said that to Kate the other day. She happened to be with me when I was buying a raincoat. I decided on an Aquascutum. 'I know it's a lot of money for a raincoat, darling,' I said, 'but it's such a good make'. And after all, my hat was expensive so the coat didn't cost all that much more."

Hilda's female friends and acquaintances usually clung valiantly to expressions of fascination, admiration, scintillation and utter agreement when she spoke like this, while at the same time suffering agonies of jealousy. They hated Hilda Malloy for constantly tormenting them about how much money she was able to spend on clothes and entertaining and how many important people she knew. It didn't help to know that Hilda had come from nothing. Her father had been a labourer in Londonderry and her mother had scrubbed out pubs in her spare time between acting as an untrained and unpaid midwife. Hilda was at the apex of the ladder that most of them were intent on climbing. Hilda Malloy had acquired everything in life their circle considered worth having. She had money and a husband with a secure position – that was, he was sure of continuing to make more money. She had a claim to fame – she had won medals at first aid and awards from the Corporation for services to the community. Their house had the best of both worlds. It was old enough to be solid and substantial with large, high-ceilinged rooms, but because Joe Malloy had a builder's business, every improvement and modernisation that could be made had been made. The kitchen was an American-style dream, white and streamlined, and it boasted what surely must have been the biggest fridge and deep freeze in Pollokshields. There was a serving hatch from the kitchen to the dining room and a folding wall that could open right up between the morning room and the sitting room, and the sitting room had a really professional-looking bar.

The other houses, although sometimes referred to as villas,

were still just bungalows. Simon had had the attics in his bungalow made into bedrooms and dormer windows added, and a smart conservatory built. He had a well-established tobacconist's, paper shop and confectioner's in town but a shop was somehow not, of course, in the same class as an expanding company like Joe Malloy's with a board of directors.

"Any more gin for the girls?" Joe asked and strutted back to the bar for another bottle.

In the silence while the glasses were being watchfully replenished, Alice suddenly giggled.

"It seems a bit daft. I mean, us meeting like this."

Joe screwed an orange-peel face towards her. He had already consumed two or three pre-dinner whiskies, several glasses of dinner wine, a couple of liqueurs, and two whiskies with his guests. Purple veins criss-crossed his nose and cheeks.

"It's you that's bloody daft, Alice!"

"Well, what's the point of it? What can we do?"

"Isn't that what I've invited everyone here to discuss, eejut!" Joe's gravelly laugh scraped across every nerve in the room.

His wife winced. For all her expensive belongings and fancy talk, Hilda could never conceal the fact that she was embarrassed by the streak of coarseness that betrayed Joe's working-class background. She believed she had managed to keep this secret of hers. Of course, Joe always tried to twist his origins into an advantage, another source of boasting and pride.

"I make no secret of the fact that I've come from nothing," Joe often boasted to all and sundry. "I'm a self-made man and proud of it."

That in fact was not strictly true. He had started at Brown the builder's as a labourer and worked his way up to manager. When Brown, an old bachelor with not a relative in the world, had died and left Joe the firm, it had helped considerably.

He banged the bottle of whisky down on the bar and selected a cigar. While he was lighting it his wife pounced on the box and began plying the men with its contents.

"Joe says they're hand-rolled Havanas. I know nothing about cigars and cigarettes because of course I'm a non-smoker, but I'm told they're the best in the world and frightfully expensive.

Joe happened to pick up a few that last time we popped over to Mexico, or was it Cuba? We went somewhere different anyway."

"Well . . ." Alice said, "to get back to the Pakistanis. I hope nobody is planning to be unkind."

"Unkind? Unkind, did you say?"

Mr Bierce suddenly spoke up. Or rather roared up, making Sissy, his timid mouse of a wife, wince and shrink into herself. "If I had my way, I'd string every dirty stinking nigger in Britain up by their filthy black throats."

"Why do you always talk like that?" Alice really wanted to know. Mr and Mrs Bierce lived across at the other side of the square and she had been struggling to psychoanalyse Mr Bierce for years. It made her feel genuinely upset to think of all the unhappy, bloodthirsty thoughts that battled around in Mr Bierce's head like a pain that was never soothed. If he had his way he would decapitate every "long-haired lout" in the country. He would shoot every politician. He would hang every criminal. He would birch every child. He would run every Jew out by the scruff of the neck. His pet hate beyond all doubt, however, was people of a different colour from himself.

Alice said, "Surely you must have suffered something terrible in your childhood to make you feel so twisted and bitter."

"Alice, please," Simon appealed, and then turned to Joe. "What had you in mind?"

Joe knocked back another whisky before commencing in a slurred voice, "Right you are, Simon, old son. Time to get down to business."

# Eleven

First there had been Anver's mendhi, or hen night. That was quite good because there was lots of dancing. But next day, the shad, or wedding, depressed Rasheeda. Poor Anver sat cross-legged on a satin cushion on the floor of the Gorbals sitting room, dressed in a scarlet lenga beautifully embroidered and edged with gold. Her face was heavily veiled. She was sobbing loudly because she was leaving her family.

All the female members of the family and all their female friends sat cross-legged around her on coloured cushions. The room was packed solid. First there was the mikah, or ceremony, with the molvi, the priest, and after Anver had taken her vows and said "I do", the molvi went to the next room where all the men, including the groom, had gathered. There the molvi would go through the ritual with the groom.

After the wedding the bride and groom sat while everyone filed past and gave them money. After that, the men all went out to a private room in a restaurant for the wedding meal. All the women had to wait in their separate room until the men returned before they could go to the restaurant. But the most depressing and upsetting part of the whole event was at the end of the wedding when there was the rucksati, the formal giving away of the bride by her father. Everybody in Anver's family was in tears then. Except her big proud father.

As was the custom an aunt or cousin from the bride's family went home with the bride and groom to stay overnight with them. The next day there was the vahina, the party given by the groom's side. Then the bride and groom came back to stay for a night at the bride's family home, before eventually returning to settle in their own house.

As well as feeling depressed by the whole business, Rasheeda seethed with resentment. She resented the swagger of the men, the way they ignored the women and went off to enjoy themselves, leaving the women to wait for what seemed an age at their convenience. She resented – no, more than that – she hated Anver's husband. He was so old. A weed of a man with moist lips and shifty eyes. What on earth had Uncle Mirza and Aunty Shafiga been thinking of, giving Anver away to somebody like that? They were ruining Anver's life. The man had a good business, but so what?

She prayed that her mother and father would never do such a thing to her. Even if they arranged a marriage to a man who was handsome as well as rich, she would have none of it. The mere idea of being given away like a parcel to a man who was not of her own choice threw her into a panic. To be tied to someone that she'd not had the opportunity to choose with freedom and love was anathema to her. It would be like putting her into a straitjacket. Or suffocating her, or condemning her to a slow death. She couldn't bear to thing of such a thing. She'd kill herself rather than allow anyone to make such choices for her.

She slipped away early from the restaurant where the women had been having the wedding meal because she'd arranged to meet Russell. Nobody noticed her go.

"Oh Rasheeda," he greeted her with his usual eagerness and sense of wonder. "How beautiful you look. You take my breath away."

"I hate being dressed like this," she said impatiently. "I'd far rather be wearing western clothes."

"You'd look lovely in them as well. But not as wonderful as you look right now in all those beautiful colours and spangles and bangles." Overcome for a moment, he shook his head. "You're so exotic, so different from anyone I've ever known in my life. You're magic. Sheer magic. Sometimes I look at you and I think I must be dreaming."

Rasheeda laughed and linked arms with him. They were in Queen's Park, walking up towards where a towering flagpole marked the highest area of the park.

He put his arm around her waist and held her close. They'd

come to this area of the park before and knew how private it could be if they sheltered from view behind some bushes. There they sat, close together on the grass.

Russell said, "Promise you won't laugh at me, Rasheeda. I want to say something very serious. At least, it's serious to me."

She lay back on the grass and gazed up at him.

"I won't laugh. I promise."

He paused awkwardly, then said with sudden firmness, "Rasheeda, I know we haven't known each other very long but that doesn't matter to me. The truth is I love you. One day I want you to be my wife. I know I won't have any money or a job for a few years yet. I'll have to go to university and take my degree. But we can see more of each other when you go there too. And then . . ."

She pulled his head down until her mouth was silencing him.

Eventually, after a long, passionate kiss, she let go of him and said, "I love you too, Russell, and now I'll look forward to going to university because I'll be closer to you there. It'll be wonderful to be free of the silly rules and regulations about the sexes that we have at the Academy."

"And will you marry me, Rasheeda? Will you wait for me?"

She gave him one of her enchanting smiles.

"Until the end of time."

He grinned down at her. "A few years will do fine, thanks. I can't wait until the end of time."

"It must be our secret though, Russell." Her voice acquired an edge of anxiety. "I don't want anyone to spoil our hopes and dreams."

"To me, they're not just hopes and dreams, Rasheeda. As far as I'm concerned, our plan to marry is a practical reality."

"Yes, but you know how I've explained about the ways of my family. They'd never allow it, Russell. It'll have to be our secret. Then, when the time comes and we both have our degrees and get jobs, we can just slip away to a register office. We can marry without them knowing. After that it'll be too late for anyone to do anything about it." She entwined her arms around his neck. "My own dearest sweetheart, I can't bear the thought of anyone coming between us. I do love you. I'd die if anyone took me away from you."

He nursed her in his arms, kissed her head and face, her neck.
"Darling Rasheeda, nobody could ever take you away from me. I wouldn't let them."

She was full of love for him but she suddenly felt aware of their youth and helplessness. Innocence too. As he continued to kiss and caress her with mounting passion, other thoughts and fears began troubling her. She knew very little about sex and how one became pregnant. He wasn't much older than her and she wondered if he was any wiser. They didn't get taught such things at school and her mother had never broached the subject.

The girls at school often whispered together about boys and how their mothers had told them that doing "dirty things" with boys would get them into serious trouble. She guessed they meant they would get pregnant. At the same time, she couldn't feel that there could be anything dirty in anything that happened between Russell and herself. Everything was beautiful between then. She melted into him with love and felt at one with him. Then suddenly he drew back and rolled away.

"Oh Rasheeda, I wish we were married now."

"Is something wrong?" she asked anxiously. "You do love me, don't you?"

"You know I do. Too much perhaps."

"How can anyone love too much?" she laughed, light-hearted with relief.

"You know how your men always say they respect women. I've heard your father and Bashir say that. Well, I want everyone to know that I respect you. I don't want anything to happen to you."

"You mean, get pregnant?" she asked.

"Yes. There's always the risk if we go too far."

"I want lots of babies. Lots of wee Russells."

"And I want lots of wee Rasheedas. But not until after we're married. Can you imagine what your family would say and do if anything happened just now?" It was, of course, unthinkable.

"That's why I said we must always be careful to keep our love secret, Russell."

He nodded and sat up. She longed to pull him down again and plead with him to go on kissing her and caressing her. But she loved him and didn't want to make more difficulties for him. She could see he was trying hard to be restrained and do the right thing. She loved him all the more for it.

He got up and put out a hand to help her. She grasped his hand and sprung to her feet.

"It's time I went back now anyway. The wedding meal will be over. Soon they'll all be on their way home."

"Do you want me to take you back to the restaurant, or straight to the square?"

"I'll just go home and say I had a headache or something, and had to leave early."

"I wish we didn't need to be so secretive and tell so many lies."

"I know. I wish I could be like a real Glasgow girl and let everyone know I was going out with you and everyone would be pleased and happy for me."

"Maybe once we're married and your family see how happy we are together, they'll be happy for us."

They began walking down the grassy bank. Rasheeda sighed. "No, they'll never speak to me again. They'll think it's terrible. The worst thing in the world. And they will be so hurt."

"Oh, surely it won't be as bad as that. I mean, they know me. Surely they'd realise that all I'd ever want to do is look after you and make you happy."

She sighed again. For a few minutes at least, she felt sad. He, with centuries of Western culture behind him, could never fully understand the very different ways of the East, the ways of her family.

"If only it was as simple as that." She tried to shake the sadness away with a toss of her head. "But never mind, you and I are happy." She laughed. "I'm so happy, I'm walking on air. I'm so happy, I want to dance."

She broke away from him and twirled around, head back, arms outstretched. He stood entranced, watching her. He'd never seen anything so beautiful. The scene literally took his breath away. The green grass, the tall trees and the brilliantly coloured vision sparkling in the centre of everything like an angel.

She began running ahead of him, laughing and he, laughing too, ran after her. It was only when they reached the park gate at the corner of Pollokshaws Road and Balvicar Street that they slowed down. They walked along Pollokshaws Road side by side, not touching, but longing to touch.

"Imagine," he said, "that we're going home – to our own house, and you're going to make my tea."

"Here," she interrupted, laughing, "I'll have none of that. You make your own tea."

"OK. I'll make the tea. You wash up afterwards. Share and share alike. We split the work fifty-fifty. OK?"

"OK."

"That's if you're out at work as well."

"And what if I'm in the house all day looking after all the wee Russells and Rasheedas and I'm exhausted?"

"Then I say to you – sit down and rest, Rasheeda. I'm here now. I'll see to everything. OK?"

She smiled round at him. "OK."

"Then after our tea, I put the children to bed and we both relax and watch television."

"With me sitting on your knee."

"Yes, and eventually we go to bed together."

"Oh yes please." She laughed, and he laughed too, both feeling excited at the thought.

"And I make love to you. I go all the way. And eventually we both go to sleep, wrapped in each other's arms."

"Promise me it'll come true, Russell," she said, serious now.

"I promise. I promise. We'll always be together. Always."

"Until the end of time?"

"Until the end of time."

# Twelve

"When neighbours come to visit with us, do not forget the Scottish tea," Sharif reminded the women.

A plate of cakes and a plate of biscuits was also important. It was the Glasgow custom. This he had learned in the Gorbals. In the Gorbals much cake and many biscuits were eaten. He had discovered too that minced beef and mashed potatoes and fish and chips were popular. (Oh, how often he'd longed for royal chicken and almond sauce. His wife, Anjum, had her dream too. She often spoke longingly about mango ice cream and milk balls made in a syrup.)

So far Mrs Alice Whitelaw was the only person to come to his house and say hello. He had seen many people walk from their houses. He had called to the mother of his daughters in great excitement.

"Quickly, be ready with the Scottish tea!"

But the people in the square had disappeared into the big villa to visit with the other immigrant family.

On his way to work, he had passed one or two neighbours. The mother of his daughters and Noor Jahan and Zaida had gone to the shops and they too had seen people.

He had warned his family, "Remember, don't smile or talk or make eye contact. It's immodest."

Bashir often contradicted him in this. "Och, that's no' the way. They'd get on much better if they smiled and said hello."

Bashir should not contradict him but he was a good man and he meant well. Eastern women were naturally shy. Except Rasheeda. Rasheeda was a big worry. For a Muslim woman she didn't behave properly.

No one had made a move except Mrs Alice Whitelaw. When

they had their first visit, Rasheeda had done wrong. She had made Pakistani tea.

Now he relaxed in his kitchen. It was warm with a large fire and his family around. Zaida had brought the gramophone from the sitting room and she was playing music from a Pakistani picture. Every Sunday afternoon in town, a small picture house showed Indian and Pakistani films. Often he took the family. It was most enjoyable. In India and Pakistan, cinema-going was a favourite pastime.

He sang along with the record in his high nasal voice as he played with Shah Jahan on the floor in front of the fire. Shah Jahan tottered towards him and with much squealing of delight, chug-chugged his wispy white beard. He continued to sing. Also he jerked his head from side to side. Shah Jahan jerked too and laughed and cried out the Pakistani word for mother's father, "Nanna! Nanna!"

Noor Jahan had the sewing machine on the table. She was making a new qamiz and trousers for Zaida. If Zaida passed her Higher examinations she would go to university. For this she must look neat.

Anjum put several teaspoons of tea into a saucepan with water and sugar and boiled it up. Another saucepan was used to boil milk. Into a large teapot she strained the sweet tea mixture. Finally into the teapot she poured the boiled milk.

"Come, Rasheeda," Anjum said. "Fetch the teacups from the cupboard. We'll drink tea."

Sharif sat up at the table and savoured the hot comforting liquid. Soon he would have to go out to work. Every day he had to walk many streets and climb many stairs. This was terrible. He was an old man. He had rheumatic pains in his knees. He became very tired. It was no good. But he needed the money.

There had been Noor Jahan's wedding. He had given her a very good dowry. On her husband, Bashir, he had showered many presents – a transistor radio, a typewriter, a camera, a telescope. Noor Jahan had received from Bashir's parents golden earrings and bangles and a most beautiful golden necklace.

He and Anjum had given her many yards of satin. She made the lenga, or long circular skirt, in which she was married. Noor

Jahan looked most beautiful. Before the wedding she and her sisters and Anjum had wailed and wept. He too had wept. His heart had been very sore. A wedding was a most sad occasion.

Noor Jahan had gone to stay with her husband's people. But she had not stayed long. He had been happy when she returned with Bashir. He told her, "You are not my daughter. You are my son."

This was the ultimate expression of love and pride in a daughter.

Now they were together in a nice place. But his old knees were stiff and painful. He had to go to bed and rest every day.

Before he went out, Mrs Alice Whitelaw came to visit again. He and his family received her in the sitting room. She brought a large bunch of flowers from her garden. This was most kind.

"We thank you too much, Mrs Whitelaw," he said.

"Oh, you might as well call me Alice," she replied. "Everyone else does."

The mother of his daughters quietly slipped out of the room. She was self-conscious and ashamed because she could speak only a few words of English. Also she was a very timid, very frightened woman. She often told him this.

"I am frightened in this country."

He apologised to Alice. "You excuse please. My wife is frightened."

"Och, nobody could be frightened of a silly big ass like me!"

A burst of laughter caught him by surprise and unsettled his glasses. He pushed at them. He tucked them firmly round his ears. He took a grip of himself and eyed his family sternly. Zaida was giggling shyly behind her hands. Rasheeda had flung back her head and was laughing immodestly. Noor Jahan's chuckle gurgled from her palate. When Noor Jahan laughed or talked, her tongue kept slipping up behind her teeth as it would to make Urdu sounds. Of all his daughters, Noor Jahan, wife of Bashir, was the least westernised.

His family subdued, he returned his attention to Alice. She lit a cigarette and puffed at it. He tried to remember that she was kind. She was their friend.

"Rasheeda," he said. "We give Alice tea."

"No, please," Alice said hastily. "I don't feel like any tea today."

"I give you the tea!" he insisted.

"No, really. No thanks."

In exasperation he thumped the air with his clenched fists and stamped his foot. "But it's my duty!"

"Oh." Alice's face fell. "All right, if you feel that you must."

"You no' worry, please," he informed her stiffly. "We give you the Scottish tea."

"Last time Rasheeda made a mistake," Zaida explained. "We're sorry." With lowered eyes Noor Jahan edged towards the door after Rasheeda. "Excuse me." Sharif spoke to Zaida in Urdu. "I must get ready for work. So too must Bashir. It is good for me that he works late shift in the shop and can give me a lift. Explain to Alice why Bashir and I must go. But tell her that she is always welcome in our house."

Zaida answered in Urdu, "I will tell her. Perhaps she will help me with my English studies. Will it be fitting to ask her?"

"No, no, Zaida!" he corrected sharply. "You may only tell of your difficulty. I'm worried about my English, you can say. But she is your elder. You must be careful not to sound cheeky. I will ask her to help you."

He turned to Alice.

"You help Zaida with English studies, OK?"

Then he went through to the kitchen for his Corporation jacket and cap. The jacket was of ill-fitting, heavy navy-blue material with silver buttons. It was shabby but warm.

Baby Shah Jahan struggled to his feet. Then he tottered forward.

"Nanna! Nanna!"

Sharif lifted the plump little figure and shook him with rough affection.

"Nanna must to go work." Then he pointed to the corner near the back door.

"See Nanna's new spade?"

He had bought the spade earlier that day. It had a long red handle but the blade was green. At present his garden was a wilderness. Many weeds choked the earth. These he would patiently dig out.

"How you dig in the garden?" Anjum had queried. "You have sore knees."

"I will dig!" he had shouted angrily. "I will plant seeds. We'll have many flowers."

It would be difficult. This he knew. But by the will of Allah he would succeed. This also he knew.

He dreamed of planting herbs as well as flowers. Most of the medicines he had used in his chemist's shop in his homeland had been made with herbs. In his homeland he had cured many people by reciting from the Qur'an. The people they had come to him. They had told him of their pain and of their trouble. He had touched them and breathed on them and recited the Qur'an.

"If you have faith," he had told them, "you will be cured."

He gave them good medicine made of herbs, as well as prayers. He could grow herbs in his new garden. He would make medicine to help his sore knees. He would help many people. In the Gorbals, Pakistani people came to him.

"My child is sick," they said. "Please will you help him?"

He had friends in Pakistan send him herbs or bring them if they visited Scotland. But sometimes he had none. Then he breathed on the patient and recited the Qur'an. He prayed most earnestly.

Sometimes Allah was merciful. Other times Allah would shrug and say, "I did not will it to cure this child."

It is written – "Such is the will of Allah. He does what He pleases."

He said to Shah Jahan, "Nanna's spade will prepare the earth. Nanna will have flowers of many colours. Herbs and plants and trees also."

Rasheeda said, "Och, daddy, you'll no' be able to grow Pakistani plants and trees in this climate. Fancy having passion fruit and mango and eucalyptus here!"

"You're far too cheeky to your elders." Sharif raised his voice sharply to her. "You're getting far too many of the Glasgow ways. It is no' good. Go at once. Take the tea tray. Serve our guest as you have been instructed."

Rasheeda sighed but did as she was told.

"She is a worry, that one," he told Anjum.

"Yes, it is the truth," his wife agreed. "It is the fault of the Glasgow school. There Rasheeda mixes with boys."

"No, no, she is taught with girls only."

"I know, but coming out of school, they are all together. I wish we had never left Pakistan."

It was Sharif's turn to sigh.

"In Pakistan could we have given the husband of our daughter a transistor radio, a typewriter, a camera and a telescope? But most importantly, could we have given our family such a good education?"

There had been much poverty and suffering in his homeland. He had been considered middle class there. But to look on the poverty and suffering of others had been terrible. Often he had prayed to Allah, "Show me the way to help these people."

He had not charged poor people for medicines. He had asked high prices from people with money. This had worked well.

He put his grandson, Shah Jahan, down.

"I go to work now." He placed his Corporation lamplighter cap on his head. The cap was navy blue and had a hard round top. It dwarfed his small bearded face.

Outside he could hear Maq shouting roughly and laughing loudly with the Glasgow boys. They were running around in Pollokshields Lane kicking a ball. He thought it was good that Maq was fitting in so well and making friends with Glasgow boys. And so he smiled and nodded in the Glasgow way at Maq and his friends as he passed by.

# Thirteen

That first meeting at Joe and Hilda's had left Alice more anxious than ever. Not that much had happened – except too much drinking – or been decided.

She didn't look worried or anxious. Appearances could be so deceptive, she often thought. Even when she felt ill, she never looked ill because she appeared so big and buxom.

Simon often said, "I wish I could be more like you. Nothing ever bothers you. You sail through life as calm and placid as you like, blissfully unaware of the wake of chaos and disruption you leave behind."

It seemed so strange that people could think she was calm and placid when she never felt calm or placid at all. It always fascinated her how different people could be behind their outside masks. Hilda Malloy, for instance, could be a pain in the neck, but when Alice had been ill, Hilda had done her shopping for her and even brought in hot soup and made her eat it to help her get back her strength.

Simon of all people, Alice thought, ought to know what his own wife was like behind her outward placid appearance. He knew she tried not to read newspaper stories of death or cruelty, especially cruelty towards children. If there was a harrowing programme on television, she made excuses to leave the room.

Every time Simon took her out to the cinema, it was to see a war picture. They were the only films he seemed to like. Especially those featuring the RAF. He had bought a television set for her sake, though, which she appreciated. She loved to watch romantic films. She went meekly with Simon to his war pictures because he didn't enjoy going on his own. He was first and foremost a family man. He just lived for her and Russell.

She warmed towards him because of this. At times they were very close, especially at the bowling club dances. They always made love afterwards and she really enjoyed it. She was a very affectionate woman and could never resist any human contact. She loved touching people and being touched. It was a constant battle to control her need for affection and her affectionate urges. Someone, anyone, only needed to say a kind word and she teetered on the verge of enveloping them in her arms.

If she met a woman friend or neighbour in the street, she would link arms with them. She did the same with men for years until Hilda Malloy said, "I know you don't mean any harm, Alice, but what will people think if they see you hanging on to Joe? The minister, for instance. Oh, and by the way, did I tell you that Joe and I entertained Mr and Mrs Beckenridge last night? Mr Beckenridge is the chairman of our local Conservative party."

Not long ago Hilda had been sitting in the doctor's waiting room talking in an affected voice to a tweedy, "county-looking" woman, probably Mrs Beckenridge. Alice's face had lit up with pleasure as she surged affectionately towards Hilda. Her feet faltered until she stopped awkwardly halfway across, feeling like a mountainous wart. Hilda had seen her but had jerked her head quickly away. Hilda looked very smart in her Jaeger coat and expensive hat and gloves. It was understandable that she did not want to be embarrassed by what she regarded as an eccentric neighbour in front of her important friend.

Alice had subsided into a chair opposite, lowered her head and stared down at her feet. She was wearing her slippers, she noticed, much to her own embarrassment. One of her hot flushes – the reason for her visit to the doctor – fired her face and made her sweat profusely. She felt ashamed not only of the old slippers she was wearing, but the faded slacks and the sweater that somehow accentuated her spare tyre. She had meant to change before she came out but had decided at the last moment not to. The doctor's surgery was only a few minutes away and the doctor was a comfortable old friend. There did not seem any point in going to all the bother of getting dressed up.

Later that evening, Hilda had telephoned and chattered on in a very bright, friendly way but made no mention of seeing her at the doctor's surgery.

"You must come for coffee tomorrow, Alice. It so happens I'm not doing anything important so I thought I might as well have a few of the neighbours in."

In her own way she's sorry for hurting me, Alice thought, and affection for Hilda brimmed up again. Alice had tremendous fellow feeling for anyone who had faults and weaknesses, or who made mistakes.

She was beginning to suspect that she was developing fellow feeling for the Pakistanis, too. She hoped the neighbours at the coffee morning wouldn't rant on about the Pakistanis again.

At the meeting Hilda said, "I'm really worried, Alice. Mr Bierce insists that Pakistanis are most unhygienic. He says they'll encourage vermin. The square could be overrun with rats in no time."

Alice shuddered at this. She was particularly terrified of rats or mice. Long-buried memories of wicked little eyes luminous in the dark of the railway bothy returned to torment her. She remembered the busy squeak-squeak of endless agonising nights.

Mr Bierce's shoulders hunched tightly. "They're vermin themselves. I heard about a house over the other side of town. The Pakis who lived in it used to keep live animals and kill them just before they ate them. Apparently the place was like a bloody slaughterhouse. The neighbours reported it to the SSPCA and the sanitary department. Eventually the Sanitary Inspector cleared out the whole crowd of horrible bastards."

There was a pause while the picture of household pets being cruelly slaughtered sunk in.

"Mr Bierce," Alice protested. "The Ali family are not like that. I've met them and they are very nice people. I'm perfectly sure they'd never . . ."

Mrs Bell interrupted with a quavering, "Oh dear, what can we do?"

It was decided that Joe, who played golf with local lawyers and councillors and knew other influential people, would ask around and discover exactly what action could be taken. Perhaps the Sanitary Inspector could be involved.

"We'd better all get together again as soon as possible . . ."

Alice's face immediately brightened.

"You'd all be very welcome to meet in my house." There was nothing Alice liked better than entertaining friends. "Yes, come to supper. We'd love to have you, wouldn't we, Simon?"

Simon agreed with less enthusiasm and it was finally arranged that everyone would come a few days later.

"Alice," Simon said once they had returned home, "it's bad enough having to work myself into the ground every day for you and Russell, without having to feed the whole square. Why didn't you just say to come later for a cup of tea and some biscuits? Think of the extra expense you'll have now."

The mention of extra expense deflated Alice's balloon of happiness. Money had always been a terrible worry. Simon was very mean with her. "If you can't afford a thing, don't buy it," he always insisted, which she supposed was fair enough. She did tend to be a bit reckless with money. Extravagant, in fact.

It could be that her extravagance worried Simon so much that it caused his meanness with her. After all, he wasn't mean with Russell. Or anyone else that she'd ever noticed.

It wasn't so much that she was extravagant with herself. She just loved to provide Simon and Russell and anyone that came to the house with the best of everything. She made huge pots of soup and thick steaks cooked in butter and Scotch trifles reeking with sherry. She always had different cheeses and coffee and lots of chocolate biscuits. She had to admit, though, that not only did she love to see everyone else enjoy their food, she enjoyed eating it herself. She particularly relished it when she knew she could not afford it.

Their friends talked about poorer people of other districts.

"There's no excuse for people getting into debt. If they budgeted what money they had . . . if they did without . . . if they saved . . . but oh no, not them. Directly they have anything they can't spend it quick enough . . ."

Alice did not know if there was any excuse for being reckless with money but she could certainly understand it.

She remembered when she was a child, there was often nothing in the house to eat. Sometimes her mother would send her to different shops with notes begging for credit. More often she was primed to plead verbally. She remembered her mother's strained unhappy face.

"Just keep smiling like a good girl, Alice, and say, 'Could you please give me bread, margarine, jam, tea, milk, sugar and two dozen chocolate biscuits. My mammy isn't very well just now. She couldn't come and she was afraid I'd lose the money but she'll pay you herself at the weekend . . .'"

The speech and the list of groceries varied but her mother always said, "Just keep smiling, Alice. Smile like a good girl, Alice." And the expensive luxury – the chocolate biscuits – were always included.

After the awful deprivation of having nothing at all, there was a need, a craving, to over-indulge. It was as if they were compelled to stock up inside with as many good things as possible while they could, in case the chance never came to them again.

Nothing would ever taste so perfect, nothing could ever be appreciated so keenly and with such gratitude as that food, especially those chocolate biscuits gobbled greedily one after the other. Alice still ate with intense appreciation and thankfulness.

She had always loathed the begging for credit of course and the continuous trek from one shop to another with her mother's purse robbing Peter to pay Paul. The strange thing was that she had never managed to free herself from this nightmare pattern. Even now in Pollokshields, she was still on the credit treadmill.

She had an account at Daggerman's, a wholesale warehouse in town which sold everything including groceries. She had to live off the warehouse grocery department for two or three weeks and use the cash from her housekeeping money to pay the last bill. Then the next lot of groceries would come due and she would suffer agonising suspense and worry trying to scramble up enough money again. And so it went on – a never-ending vicious circle.

Yet she knew that on this occasion, as on the others, as soon as she managed to pay one bill and filled her larder with more food, the relief would be intense, she would thank God and she would be happy. And she would enjoy another eating binge. No wonder she was overweight.

She would have to go to the warehouse and get food for the neighbours coming. How else would she be able to buy a turkey or a chicken and all the trimmings to feed them? The money Simon gave her would barely pay for the basics. This would mean a much bigger bill than usual. She felt a momentary flutter of panic but soothed it away by thinking of the fabulous meal she would have. What a party it would be! What could be happier than a house full and brimming over with friends?

"All I hope is," Simon said, "that something can be done about the Pakistanis. I can't afford to lose money on this property. And that's what'll happen, believe me. I think I'll go straight to bed. I'm exhausted with worry."

Alice had completely forgotten about the reason for her supper party. She had even been thinking of inviting the Alis.

# Fourteen

The whole family was delighted with the flowers. Alice felt quite important, as if she had achieved something special in producing the gift. Usually a present of flowers only stimulated a quick sniff and an automatic cry of, "Darling, you shouldn't have. Aren't they gorgeous." Then the flowers were whipped away.

Instead the Pakistanis brought a vase of water from their kitchen into the sitting room. The vase was green and decorated with hand painting, on top of which silver glistened like a Christmas tree. They seemed to like sparkly, tinselly things and bright colours.

While the flowers were being arranged in the vase with much talk and interest and everyone was milling around like a rainbow in their coloured clothes, touching the flowers and admiring them, she noticed another odd-looking ornament on the mantelpiece. It was flat and pale green, decorated with pink painted flowers. She pointed to it and asked, "What's that?"

Zaida picked it up and with a quick tug opened it into a little cross-legged stand.

"It is a Raehill," she explained. "It is the stand for our holy book. It holds our Qur'an while we say our prayers."

Alice put out her hands for it but Zaida immediately shrunk back and returned the Raehill to its place on the mantelpiece.

"It is the plastic." She pushed at her spectacles, her voice attempting to sound casual and normal. "Once the Raehill, it was made of wood. Now everything is the plastic, even in Pakistan."

"Oh yes?" Alice smiled and feigned interest. Inside she felt deeply hurt. She suspected that because she was a Christian, they would consider her an unbeliever and were afraid her touch would defile their Raehill and their holy book.

Hopelessness swamped her. How could she or anyone else have any kind of relationship with these people, if they felt like this? But what about some Christians? Wasn't there a sect called the Closed Brethren among Scottish fisher folk? Many of them would not even eat with or speak to members of their own family who had not joined the Brethren. Then there were the Jehovah's Witnesses who believed no one would be saved. According to Jehovah's Witnesses, everyone was going to burn in hell except them. Many Catholics did not think much of Protestants and vice versa.

When the excitement about the flowers had settled down, Zaida told her how worried she was about her English.

"What a shame," she sympathised, and Zaida bowed her head.

"You speak the truth. I have shame."

"Oh, I didn't mean that . . ." Alice was taken aback. "That's just a saying we have – an ejaculation. You know what that is. No? Well, I mean, I didn't mean to say you had shame. I suppose I meant – what a pity. I mean, I was just sorry to hear that you were worried."

Alice groaned inwardly. There were probably a million sayings in the English language that had come into common usage and British people took for granted, but foreigners would completely misunderstand. It was a crushing thought.

"Maybe I could help," she offered, carefully watching each word. "Russell, my son, has good books and notes and examination papers. Perhaps you could come next door and get them. Come one afternoon and have tea with me. Perhaps Russell could help you. He's very clever."

"Thank you. We would be most pleased."

Alice's mouth remained stretched in a smile but her face emptied of everything except puzzlement. Was Zaida's use of the plural just another little example of her difficulty with the language? Or did she actually mean "we"?

Anyway, arrangements were duly made.

Earlier Zaida's father had mentioned that his wife was afraid. This was another thing that perplexed her. She was so obsessed with her own fears, the thought of the Pakistanis feeling frightened had never entered her head. She decided to ask Zaida about this.

"Your father said your mother was frightened. I don't understand. I mean . . . why should she feel frightened?"

"My mother thinks women are too free here. It is very different where she comes from."

"Hasn't she ever had to manage on her own, go on buses when she had to do any shopping in town? Having to ask for a ticket on a bus or ask for things in shops is one way of mixing and learning the language, I suppose."

"Oh no, my mother could not do such a thing. Our custom is woman never to speak to stranger. Some people are so strict that they are not so free with their relatives even. But my uncle, who is an inspector on the buses, has told my Aunty Shafiga to learn my mother to become more Scottish in her ways."

"I just can't imagine . . ."

"In Pakistan, my mother wear burkah. Would you like to see burkah? I fetch to you from cupboard."

Alice examined the heavy, tentlike garment Zaida produced.

"Can I try it on?"

Rasheeda entered the room as Zaida was struggling on tiptoe to drape the burkah over Alice's head. Alice helped her pull it down, then peered out at both girls through tiny slits for the eyes.

Rasheeda's laughter rejoiced around the room like bells.

"My God, Alice, it's far too wee for you. Your legs are sticking out."

Zaida laughed too but tried to stifle her merriment behind apologetic hands.

Alice was fascinated by how it felt to wear the burkah. It was a dark retreat inside which there was no need to smile. Her face could be forgotten, her cheeks and mouth allowed to sag. No one could see. There was no need to feel conscious of how she looked or to hold her facial muscles at the ready to cope with the ever-changing sophisticated range of expressions western society had learned to acquire.

She tried to imagine what it must be like to be hidden inside this garment for a lifetime, then suddenly to have it ripped away and be exposed in a strange and alien land.

She suddenly understood Mrs Ali's guarded expression and sagging muscles that looked like a bad-tempered scowl, and the self-conscious way she had of rubbing her hand over her face.

Helped by the girls, Alice funnelled the burkah over her head and off. "It's hot in there." Her cheeks were flushed bright crimson and her hair fell down over her eyes. "Phew!" she gasped, parting the curtain of hair with her fingers.

Zaida said, "To be wearing the burkah and to be shut away is to be in purdah."

"It feels more like being in purgatory!"

The girls laughed again and Zaida said, "A friend in Pakistan, she was wearing burkah and boy followed her in street. He was making with the eyes. My friend could see that boy was her brother. But brother could not see her. When my friend say, I am your sister, he was so ashamed."

This fascinated Alice.

"It's a wonder anyone ever manages to get married, or even find a boyfriend or girlfriend."

"Oh, we never have boyfriends. Our parents arrange marriage of son or daughter with other parents. Sometimes young couple never see each other before wedding."

Alice's eyes widened with horror and sympathy.

"That's terrible!"

Zaida looked surprised.

"Why you say that's terrible?"

"Well, I mean . . . It is terrible, isn't it? It should be your choice. You should choose your own husband, shouldn't you?" Her expression meandered between earnest condolence and polite smiling enquiry.

Zaida pushed her spectacles up to gaze curiously at her.

"How can this be? Is it possible that I am wiser and more experienced in these things than my parents? My mother and father love me and know what is best for me. I trust my parents."

"Fancy!"

Alice's mind boggled at the thought of who her drunken old dad would have chosen for her

"But . . . but I mean . . . What if, after the marriage, the young couple find they're incompatible? What if they don't get on well together?"

Zaida shrugged.

"If there be something wrong with a wife, the husband can soon teach her proper ways. The wife, she will understand and change. Pakistani women are very reasonable."

Alice teetered on the verge of asking what would happen if there were something wrong with a husband but suspected that this line of thought would be beyond Zaida's comprehension.

"When you go to university, you'll be in the same class as white men. What if you take a fancy to one of them? I mean, you're only human . . ."

"I can feel I like that man. But immediately I must say to myself – this is not possible. I must not think of that man."

Rasheeda groaned. "You're as bad as Mammy and Daddy. You're so old-fashioned."

"What do you mean," Zaida cried out. "What is this old-fashioned?"

"Och, never mind," Rasheeda said.

Alice sighed. "It seems a pity in a way. Everybody being so different and not being able to get together."

Zaida spread out her hands.

"We are getting together, you and I. Your family and my family. This is all right. It is only when marriage is in question. For instance, young white man would be Christian. We are Muslim and we could not change. Very seldom any Muslim turn his back on Islam. In Pakistan people no like that. If daughter turn Christian, she must leave home to go to church mission or some missionary people for protection. People say to her, 'How could you leave Islam to become low-caste Christian? We never heard of such a thing, no, not even in our dreams.' They whisper to each other, 'She must have done something very wicked in her home and her family has put her out. No one would leave Islam for any other reason.' And they shout at her, 'God's curse upon you. You have sinned a great sin.' And they exclaim over her defection from the faith of her fathers."

"She keeps forgetting this isn't Pakistan, and this is the 1950s, not the 1850s," Rasheeda said to Alice. "Mammy and Daddy are the same."

Alice lit up a cigarette and puffed at it without shifting her concentrated attention from Zaida's brown bespectacled face. Zaida threw Rasheeda a disapproving look but continued, "If I want to make any love marriage, my parents would be most upset. But if I say I want to marry a white Christian boy . . ." Her eyes widened dramatically. "Oh, it would be terrible. A terrible thing for me."

"Fancy!" Alice allowed all this to sink in for a minute. Then she said, "Of course, I suppose there are lots of arranged marriages in western countries too. I've heard they do it in France. Even right here on our doorstep, there's a bit of matchmaking going on because Joe Malloy and my husband Simon are keen for Kate Malloy and Russell to hit it off."

"Hit it off?" Zaida repeated in astonishment.

"Eh, I mean, well . . . get married eventually, I suppose. They've always been fond of each other. Kate's quite a little tomboy. That means . . . that means, playing with boys, acting and seeming more boyish than girlish. If you know what I mean?"

Zaida had been patiently following every word. Now she waited until Alice plunged on again.

"When Russell was younger he used to play down in the field with a crowd of his pals and Kate used to tag along like a wee dog. If the boys climbed trees, so did she. She was game for anything, Russell used to say. She was the only girl they allowed into their den." Her face screwed up. "Den means . . . you know, the lion's den. Well, it's not that . . . I mean, it can just be any old place where boys like to have as their own. Anyway, Kate's an only child and as far as Joe especially is concerned, the sun just rises and sets on that girl. Long ago Joe said, 'Kate tells me she wants to marry your Russell when she grows up and if that's what she wants, she will!' I laughed at the time and said, 'Maybe Russell will have something to say about that.'"

For no apparent reason, Alice suddenly felt tired and depressed. The coldness and the desolation of the railway bothy sprouted up like a giant tumour from the past and overwhelmed her. The railway lines, overgrown with weeds, rusted and useless, pointed to an empty future. It was as if Simon and her son had never happened. Panic assailed her quite often now. Sometimes she gazed in the mirror at the broadening and sagging flesh of her jaw and the wrinkles spreading out like cobwebs from each eye and she repeated to herself incredulously, "You're forty! You're middle-aged. You've lost your youth. You're getting old."

Soon Russell would leave the nest. That wouldn't be too long now. Soon there would be university for him. She was not important or necessary to him any more. But she still ached to touch him and cuddle him and kiss him as she had done when he was a baby. She controlled the urge, of course.

She had no baby. Nor could she have any others. Her periods had stopped. "Start late, stop early," the old wives' tale said, and as far as she was concerned, it was true.

"Is something wrong, Alice?" Zaida asked. "You look sad. Did I say something cheeky?"

Her mother always said, "Just keep smiling like a good girl . . ."

"No, no," Alice said, smiling. "Nothing's wrong."

# Fifteen

Constance McFarlane walked past the office of the detective agency several times. It was up a close in St Vincent Street, not far from John Smith's bookshop. Smith's was her favourite bookshop and she was a regular customer, both for books and for stationery. It was the oldest bookshop in Scotland, probably in Britain. Will claimed it was the oldest in the world, but sometimes Will's imagination tended to run away with him. Certainly Scotland's national bard, Robert Burns, had shopped there in the early eighteenth century.

She kept adjusting her glasses and pretending to study the books displayed in the window, but all the time her mind was in turmoil. She kept imagining herself going into the close and up the stairs, and actually walking into the office of the detective agency. Her heart raced in panic. But she had to do something. She had to know.

She walked back to the close again and, in a surge of recklessness, entered it and began climbing the stairs. It was shadowy place smelling of age and dampness. The green-tinged brass name plate on a door on the first landing said "Wylie & Baines – Private Detectives". The door had an amber glass top. She rang the bell. No one answered. She tried the handle of the door and it squeaked open.

"Come in," a man's voice called. A dark hall was covered in brown linoleum. There were three doors leading off the hall. One of them was open and she could see a man sitting at a desk. He beckoned to her and, even more nervous now, Constance entered the room. Like the hall, it had brown linoleum and wallpaper that looked as if it has been there since the house was built. The man indicated a chair in front of the desk and she was glad to sit down. Her legs had gone weak.

The man, however, wasn't a bit like any of the tough detectives she'd seen in films. He looked like a perfectly ordinary middle-aged, overweight Glaswegian.He had a bald patch on top of his head. He tipped back in his chair and gave her a fatherly smile.

"And how can I help you, Mrs . . .?"

"McFarlane."

"Mrs McFarlane, I'm Charles Wylie. Would you like a cup of tea? The kettle won't take a minute."

"Oh, no thanks."

"Sure?"

"Yes."

He clasped his hands over his beer belly and gazed at her in silence. Eventually she burst out, "It's about my husband."

"You want us to keep an eye on him and see if he's got a lady friend?"

Startled, she stared back at him. "Something like that, yes."

The chair tipped forward and he picked up a pen. "His name?"

"Ronnie."

"And you live together at . . .?"

"Pollokshields Square."

"And what does your husband do for a living?"

"He's . . ." She flushed and silently chided herself for being so stupid. "He's a travelling salesman of ladies' underwear."

"Uh huh . . . So he's away from home a lot?"

"Yes. I've probably no need for concern. I'm probably just being foolish. But somehow I can't seem to help worrying. He's with women so much, you see. I wish I just knew for certain that there's nothing going on. Just for my peace of mind, you see. But probably there's nothing you can do."

"Of course there's something we can do, Mrs McFarlane. It's our job."

"How . . . I mean . . . will it not be terribly difficult with the kind of job he's in?"

"We have lady assistants. We can tackle any kind of case, I assure you, Mrs McFarlane. And with the utmost discretion."

She wanted to ask him what the lady assistant he would put on the case would be like. Would she be a pretty young woman? Could she trust a lady detective? She was worried about that now. Ronnie had such a charming and persuasive manner. And he liked women so much. Maybe all she was doing was putting more temptation in his way. She felt sick with worry. She wished she'd never come.

She hardly heard the rest of Mr Wylie's questions, and was barely aware of the answers she gave him and what arrangements were made. She kept asking herself, What am I doing?

At last she was returning down the dark stairway and had escaped on to St Vincent Street. She felt on a slippery slope that would end in terrible trouble for herself as much as Ronnie. If he was having an affair, what good would it do her to find out? Would it give her peace of mind? Could she keep her mouth shut about it and go on happily living with Ronnie? There would be no happiness left. Yet she could never leave him. The danger was, of course, that he could leave her. That had always been what she was afraid of.

"Hello Constance, dear."

Oh God, Constance thought. Not Hilda Malloy! But it was – wide-brimmed hat over blue rinse, three strands of pearls, long gloves.

Constance tried to smile, while nervously pushing at her spectacles.

"Hilda, so nice to see you!"

"I'm so glad we bumped into each other like this, Constance. You didn't make it to our last little get-together."

"No, I'm sorry about that."

"Well, you must come to our meeting at Alice's. You'll be getting an invitation."

"Well . . ."

"Now, dear" – Hilda wagged a long, gloved finger – "I think you'd better. I'll have something to say about you if you don't."

Constance went cold with shock. Had Hilda seen her coming out of the detective's close? Of course she must have. Even now, she was only a few feet from the place. Hilda was blackmailing her. Subtly, emotionally, in order to get her own way. Oh God! She gave Hilda a bright smile.

"Well, of course I mean to go to Alice's. I'm very fond of Alice."

"Oh, aren't we all?" Hilda was smiling too. "Aren't we all?"

"Well, I must go. I've some books to pick up at Smith's."

"See you at Alice's, dear."

"Yes, 'bye," Constance called as she rushed away. She nearly passed Smith's, she was so distracted. Just in time, she turned into the shop.

She must try to be sensible. She might be imagining this about Hilda. She was getting really neurotic. Paranoid. It was time she got a grip of herself. Even if Hilda did know about her going to a private detective, so what?

Hilda was an interfering, manipulative do-gooder, that's what. It would be perfectly obvious to Hilda why she was hiring a detective – knowing the circumstances, knowing what a charmer and ladies' man Ronnie was. So what if she dropped a hint – or worse – to Ronnie? Or to anyone else, and it reached Ronnie's ears? He would never forgive her. Never.

No, she wasn't just being neurotic or paranoid. All right, Hilda hadn't actually said anything. But she hadn't needed to. That wagging finger had said it all. Hilda was always after her to join in her stupid coffee mornings, afternoon teas and dinners and soirées and God knows what else that went on in the square. But when Hilda had asked her before, there had not been any wagging finger.

Oh God, she kept thinking. Oh God. She blindly picked up a book. But why should she mind going to Alice's? Alice was somewhat eccentric but there wasn't any harm in her. She mustn't allow this to get out of proportion. Maybe she ought to get out more, mix more with the neighbours. Become more sociable, like Ronnie. Yes, she must keep calm and not allow her silly fears or imagination to run away with her.

She bought a book of poetry, paid for it and emerged somewhat apprehensively from the shop. There was no sign of Hilda. She felt relieved, then worried about herself. The real trouble with her was she'd been overworked for so long. That was it. The school was the toughest in Glasgow. It was one long battle to keep on top of everything. She spent as much time quelling riots as she did teaching. It was getting too much for her, affecting her ability to cope with the rest of her life. Perhaps it was high time she thought seriously of asking for a transfer or even early retirement. Yes, that was definitely the trouble. She was overworked and overstrained. She would have to go to the doctor and get something for her nerves.

Her sudden wave of fatigue and the band of steel tightening around her head confirmed the need for medical help. She was glad to get home to lie down on the sofa.

"Are you all right, Mum?" Emma asked. "You look awful pale."

"I'm a bit overstrained. Things are getting worse at school. All that hassle. It's beginning to get me down."

"Didn't I tell you? You need to get out of that place, Mum. For all the thanks you get, it's just not worth it."

Constance sighed. "I used to think it was."

"It's high time you faced it, Mum. You're not as young as you used to be. You're nearly sixty, for goodness, sake. It's ridiculous for a woman your age to be struggling with a crowd of thugs and tearaways every day. No wonder you're cracking up."

Constance felt a terrible sinking in her heart. But she tried to rally some spirit.

"I'm not cracking up, Emma. I'm only a little tired."

"Mum, you can't fight it all your life."

"Fight what?"

"You know perfectly well what. I'm not daft. I don't know why you worry so much. After all, Dad knows your age."

Constance felt a flush suffuse her face.

"Oh Emma, am I making an awful fool of myself? Mutton dressed as lamb, and all that?"

"No, no." Emma rushed over to the sofa, knelt down beside it and gave her a reassuring hug. "You always look lovely, Mum. Honestly. All I'm saying is I'm sure it wouldn't matter to Dad whether you were wearing your old skirt and cardy or your Dior dress. He'd love you just the same."

"Darling," Constance lovingly stroked Emma's short curls, "you're a very kind and lovely girl. Never mind my problems. Have you found another job yet?"

"Yes. I went for an interview today in Newton Mearns. A doctor and his wife. She's a physiotherapist. They have one girl of two and a half. They seem a very nice couple. And the girl's a sweet wee thing. It'll be daily. That's what I wanted."

"Oh good, dear. That'll mean we'll see more of you."

"Yes, and I'll be able to keep a better eye on you. Make sure you behave yourself."

Constance couldn't help laughing.

"Yes, nanny."

She felt cheered. Her spirits lightened again, although her body still felt heavy.

Emma said, "I'll go and make you a cup of tea."

"Thank you, dear."

Constance sank deeper into the cushions of the sofa, closed her eyes and tried not to think of her crazy visit to the private detective.

# Sixteen

"You were talking to Rasheeda for a long time at the back gate, son," Alice greeted Russell.

He groaned and rolled his eyes. Then he pushed past her to clatter down at the table. She felt hurt.

"What have I said?"

"Oh, Mum, I wish you'd get off my back. You worry about me too much. I'm not a child any more."

"I never said you were. I mean, you come crashing in here and nearly knock me down . . ."

"Oh, for pity's sake! You're always exaggerating. It's ridiculous the way you go on. If it's not one extreme, it's another."

Inside her chest, something rapidly folded up for protection. She smiled and said airily, "Gosh, what a fuss about a perfectly innocent, casual remark. Eat up your soup. It's a cold day, you need something warm inside you."

"You were watching me. I'm a man, remember. I'm sixteen. I can do what I like."

She sighed. "I suppose we all think we know everything when we're young. But Russell, nobody can just do as they like. I mean, there's always other people to be considered."

"You and Dad are smug, middle-aged, middle class and colour prejudiced, that's all."

She flashed up. "As far as I'm concerned you can talk all day to Rasheeda if you like. Only don't blame me if your lunch gets ruined." She subsided as gracefully as she could into a chair and fumbled with a trembling hand for her soup spoon.

Russell grimaced.

"I'm sorry, Mum." He leaned across the table and gave her a quick peck on the brow. There was a pause after he sat down again. Then he mumbled, "Rasheeda's fantastic. I don't care what anyone says. But I didn't mean to upset you."

She kept her attention on her soup and fed herself with regular, dainty spoonfuls. Russell was a good boy. Her love for him had X-ray eyes that saw his inner core of decency, his capacity for generous and passionate involvement.

"That's all right, son."

Her mind slowed down and wound itself into a fuddle. A problem confronted her and it was her duty to tackle it. She felt that every empty movement decried her stupidity and ineptitude and accused her of failing her son. To allow a relationship to develop between Rasheeda and Russell meant nothing but trouble.

"It's not your dad or me you'll have to worry about. The thing is, Russell, I don't think you realise . . . few people do, I suppose, but they have objections to us. I'm not trying to criticise them, son. I'm just . . ."

"Who's 'they' and 'them'?"

The wrinkles at the sides of her eyes deepened.

"You know who I mean. Pakistanis. The Alis. It's their religion, you see, and their customs. That's what's different."

"To hell with their religion and their customs." Russell's eyes bulged and his voice loudened. "Rasheeda and I will see each other and talk to each other as often as we like."

"Oh now, Russell, that's not fair. Surely they're as much entitled to their religion and their customs as we are to ours."

"To hell with *our* religion and *our* customs. What do I care about the superstitious and compulsive habits of a selfish, hypocritical generation that's made such a mess of the world?"

"Oh, thank you very much," Alice said.

"What's for lunch? We're not just having soup, are we, Mum? I'm starving."

She dished up his pork chop and beans, wrestling with herself in an effort to press on with explanations. But Russell, who was cutting up his chop with energy and enthusiasm, went on, "When you meet a girl, you either go for her or you don't. Who cares about background except—"

"Don't tell me!" she interrupted. "The smug, middle-aged middle class."

"You said it. I bet I know more about their customs and religion than you do anyway. They don't eat pork for a start."

"Don't they?" Alice was grateful for discovering this in time. She might well have decided to have roast pork sandwiches later in the day when Zaida came.

"They think everything from a pig's dirty. Come to think of it, they may well be right."

"Now, don't start trying to put me off my pork chop," Alice warned. "You know how squeamish I am and chops are too expensive to waste. Is there anything else they don't eat? I don't want to offend Zaida. It's today she's coming for tea after school and you said you'd help her with her English."

"Yeah, yeah." He switched on his radio. "They're the same as the Jews with meat."

"How do you mean?" Her voice strained to compete with Elvis Presley.

"They have their own special butchers because they believe when the animal's killed, it must have God's name recited over it and it must be bled. They cut their throats and let them bleed to death," he finished cheerfully.

"That's horrible and cruel."

"That's religion for you! Don't worry, Mum." He grinned. "The animals don't feel anything. They just get weaker and sleep away."

"That's terrible!"

"What about our slaughterhouses? There's a few practices . . ."

"No, please, Russell," she cried out. "Don't tell me. I can't bear to know."

"That's another thing I can't stand about the older generation. What a hypocritical head-in-the-sand attitude to life! You eat meat but you can't bear to know how it was killed."

"Oh, all right. What am I supposed to do? Turn vegetarian?"

Russell shrugged. "It's your life. I'd better hurry. I don't want to keep Rasheeda waiting."

He went away, his black hair flopping forward, the fingers of his hand snapping, his body jerking in what looked like a tribal dance.

The house was deathly quiet after he had gone. She lit a cigarette, puffed at it and gazed absently around. Then she succumbed to the temptation of peering out of one of the kitchen windows. From it she could see the side of the Alis' bungalow and, pressing her face close to the glass, she could also see down their garden. She tiptoed slowly and heavily through to the scullery window for a better view.

Out of the Alis' back door emerged Rasheeda. Never had Alice seen such a straight back and a head poised in so effortlessly royal a way. Her coat flapped open to reveal a navy skirt and white blouse and Pollokshields Academy tie. Under the conventional skirt she wore tight white satin trousers. The effect was startling. She had a glamorous woman's head with long hair like black wings, a schoolgirl's body and mysterious eastern legs.

"Hey there, Russell," she called and waved.

Alice saw Russell's expression as he watched Rasheeda approach him, and she groaned out loud, "Goddammit! What am I going to do?"

Then she remembered the first thing she had to do was tidy the house and prepare afternoon tea for Rasheeda's sister.

"Oh hell, what next?" There was somebody at the front door but it couldn't be Zaida already.

She discovered with sinking heart that it was old Mrs Bell who had come to relate the distressing tale of how a ball had been kicked into her garden, and bounced off her window. Then she'd seen a black face leering at her.

"It was that boy next door to you."

"Maq."

"He nearly frightened the wits out of me. I'm on my own, as you know, and with all these people milling about, I haven't been able to sleep a wink, Alice. It's bad enough an old person like me living alone at the best of times. I'm eighty-six after all. You know how nervous I am. I've always been highly strung, but now I feel really ill."

"Come away in. I'll make you a nice cup of tea," Alice soothed. "But there's nothing to be nervous about. Maq wouldn't mean you any harm. You know what boys are like.

Always kicking a ball about. I bet he was just having a game of football with Russell."

"Oh no, Alice. It wasn't Russell looking in the window."

Alice felt sorry for Mrs Bell whose frail body was trembling with genuine distress.

"Maybe what you need is a wee sedative from your doctor," she advised later over some tea.

She began to feel in need of a sedative herself. Time was passing. If Zaida arrived while Mrs Bell was in, the old woman might never reach her eighty-seventh birthday.

# Seventeen

All morning, Bashir painted the dark brown woodwork white. Everyone was very busy in the house. In the afternoon they stopped to get ready for the visit with their friend, Alice. All his family were happily looking forward to it.

He was worried about what would be the most fitting wallpaper to buy.

"We will study the house of our friend Alice first," he told Bashir.

To integrate properly into a new community was not easy. There were many things of which he could not be sure. Not only were there plenty of differences between Pakistan and the Gorbals, but plenty of differences between the Gorbals and Pollokshields.

In Pakistan, walls inside and out were whitewashed or painted green or grey or blue or red. In Pollokshields red walls might cause offence. No doubt in Alice's house they would learn much.

Anjum did not want to come.

"You will come," he insisted. "You will not offend our neighbour."

So she had come. They all crowded into Alice's porch. All were wearing their best clothes. His baby grandson Shah Jahan had a new blue coat lined with white nylon fur. The coat had a fur-lined hood also. Anjum wore a brown coat over her cream salwar qamiz. Her daughters Zaida and Noor Jahan were very resplendent. Long gold or silver earrings dangled from their ears. They wore many golden bangles and silver rings also. Zaida's salwar qamiz were of blue satin. Noor Jahan glistened in silver. Rasheeda had changed quickly out of her school clothes. She wore golden salwar qamiz.

Most of the salwar qamiz were as they should be – trousers worn under a long, loose, knee-length tunic so that no shape of breasts or any feminine shape was visible to cause chaos among men. But Rasheeda's shape could clearly be seen. She had done something with the sewing needle. As usual, he felt angered by Rasheeda. Many times he had warned her about her immodest appearance. Many times he had chastised her about having hair swinging loose round face and shoulders.

"What is wrong with plaiting your hair like Zaida?" he complained again.

"Och, Daddy," she flung at him impatiently, "you don't understand. This is the fashion."

"Fashion? Fashion? What is this fashion you keep saying?"

"Everybody wears their hair loose."

"No' Pakistani woman."

"Och, Daddy!"

"Never mind och daddy! I will speak to you later."

Alice opened the door. Her features collapsed with astonishment. Sharif Ali thought it must be with wonder over their splendid appearance.

"Don't you look grand! Come away in. Oh, a baby too. Gosh, isn't he lovely!"

They crowded after her and round her into the hall. She towered above them, for even Sharif Ali was not tall. Rasheeda was the tallest in his family.

Alice smiled vaguely.

"Well, we'd better go into the sitting room. But first, would you like to take your coat off, Mrs Ali?"

Anjum paid no attention. This was because she did not know to whom Alice spoke. Pakistani women did not take their husband's name on their marriage. In Britain names were too important and became a point of terrible confusion. There were plenty of things Sharif Ali did not understand yet. In Britain they called names Christian and second. But people with the Christian name often did not go to the prayer houses, and the second name often was not the second. For some people had three names.

He spoke sharply in Urdu, "Alice say take your coat off."

Anjum looked most wretched. She did not like to take her coat off. She handed the coat over to Alice with much reluctance.

Alice said, "Let me take your scarf as well."

Anjum jerked the piece of chiffon back from Alice's hands. Desperately she clutched it beneath her chin while one palm massaged frantically all over her face.

Noor Jahan forgot her shyness to explain.

"Excuse my mummy, please. It is our religion that women must be covered from head to toe. That is why my mummy and my sisters and I wear the doputta or scarf."

"Except me," Rasheeda laughed. "I'm a bad girl."

Sharif eyed her sternly. "You are indeed. Why you laugh? You cheeky girl. You are the big worry to me."

Alice shepherded them into the sitting room. She was always smiling, that Alice. A very nice woman.

"Sit down, please," she said. "I mean, just make yourselves at home. I'll go and fetch the tea and tell Russell you're here."

"Zaida, you go and help Alice."

"I'll go." Rasheeda jumped up.

"No, you'll no'," Sharif Ali snapped. "Sit down."

Pouting with displeasure, Rasheeda bounced down again on her seat. Zaida trotted away after Alice.

Sometimes Rasheeda appeared to have no bones in her arms and legs. She draped over a chair with long limbs dangling loose. Sometimes she moved and walked with much grace and beauty. Other times she pranced energetically about like a young colt.

She said, "Isn't this a fantastic house?" Springing to her feet, she whisked back her hair before examining the ornaments on the mantelpiece. She lifted things. She felt them. She turned them round and round.

Sharif patted the arm of his chair and spoke in Urdu to Bashir. "These are very nice chairs, very comfortable. I like these chairs. What do you call this material?"

"I think it's called moquette."

"Moquette," Sharif repeated carefully. "Moquette."

They all got up and began milling around the room, chatting in Urdu and admiring the wallpaper, the curtains, the carpets. Then

Alice and Zaida came in with the tea. Alice's son entered also. He carried a small table. On the table were cups and saucers.

"Careful now, son," Alice murmured.

Once the small table and a tea trolley were in position, she spread a big smile around.

"Has everyone met Russell? Anyway, he's my son. Russell, this is Mr Ali and this is Mrs Ali."

Anjum lowered her eyes, one hand twitching at her headscarf.

When Alice introduced Noor Jahan, she remarked, "Noor Jahan's a lovely name."

Sharif explained proudly that it meant "Light of all the world."

Zaida said, "I have seen Russell at the Academy."

"Oh yes, of course," Alice said. "He knows Rasheeda as well."

Alice and Russell handed round cups of tea and biscuits and cakes. Then Russell sat down on the carpet near Rasheeda's chair.

This made Sharif Ali feel embarrassed and uneasy. He was not angry with the boy. There were plenty of differences in customs. The boy would not know. Many things shocked him about British customs but none more than the freedom of the young men and women. Women walked about with naked legs.

Alice said politely, "What's it like? Your own . . . I mean Pakistan? I've never been there."

He shrugged and spread out his hands.

"I have language difficulty. I can't help Zaida so I am most grateful for your offer to help be a teacher for Zaida with your books, Russell."

"That's OK," Russell said.

"I cannot explain everything, Alice. I'd like to take you to show you my own country. But I am sorry. I haven't enough money. That is big trouble. Otherwise I go to Pakistan with you, or with Russell, or with any other. We travel by car. Up to Japan. Up to China."

Alice was most impressed.

"Japan? And China?"

He made another grand gesture. "Of course."

Noor Jahan's shy smile widened with pride.

"We travel seven countries to come here – Yugoslavia, Turkey, Bulgaria, Greece, Austria, Germany, Belgium."

"And were you all covered up before . . . Did you wear the burkah?"

"Yes. I was most surprised when I saw women here."

"I'm sure I've seen Pakistanis in town wearing western clothes – skirts."

Sharif scratched his beard.

"They must be Indian women. Hindu women wear salwar qamiz or sari or western clothes. Muslim women wear salwar qamiz or sari but no western clothes."

"Are Hindus different then?"

"Oh my!" Sharif let out a loud yelp. "You no' know about the Hindus? If I a Hindu I make a statue with my own hands." He gesticulated and made statue shapes in the air. "And I keep it on table here and I say" – he leaned forward with his palms together in mock prayer and with face screwed up in ridicule and mimicry – " 'Oh my God, give me money! Oh my God, give me son.' So I made God with my own hands and I say 'God give me money! God give me son!' " He flung his hands to one side in disgust.

Noor Jahan's smile erupted in a throaty gurgle.

"Hindu say caw is our mother."

Alice peered at her.

"Caw?"

"Yes." Noor Jahan nodded for emphasis. "Hindu say caw is sacred. They don't eat."

Her father's voice proclaimed it loudly.

"Caw – caw! It is true."

Rasheeda laughed. "They mean cow."

Sharif's hands shaped the air again. "They take . . . bowl. Cow makes water . . ."

"Yes?" Alice's smile struggled to encourage him on.

"They put in bowl. They put their hands in cow's water in bowl and they sprinkle in their kitchens."

Alice's smile collapsed.

Noor Jahan said, "Hindu house has a bad smell."

"When baby born," Sharif continued, "they give baby one, two, maybe three drops of cow's water. I cannot speak English properly because in my old age I came here. I cannot explain properly. Otherwise I explain to you all about Hindus, Sikhs, Mohammedans, Christians." He sighed. "British people don't know the difference. I fill in form at work and boss get most angry and shout very loudly at me, 'That spelling wrong. This no' bloody good enough!' And he thinks coloured men are stupid because of mistakes in speaking and spelling. But I ask myself – how many words can that boss speak or spell in Urdu? I make mistakes but I'm no' stupid, Alice."

"No, of course not," Alice warmly agreed. She was a nice woman. They were lucky to find such a friend. He felt he owed it to her to make the effort to explain.

"I am Muslim. I believe only God. God he has no son. No daughter. No mother. No anything. But God is one in the world. And everybody is coming from God. And everybody will be go to God. That's all. I believe this. And Mohammed is the messenger of God. He gives the messages to us. Just like Jesus bring the message from God and he give it to the Christians."

"I see."

"When we came here first, I took my family to see picture. You see picture called *The Bible*?"

"Oh!" Noor Jahan gasped. "It was very good picture."

Alice shook her head.

"No, I must have missed that one."

"You no' see *The Bible*?" Sharif cried out incredulously. "My God, you no' see *Ten Commandments*? You no' see *Adam and Eve*?"

"Eh . . . no, I don't think so."

"Oh my God!" Sadly he shook his head. "Adam a pile of sand. Then wind blow and aye!" He flung up his hands. "Very strong wind. Sand come here and make small hill. Again wind blow strongly. All sand blow away and statue come out. After that God gave the air in his body and he moves and he is Adam. Then Adam walking along this way and that and no' having any enjoyment. Tigers came and sat on his feet. Elephants came and sat on his feet. But he didnae enjoy it. So God made Eve."

Alice's eyes grew very large.

"Fancy!"

It had been a most pleasant afternoon. Soon, however, Sharif Ali realised that he must get ready to go about his duties. Bashir was already at work and was sorry he had missed the visit. Sharif Ali and his family said goodbye most politely. Except Rasheeda who waved her hand and called out, "Cheerio."

Tomorrow was his day off. The father of Bashir and his family were coming to visit with them – Mahmoud and his wife Shereen and the brothers of Bashir who were students at Glasgow University. The brothers were as Scottish boys and fitted in well. Yet they were also good Muslim boys. Mahmoud told him they said their prayers very conscientiously. Mahmoud was very proud of his sons. So too was his wife Shereen. But when the sons heard of Sharif Ali's bungalow in Pollokshields they had prophesied: "You're going head on into trouble. You obviously don't know the reputation of that place. They won't think much of you there!"

Now he looked forward to correcting Bashir's brothers.

"I have always been happy with Glasgow peoples," he would say. "And the Pollokshields peoples are most impressed by me."

# Eighteen

"Oh please, Russell, let me laugh!" Alice clutched at her large bosom and closed her eyes.

Her son trembled with fury.

"It's a typical side-effect of corrupt bourgeois society . . . laughter becomes cruel and warped."

"I don't want to be cruel. I just want to laugh."

"Why should you laugh?"

"Goddammit, it was funny."

Russell began to shout, "You wouldn't want to laugh if they'd been white people. It's just your rotten colour prejudice again!"

"That's a silly thing to say and you know it. I'm no more prejudiced than Mr Ali. Did you not hear him about Hindus?"

"Why should prejudice be the monopoly of the white man?"

"Why indeed? Obviously we're all basically the same underneath. I don't claim to know everything, Russell. I never took my Highers at school. But I don't need Highers to know when something's funny."

"They're good people. I'm not going to allow you or anyone else to make fun of them."

"Russell, I know they're good people. I've come to like them very much. Please believe me. And I think Rasheeda's fantastic. I mean, I've never seen anyone so beautiful."

He flashed her a quick look of gratitude. Then his mouth suddenly quivered as he chanted, "Elephants came and sat down on his feet. But he didnae enjoy it. So God made Eve!"

"Oh, don't," Alice pleaded as she suddenly rollicked across the room to collapse into a chair. "You've made me feel guilty about laughing now."

"I suppose there's laughter and laughter."

Alice wiped her eyes. Mascara was etched over her freckled face like bird prints.

"I do like them an awful lot. I really do."

"What's for dinner?"

"Russell, you've just had an enormous afternoon tea."

"I'm starving. Anyway, I'd like my dinner early because I've promised to go next door and help Zaida with her English. Noor Jahan might join in. Although it's not her that needs to worry about exams."

"And Rasheeda perhaps?"

He grinned.

"I might as well treat her to a share of my valuable brain power while I'm there."

"She talks as good English as you do."

"She's had her difficulties."

"You'll both be having difficulties if you don't watch out. I mean, the old man sounds a bit narked with Rasheeda as it is. And did you not see the expression on his face when you sat at her feet? Oh no, of course you wouldn't. You were too busy gazing adoringly up at her!"

"Oh Mum, cut it out! Can I have my dinner early? There's nothing else happening, no one else coming or anything, is there?"

"No, not tonight. I've all the other neighbours coming tomorrow, though."

Remembering about the other neighbours, she did not feel like laughing any more. They would be arriving the next evening all intent on doing the Pakistanis as much harm as possible. She tried to banish the impending supper party from her mind but failed.

Sleep evaded her for hours that night. The whole thing was a terrible worry. She wished her neighbours would disappear. If she took ill and stayed in bed perhaps they would cancel the meeting. But she didn't believe they would. Anyway she would be in an agony of curiosity to know what plot they were hatching and what was going on.

She really did feel ill the next morning. Lack of sleep caused a thumping headache and hay fever erupted unexpectedly to torment her with sneezes and watery eyes and nose.

Simon shook his head. "You would have to be like this, of course, when we're having the whole square in for a meal." But he gave her his usual affectionate kiss before leaving for work.

She longed to beg a lift into town but she was afraid in case he asked why she was going. He knew nothing of her sorties to Daggerman's Wholesale Warehouse, although she feared he suspected. Often he worriedly questioned her about how she could afford this, that or the other.

She made a wretched, bleary-eyed journey by bus with a zipped holdall and a tartan trolley on wheels. Both bags were soon bulging with tins, jars and packets and, laden like a camel, she made the slow and breathless trek to the bus stop for a bus back to Pollokshields.

Her purchases included a chicken, a tin of cooked ham, asparagus tips, celery hearts, petit pois, chutney, pickles, tins of fruit, table jellies, cartons of cream, a cherry cake, a fruit cake and a tin of assorted chocolate biscuits.

With great difficulty and sweating profusely, she managed to heave her shopping bag on to the bus. It seemed to weigh a ton and she kept imagining she was going to slip a disc or do herself some serious mischief. The hair that she had pinned on top of her head now spilled down to one side and kept slithering down, giving her an air of harassed helplessness.

For the whole bus journey she dreaded the struggle to get off again. Eventually she tottered into the square, willing herself to bear up until she reached her house. Before she started preparing the chicken and cutting meat and making trifles, she treated herself to a big glass of whisky, four chocolate biscuits and a cigarette.

Russell was out, she knew not where. Perhaps trying to console Zaida. Zaida had been too late to get a place at Glasgow University. Everyone was devastated by the turn of events.

"My father depends on me to get my Pharmacy degree," Zaida had wailed.

Alice had promised to help her make enquiries at every college in Scotland if necessary.

"Don't worry," she had assured the distressed girl, "there'll be a place for you somewhere."

Constance McFarlane arrived first with a bottle of wine, looking very nice in a pencil-slim dress in blue linen with a fashionably high waist. Alice gazed at Constance's hairstyle in admiration.

"How do you manage to get your hair to stay like that?"

"I go to a good hairdresser. But I've got quite professional now at back-combing it myself."

She accepted the glass of wine Alice gave her.

"This is very nice of you, having all the neighbours, Alice. I'm afraid I'm not very hospitable these days."

"You work full time, Constance. No one expects you to be able to have the time or the energy to organise dinner parties." Alice hesitated. "I feel a bit guilty about this one."

Constance stared at her in surprise. "Guilty? Why should you feel guilty?"

"Oh well, they're all up in arms about the Pakistanis moving into the square. It's really a kind of meeting about that. I keep hoping, of course, that it'll just turn into a nice sociable evening, but you never know. I'm sorry, Constance."

"Oh, I understand, don't you worry," Constance said with feeling. "I was speaking to Hilda. I bet it was her idea. I was glad I missed the last one."

"Well, more Joe's idea, I think. Then when they wanted to have another meeting, I thought if they met here over a nice meal and I tried to explain about the Pakistanis . . . They're really a very nice, respectable family, you know."

"Oh well, I'm sure you'll do your best, Alice."

Kate Malloy showed keen disappointment when she came with her parents and discovered that Russell was not present. She was a plump girl who looked as if she was going to grow up in the same mould as her mother. Her wide, flounced dress didn't help any.

"Didn't I tell you, Daddy?" Kate looked up at her father with tragedy in her eyes. "I hardly ever get a chance to speak to him now. That horrible girl next door's always got her claws in. She just can't leave us alone. My life's a misery. I can't bear it any more!"

"Oh now, Kate," Alice protested half-heartedly, "don't be so melodramatic. I'm sure you're all good friends. I was just saying to Constance—"

Tears sparkled in Kate's eyes as she interrupted, "I'm not good friends with her. I hate her."

Joe hooked a comforting arm round his daughter's shoulders. "Why the hell did they have to come here?"

"I've quite a few Pakistani children in my class—" Constance began.

"Have you, dear?" Hilda Malloy interrupted with a smile, before turning to Alice. "The poor darling is quite inconsolable. Her whole world has come crashing down. I bought her the most beautiful little fur hat to try and cheer her up but without the slightest success. It was white ermine and frightfully expensive too. My dears, I just daren't tell you the price. But I will say this – my last hat was expensive enough but in comparison with the ermine one it was a mere trifle."

Alice felt like saying, "For goodness' sake, why doesn't she pull herself together? You as well." But she felt too miserable with her hay fever to bother.

Simon came into the room and after all the friendly hellos, he began pouring everyone a glass of whisky.

The meeting had just got under way and it was regrettably established that there was nothing legally anyone could do about the Pakistanis at this juncture. Joe Malloy quickly assured everyone, however, that a friend from the sanitary department had made some very interesting and helpful observations. Before he could elucidate on these, Russell breezed in. He grinned.

"You lot look awful serious. Is it Mum's cooking?"

Joe said, "We're discussing what can be done about that lot next door."

Old Mrs Bell quavered, "I saw a whole crowd of them going along the square tonight. Oh, what are we going to do? How can we make them go away?"

Russell immediately turned white-faced with anger. His eyes bulged.

"It's too bloody bad if they can't have a few visitors. Look at the crowd of you."

"This is our square, our country," Mr Bierce shouted, making Mrs Bierce wince.

Russell rolled his eyes.

"U Thant must have had you lot in mind when he said, 'The single most important impediment to global institutions is the concept of My Country, right or wrong." It's an impediment to any kind of logical thought or objective behaviour."

Joe shook his head at Simon. "See the kind of education you pay for?"

"Well, you know," Simon said mildly, "he's young. At that age, we all . . ."

"Go and get your hair cut," Mr Bierce bawled at Russell. "You're a disgrace!"

"You're a crowd of mangy wolves and dirty two-faced hypocrites!"

"Russell, please," Alice appealed. "These people are our guests . . ."

He turned on her.

"You're the worst of the lot. How could you? How could you, Mum?"

"All I wanted was to have some friends in for supper."

"Russell," Simon said, "that's enough. You're upsetting your mother. Just be quiet."

"No, I will not be quiet. Nothing will make me be quiet."

"Would you listen to the saviour of our nation," Joe said to everyone in general, and then, to Simon, "And you're the one who's to do all the dirty work to pay for him being taught all this."

"What dirty work?" Russell shouted. "This tonight, you mean? You keep me out of this. Don't you make me an excuse or a party to your filthy racialism."

He slammed out of the room. Kate Malloy started to cry. Her plump chest bounced with sobs.

"It's that horrible girl who's made him like this!"

"Rasheeda isn't horrible," Alice said firmly. "She's a very nice girl."

They'd gone far enough, she decided. Time for some straight talking.

# Nineteen

Russell saw Rasheeda in the next-door back garden as soon as he strode from the house. He leapt over the fence, rushed over to her and grabbed her in his arms.

"Russell!" she gasped in surprise before he silenced her with a hard, determined kiss.

Eventually she surfaced and, punching him away, she hissed at him, "Have you gone mad or something? Do you want my father and mother to see us acting like this?"

"I love you."

Rasheeda's eyes continued to flash.

"Do you want to ruin everything?"

Russell was beginning to calm down.

"I'm sorry. I was just so angry. There's a bunch of stupid bigots in there." He jerked his head towards his house. "I just thought – to hell with them."

"You've a terrible temper, Russell."

He shrugged. "A bit quick sometimes. I'm sorry."

She looked round at the windows of her own house. "If anyone of my family saw you . . ." She turned a tragic gaze on him. "You don't know what they're like."

"They can't be as bad as that lot next door. But I don't think anyone saw us, Rasheeda. Do you want me to come into the house with you just now, just to make sure? I could say I've come to ask Zaida if she needs any more help."

She nodded, then strode in front of him into the house, head held high. He saw the courage and dignity of her, loved her all the more, and hated himself for causing her distress.

Sharif Ali's black face lit up at the sight of Russell.

"Ah, Russell. You are like a son of my house."

Russell smiled. "You mean I'm here too often."

"No, no. You are always welcome."

"I just wondered if Zaida and Noor Jahan would like to practise English conversation. They've got a basis of grammar and all the theory. It's practice at conversation they really need."

"You're too kind! But Noor Jahan and wee Shah Jahan and Zaida have gone with their mother to the shop of Bashir to choose their messages." Messages, the Glasgow word for shopping, sounded funny coming from Sharif Ali. "I'm here alone."

"I'm here," Rasheeda said, adding with a twinge of bitterness in her voice, "but of course I don't count."

"Go and make tea and don't be cheeky," her father snapped. "It's stopping your English conversations we need."

"No thank you, Mr Ali," Russell said. "I can't wait for tea. I said I'd meet Maq and Will and some of the others in the park for a game of football. Maq's away, is he?"

"Aye, he said to the park, right enough."

"OK." He gave the old man a wave but didn't look round at Rasheeda. "Be seeing you."

"Aye, OK, Russell. You're always welcome, mind."

Russell felt miserably guilty as he walked down Pollokshields Lane and out on to Pollokshields Road. He stood for a moment before crossing over to the park. He hated being deceitful and having to lie to Rasheeda's family, especially to Mr Ali who was always so nice to him. He wondered if Mr Ali would really want to spoil things between Rasheeda and himself. He was sure the old man liked him. And if Mr Ali could be assured that he'd always love, cherish and respect his daughter, how could be object?

A popular song suddenly came into his mind, one about being too young to be in love. Maybe their age would be the objection. It certainly would be from his family. Well, he could allay their fears about a rushed teenage marriage. He could assure them that he and Rasheeda had every intention of going to university and taking their degrees, and then finding good jobs. But while he was thinking all this, he knew he was kidding himself. It wasn't just their youth as far as the Ali family was concerned. No, it was centuries of religious indoctrination. What chance had his love for Rasheeda and her love for him against that?

He trailed across the road, numbly kicking a stone along in front of him. Inside the park he caught sight of Will and Maq and went over to join them. They were on the hilly side of the path opposite the swings and the ball they were kicking from one to the other kept rolling away from them. Russell caught it with his foot and flicked it back.

"Where are the Lewises?"

"Locked in their room," Will said.

The Lewis boys were twins, a year younger than the rest but still too old to be locked away.

"For goodness' sake, I thought my parents were bad enough but they wouldn't dare do that to me. That's ridiculous. What crime are they supposed to have committed anyway?"

Maq said, "They were arguing and Benny said, 'If you do that again, I'll fuckin' kill you.' And Dan said, 'Not if I fuckin' kill you first.' It wasn't them threatening to commit bloody murder that got their mum and dad angry, of course. It was saying fuckin'."

They all laughed. Then Russell said, "I felt like murdering all the white gits in the square today."

"How?" Will asked. "What happened?"

"Not your mother," Russell hastily added. "Mostly old Malloy and Bierce. Hitler would have loved them. Bloody fascist bigots. How about going round to the chippy? I marched out without my dinner and I'm fuckin' starving."

They all laughed again and Maq picked up the ball.

"I don't think my dad knows how to curse. Not in English anyway. I could say fuckin' until the cows come home and he'd probably think I was really clever at speaking 'the Glasgow', as he calls it."

"I wonder what the Pakistani curses are," Will said.

Maq shrugged. "Haven't a clue."

They sat in at the chip shop and ordered fish suppers and glasses of Irn Bru. Enthusiastically they shook salt and vinegar on to their plates. Russell fed the juke box before settling down to enjoy the food and gulp down the Irn Bru. He'd chosen a record of trad jazz, the music of the Ban the Bomb protesters. It triggered a discussion between the boys.

"It just shows the madness of the older generation," Russell said, "to be going on with the production of the bomb after that appeal to stop it was signed by fifty-two Nobel Prize winners and top scientists. It could wipe out whole nations, they said, neutral or belligerent."

"I know," Will said gloomily. "That bloody thing's going to wipe out the whole human race. And they've the cheek to criticise us. My dad's a bloody Tory. All he cares about is silly, stupid stuff."

"I know what you mean," Russell agreed. "It's money, money, money all the time with my dad."

"Same with mine," Maq said. "He works in that shop in bloody Maryhill from the crack of dawn till late every night. It's a miracle when he manages to come home a wee while during the day that he and my mam recognise each other. Thank goodness I'll escape to the university. But what do you bet they'll still have me working in the bloody place every free minute I get."

Russell rolled his eyes in sympathy and went over to put another coin in the juke box. This time he chose a Bill Haley and the Comets number which belted out with deafening vigour. The three boys stamped their feet and banged the table with their fists in time to the beat. It cheered them up, made them feel better and more positive. It put them into a "to hell with the lot of them" mood.

Outside in the street again, they wondered what to do next and where to go. A couple of girls passed, all done up in bouffant hairstyles and dresses made to stick out with layers of stiffened petticoats. Will knew about this because of his mother's dresses and petticoats. His mother was such an embarrassment at times. She was far too old to dress like that.

They whistled and chirped at the girls, who passed them with their heads in the air.

"Huh!" Maq said. "Think they're somebody."

Russell said tentatively, "Have you two ever . . . You know, ever done it? Confidentially," he added. "Strictly between us."

Maq shook his head.

"Not interested at the moment. I mean, I don't mind fooling

around a bit. But I've got to concentrate on my exams and on getting to the university and then more exams, I suppose. If I don't, my folks'll kill me. They've probably got a wife lined up for me already – for after I leave university. But I'm having none of that. I choose my own wife."

"Good for you," Russell said. "It's time all this traditional stuff was done away with. How about you, Will?"

Will said, "No. You'll never guess, though."

"What?" the other two cried out in eager unison.

"My mother and father are always at it."

"You're joking," Russell said.

"I hear them. It's disgusting at their age."

Maq made a face. "It's enough to put you off. What started all this anyway?"

Russell shrugged. "I just wondered. I haven't yet."

"Do you know big Bert Sharkey?" Will asked.

"Who doesn't?"

"Well, he said it was a hell of a job."

"What did he mean?" the other two wanted to know.

"He says there's an armoury of assorted underwear to get through. He says there's girdles so tight they never yield an inch. They're made so that nobody can bypass them – like a fortification. By the time you've struggled with these girdles you're knackered. The best you can get, he says, is petting. Some of them allow petting but keep refusing to go all the way."

"A lot of good that is," Maq said.

"I know."

"That'll be the only consolation," Maq said, "if I go with a Pakistani girl. At least she'll not wear a girdle."

"How do you know?" Russell asked. "Maybe they do."

"No, I've never seen any girdles in our house. Pakistani girls are supposed to cover themselves up in loose clothes. It doesn't matter if they've got big bellies. Nobody sees them."

"Here," Will said. "I've just remembered. I pinched some of my dad's cigarettes. Do you fancy a smoke?"

"You bet!"

Automatically they returned to the park and made for the shelter of the bushes where they would not be seen.

# Twenty

Alice secured some long tendrils of hair behind her ears as she continued to speak.

"I know you're worried, to say the least, about the Alis coming to live here. But it's because you don't understand them. I think it took a big heart and a lot of guts to calmly march into a middle-class fortress like this. I mean, he's not just a lamplighter but a coloured one! Didn't that take nerve? Surely you've got to admire it."

"Bloody hell!" Joe gasped. "I know they've got a nerve. Isn't that what I've been saying all along? Now you actually expect us to admire them for it!"

"Well, think of yourselves going to live as the only white family in a whole neighbourhood of coloured folk. How would you feel?"

"I wouldn't be such a damned fool. I'd stay among my own kind where I belong."

She would like to have said, "Oh, but I thought you belonged to Ireland." She resisted the temptation, however. It was no use trying to score points for oneself and embarrass other people. That only made them all the more bitter and resentful. Instead she continued mildly, "I suppose it's a natural instinct. I mean, when Scottish people go abroad, the first thing they do is to get in touch with other Scots and form Caledonian societies and Burns clubs. And they try to settle alongside other Scots folk. It's the same with everybody. But surely it's an instinct we must try and overcome."

"Why should we?" Joe was turning purple-faced with exasperation. "Why should we go against the most basic instinct to keep with our own kind?"

"Because it puts barriers up."

"There was no trouble at all here until they came. We were all perfectly happy."

"But it couldn't last, Joe. We've got to face facts. It's a multiracial city now and it seems to me we should try to get to know one another better. I believe there ought to be classes in every school to teach children of different races all about each other."

"There's quite a few Pakistani children in my school—" Constance began again but Joe interrupted her.

"You've got a nerve to sit there telling me or any of us the right way to do this and that. I'm a successful businessman, Alice. What have you ever done?"

"I suppose it depends on what you're successful at," Alice said. "You and all your friends are good business people. You're all successful at making money. But surely there's more to life than that?"

She lit a cigarette. "Life's so short," she wanted to say. "Surely we should at least try to understand. I've seen my mother die, and my father . . ."

A sluice gate opened and allowed pain to flood free. Had she been patient with her father? Had she tried to understand him?

She remembered him at her mother's funeral – gawky, lanky, grey-faced and sober. Afterwards he had wept and reached out to her for comfort but she had been bitter in her twelve-year-old grief and had turned away.

For a long time afterwards he had sat in the house, sunken-eyed, silent and sober. At other times when she returned from school, he would be fussing clumsily around the bothy trying to tidy up or make the tea.

It would have fitted him better, she used to think, if he had behaved himself and helped her mother. But often since, she had thought – who was she to pass judgement on her father?

That last night he had come home drunk, had she heard him in her nightmare sleep? After he had fallen across the railway line, had he called out to her?

She knew the heart of her son and would forgive him anything. What was the core of her father? She did not know. She had never reached out, never looked.

Now she gazed around at her neighbours.

"What harm have Sharif Ali and his family done to any of us?" she asked. "Why don't we at least try to be honest?"

Joe said, "We're the honest-to-God practical ones around here. Not you, Alice. You're away in a daft world of your own most of the time."

"Yes, dear," Hilda said. "We're just trying to keep the square the nice happy place it's always been."

"But none of you have met the Alis. You've never spoken to any of them."

"I have," Constance said. "Maq seems a nice enough boy. My son, Will—"

This time it was Mr Bierce who interrupted her. "I don't need to talk to the bastards."

Alice was fascinated to see that Mr Bierce had begun to tremble as he went loudly on. She wondered why on earth he felt so strongly about this.

"I know them a hell of a lot better than you. I was brought up in India as a child. My father worked over there. I remember it only too well. The whole country was filthy and diseased and stinking. You'd see lepers and all sorts of horrors lying around begging in the street. They cut the fingers off their children so they could beg."

The women gave little shrieks of disgust. Only Sissy Bierce put her hand over her mouth and made no sound. Words flurried indignantly around the room.

"Isn't that dreadful?"

"There's no excuse for anybody being like that!"

"They're simply not like us at all."

"Oh, I don't know . . ." Constance began again but was defeated by Mr Bierce who was now really getting into his stride. Alice closed her eyes. One of these days she would have to find out why he was like this.

"And they're not to be trusted. My father had to pay men with guns to guard our house. They walked around our house all day and night keeping everybody back with their guns. And you've heard about their so-called holy river, the Ganges? My God, it's stinking!" He knocked back his whisky as if to drown the memory of it. "It's stinking, and they bathe in it and do everything in it. And they worship cows. Cows are the only bloody things that are sacred to them."

"No, no," Alice protested. "Hindus are the ones who think the cow is sacred. The Alis are Muslims."

"I don't bloody care what they call themselves. I'm not having any of the ignorant heathens living anywhere near me!"

"But they're not." Alice raised her voice in exasperation. "They're more devout and religious than we are. And it's no use generalising about Muslims or Hindus or anybody. Look at some British people. Look at some of the recent cases – people knifing and slashing each other, beating up and robbing people, neglecting and murdering children. Would you want foreigners to lump everybody in the British Isles together and say – Britishers are all child beaters, murderers, gangsters and thieves?"

"In my school, I have to deal with a pretty rough crowd, I can tell you," Constance said, "but it's amazing what one can do with a bit of patience and understanding."

"If there's one thing I despise," Joe pushed his words out from between clenched teeth, "it's bloody airy-fairy idealists. It'll be a different story when the bottom drops out of the property market here."

Alice tutted with exasperation. "Everybody keeps saying that but the only thing that's different now is the fact that the Alis are improving the house. That bungalow was horrible and that's a fact. Goddammit, Joe, the place was filthy long before the Alis came."

Simon said quietly and patiently (the others regarded him as saintly), "Alice, how do you know what the bungalow was like? You were never inside it when Mrs Ogilvie lived there. Everybody knows the old woman liked to keep herself to herself."

"She went queer." Alice was beginning to feel far from normal herself. "I used to worry about her. I used to be frightened all the time in case she would be lying dead behind the door."

"That old woman was perfectly happy in that house, perfectly happy just minding her own business. Until you wrote to her son and stirred things up and got her put away in a home."

Alice puffed at her cigarette for comfort.

"I never!" She gazed around like an injured doe. "I was just trying to help. Her son didn't know how she was. I mean, he never came to see her, did he?"

"You soon sorted that, Alice." Joe pushed his glass in front of Simon for a refill of whisky. "This whole thing is your fault. These Pakistanis wouldn't be here now if you were like everyone else and minded your own damned business. Selling her house to a crowd of Pakis is the old girl's revenge. But I don't see why we should suffer for your mistakes."

"Suffer what?" Alice gasped helplessly.

"The Pakis are the ones who are going to suffer." Mr Bierce riveted Alice with snake-eyed hatred. "We'll make it so hot for them in this square, they'll be glad to get away."

"Oh, for goodness' sake," Constance gasped. "You know perfectly well Alice is right. Mrs Ogilvie's bungalow was a mess. The first thing the Alis did was to clean the whole place up. So what on earth can you have against them?"

"Yes, and that's a horrible, wicked way to talk, Mr Bierce!" Alice cried out. "Wicked and cruel."

"Oh, I'm sure Mr Bierce doesn't mean that, Alice," Hilda said, patting her sparkling blue hair. "Nobody wants to *hurt* them."

Simon said, "Alice, please calm down. You're just upsetting yourself."

But Alice was really angry now. "Call yourselves Christians? Well, Christ was from the East. He must have been coloured – a coloured Jew. No one ever mentions that fact. That's the most untalked-of fact in Christendom." A wild fit of sneezing attacked her and her eyes began to water but she blustered on, "And what's supposed to happen after you all die? You believe in heaven. Do you really think coloured Jesus is going to operate a colour bar up there? Does he believe in segregation? You accuse me of being daft. Well, if I'm daft, you're dafter!"

She had gone too far. They would be angry with her. She feared the hurt of snubs to come, eyes averted, heads turned away. The unknown future merged with the forgotten past, and lapped backwards and forwards like an icy sea. Shopkeepers' rolling eyes, impatient, unloving, unbelieving.

"It's the Parish kid again trying to get credit . . ."

"If your mother and you budgeted properly, and saved your money, and were more economical . . ."

She sneezed and sneezed again. Tears streamed down her face. She groped behind a cushion for the roll of toilet paper she had been using to blow her nose and mop her eyes – one of her many attempts to please Simon by being economical. With a tug it leapt out. She clung to one end of it but the rest shot across the floor and snaked away among the feet of her guests.

Everyone gazed in horror at the toilet roll. Simon closed his eyes.

# Twenty-One

"You were lucky you weren't there," Constance told Jenny. They'd bumped into each other in the supermarket.

"That bad, was it?"

"I couldn't get a word in edgeways for that horror Bierce. Alice tried her best but she got all upset. You know how she keeps getting too emotionally involved with people."

Jenny smiled. "You're a fine one to talk."

"In my job, yes. It helps the young people I teach if they know I really care about them."

"I didn't lie to Alice, you know. I really did have a rush job that I had to work all evening on."

"It's Sissy Bierce I'm sorry for."

"Who isn't?" Jenny said. "They're always together too. As if they're joined at the hip."

"I know. Can you imagine any woman marrying somebody like that in the first place?"

Jenny could, but she shook her head. "Talk about losing one's identity. I bet poor wee Sissy has forgotten she ever had one."

"Put your stuff in the car," Constance said. "I'll give you a lift home."

"Thanks."

During the drive Constance broke the silence with, "Ronnie keeps nagging at me to ask the Alis round for dinner one evening."

"I suppose I should do something as well. I'm not up to dinner, though. But maybe the mother could pop in for coffee. There's a married daughter in the house as well, isn't there?"

"So I believe. I get kept informed by Will. He's friendly with Maq, the grandson. I don't think you'll have much luck with the old woman. Maq says she can hardly speak any English. That's one of the reasons I keep putting this dinner idea off. Along with not knowing what to say to them and not being sure about what I should give them to eat. I don't know why Ronnie's so keen." She laughed unconvincingly. "Unless he's after one of the daughters. You know what Ronnie's like."

Jenny stared round at her.

"I know he's very pleasant and friendly. A really nice man, I've always thought."

"Oh, he's friendly all right, and nice." She laughed again. "Too nice at times."

Jenny said, "You surprise me, Constance."

"Oh? Why?"

"I never guessed you were so insecure."

"Insecure?" Constance said. "Me? What on earth gives you that idea?"

"Never mind. But just you think about it."

Now Jenny understood the mutton-dressed-as-lamb tendency. Constance was older than Ronnie and afraid she would lose him. Poor Constance.

"I don't think you've anything to worry about with the Pakistani women."

"I'm not worried about them. Why should I worry about them? For goodness' sake, Jenny, you'll be getting as bad as Alice, trying to psychoanalyse people."

Jenny didn't reply. There was silence until they arrived at the square and were removing their shopping from the boot. Then Constance said, "One Alice in a small place like this is more than enough."

I've hit a raw nerve, Jenny thought as she gave Constance a wave and called out, "Thanks for the lift."

Emma met Constance at the door and carried in a couple of the shopping bags.

"Jenny always looks so smart, doesn't she? I like her tailored skirts."

"Oh yes, very smart. Pour me a drink, darling."

In the sitting room Constance slopped on to the sofa, accepted a gin and tonic and asked, "Has Daddy phoned?"

"I'm not long in myself and I don't know where Will is. Probably at Russell's or Maq's. Were you expecting a call?"

"Not really. Just hoping."

"He'll be on the road somewhere. He'll call as soon as he's able."

"Yes, of course. I'm not worried."

"I'll go and make the tea."

"It's all right, darling. Just give me a minute."

"No, you just lie there and enjoy your drink."

Constance watched Emma's slim, efficient figure leave the room. Any employer was very lucky in having such a nanny in charge of their children. And she was luckier still to have her as a daughter. Emma was far more mature and well-balanced than her mother. She definitely looked more sensible with her short brown naturally curly hair, no make-up face and her nanny's uniform.

It was true what Jenny said, Constance suddenly thought. She was insecure. She wondered why. But deep down, of course, she knew. She just never allowed herself to think about it. It was safer to think of other people's problems. Now, painfully, her mind opened to the memory of her father. She had adored him. He had been such a charming man, handsome and loving. She had believed he adored her too. Then she'd come home from primary school one day, and found he'd disappeared. She'd never seen him again. He'd gone off with his boss, a wealthy widow who owned a chain of fashion stores. She had been devastated. Now, a lifetime later, she realised she hadn't got over it.

Rasheeda and Russell climbed up the hill to their usual place near the flagpole. For a few minutes they stopped to gaze back down at the long elegant stretch of Victoria Road and, away in the distance, beyond the rooftops of the city, to the hills. They loved this view of the city to which they both felt they belonged.

Eventually they lay down on the grass behind some bushes. They cuddled their arms around each other and spoke of the future.

"Think of it, Russell," Rasheeda said with wonder in her

voice, "once you're an architect, you can design your own house."

"I know," Russell said, full to overflowing with pride and happiness at the thought. "But not my house. *Our* house."

His hand began caressing her cheek, her neck and then gradually slid down to cup her breast. She did not resist him and oh, how soft and sweet she felt. He wanted to touch and see every secret part of her, to feel closer and closer to her. His hand slid further down and began easing up her clothes.

Then suddenly, horrifyingly, a voice bawled out, "You white bastard!"

Both Russell and Rasheeda struggled to their feet. A Pakistani youth was now shouting through the bushes to the other side.

"Come over here, you lot. There's a white bastard needs teaching a lesson."

Rasheeda grabbed Russell's hand. "Come on, run."

"I can handle myself." Russell resisted her frantic pulling.

"Russell, for goodness' sake," she shouted at him. "I'll never speak to you again if you don't run. Right now. I swear it."

So they swooped away down the hill like a couple of wild birds.

Once out on Pollokshields Road, Russell gasped breathlessly, "It's never any use running away, Rasheeda. It makes you look as if you're afraid – a soft mark. And I'm not."

"I know, darling. But I saw a whole pack of them coming. It was the only sensible thing to do. I know how they think, you see. It's not just my family. There isn't a Pakistani in Glasgow who wouldn't be shocked at me, who wouldn't condemn me." She sighed. "Now our lovely private place is spoiled. We'll not be able to go there again."

"We'll find somewhere else."

"It was so lovely there."

"It's a big park. We'll find another private corner of it – just for us."

She nodded and smiled up at him. How lucky she was, she thought, to have met him. She was sure she would be the envy of every girl in the school if they knew. One girl who was obviously jealous of her was Kate Malloy. She was too young for Russell for a start. But she wanted him and the spoiled brat was used to getting what she wanted. Well, not this time, Rasheeda felt like telling her. Apparently she had once followed Russell about like a pet puppy. Now she never got the chance. Rasheeda smiled to herself and hugged Russell's arm.

"I thought you were afraid your family would see us," Russell said.

"Oh, I'm forgetting." Quickly she withdrew her arm.

Russell said, "I wish we didn't need to deceive them."

"So do I, Russell. But believe me, we've no choice."

They parted just before turning off Pollokshields Road into Pollokshields Lane. Rasheeda went first and Russell watched her slim, erect figure stroll nonchalantly along between the lines of trees, every now and again tossing back her long cloak of black hair. He caught glimpses of her between the trees as she crossed into the square and over to the bungalow next to his. Then she disappeared inside.

He was just turning into the lane when he heard shouts behind him, "There's the bastard!"

Russell stopped and looked round. The crowd of Pakistani youths was racing towards him, dodging in and out of the traffic. Before he could decide what to do, a taxi pulled up in front of him. Sharif Ali was rapping on the taxi window at him. Then he emerged.

"Ah, Russell," Sharif greeted him in some agitation. "Rasheeda was supposed to be in the house of relations but she wasn't there and I can't find her. She's always a big worry to me, that girl. Have you seen her at all?"

"Yes, I saw her go into the house a few minutes ago."

They walked down the lane together and, glancing round, Russell was relieved to find the gang of youths had disappeared.

"Noor Jahan never a worry," Sharif was saying. "Zaida never a worry. But that Rasheeda! Oh!" He flung up his hands in despair. "I don't know what to do with her."

Russell felt a stab of annoyance at the old man. Sharif Ali was lucky to have such a beautiful daughter. Rasheeda was far lovelier than her sisters. Intelligent too. After all, Zaida hadn't even managed to get a place at Glasgow University. Rasheeda could speak perfect English, far better than the studious-looking, bespectacled Zaida. As for Noor Jahan – well, the least said about her the better, he thought. In a few years, she'd look just like her mother and she'd still be as inarticulate, in English at least. He felt angry and resentful on Rasheeda's behalf. How dare anybody criticise her?

It was a late summer's evening with only the slightest breeze rustling and sighing through the trees. He longed to be walking with Rasheeda by his side. Every time they said goodbye, he missed her. Every time it was as if part of himself was wrenched away. He barely managed to bid Mr Ali a polite goodnight as they entered their respective garden gates.

"Hello, son," his dad greeted him. "Your mum's in the kitchen making a cup of tea."

"Fine." Russell slumped down into a chair.

The news was on the television. He stared gloomily at it. There was still a disgraceful carry-on in America with white men and even the National Guard in Little Rock, Arkansas, trying to stop black children going to school with white children. Apparently black and white kids weren't even allowed to play together. Now two black and two white church leaders had walked with the nine black pupils – three boys and six girls – to school. The National Guard had turned them away so they walked calmly and bravely through a huge mob of jeering whites. Americans in more liberal states, the announcer said, were ashamed of the whites' behaviour.

And so they should be, Russell thought. He could just imagine old Bierce in among that lot. He'd be in his element – bigoted, fascist pig. He trembled inside with the strength of his emotion.

The black children in Arkansas were behaving with great courage and he could imagine Rasheeda in the same circumstances behaving with equal courage and dignity. He felt a rush of protectiveness towards her again as if she were at present in such dangerous circumstances.

"Oh, there you are, son." His mother's face lit up at the sight of him and now he felt a pang of guilt. It wasn't just the Pakistani family he was deceiving. It was his own parents. Maybe there would be no harm in telling his mother that he and Rasheeda were now more than just friends. They were promised in marriage. His mother would use the old-fashioned word "betrothed". He toyed with the word in his mind. Betroth – to pledge oneself. Betrothal – an engagement to marry.

"Russell!"

"Eh?"

His mother was smiling down at him. "You were miles away, son. I was saying I've just brought some biscuits through but I could make you a spam sandwich if you'd rather."

"No, a biscuit'll do fine, Mum. Thanks." He accepted a custard cream from the plate she held out.

His dad said, "There's a grand war film coming after the news."

Russell groaned inside. That was typical of the older generation. Them and their stupid wars. Even the most recent Suez débâcle hadn't cured them. Even if his dad read Nevil Shute's scarifying novel, *On the Beach* (which he hadn't, of course), it wouldn't change him or make him see sense. All dad cared about was "his finest hour", flying his stupid planes and dropping bombs that killed and maimed his fellow human beings. His usually patient dad had no time, no patience, for the solitary Quaker couple who'd volunteered to make a suicide voyage into the H-bomb test area on Christmas Island.

Right there and then, Russell decided that as soon as he got to university, he'd join CND. It gave him a perverse satisfaction thinking about how his father and probably his mother as well would be shaken to their thoughtless unimaginative roots. He suddenly got up and announced, "I'm going to bed."

Alice and Simon looked at each other after Russell's sudden march from the room. Simon said, "I was never prey to moods like that when I was his age. Were you?"

"No," Alice said. "I don't think so."

"Young people are so unrestrained and violent nowadays," Simon said, and then with sudden urgency, "Oh good, there's the film coming on."

# Twenty-Two

Chewing her tongue and peering earnestly at Bashir's typewriter, Alice typed Zaida's letters to the colleges. She used two fingers because she had never been a professional typist.

After her father had died, she had been forced to find a job that would also provide a home for herself. She had answered an advert in a newspaper for a young girl to train as a children's nanny.

She would never forget the shock of seeing inside her employer's home for the first time. It seemed incredible that some people were living in such an overabundance of luxury while others could die of not having enough.

Another thing that astonished her was that none of the household appeared happy. The woman, Mrs Livingstone, was skinny and neurotic and never at peace for one minute. Every meal was a pointless race against the clock. Mr Livingstone, a tall, quiet, gentle man, spent a lot of time at his club and Alice did not blame him.

Mrs Livingstone had a thing about germs and everything in the nursery – toys, clothes, dishes – had to be religiously boiled and sterilised. If her four-year-old son, David, could have been boiled, she would have ordered Alice to sterilise him too. As it was, Alice had to strip and put all her clothes in the wash after she had been off duty. Before she went near the child, she had to bathe and change into freshly laundered underwear and uniform. The white uniform dress had been bought for her, along with a black military-style coat and hat for out of doors.

She had felt sorry for the silent, pale-faced little boy and tried to liven him up and instil into him some warmth and cheer. Every time his mother went out they immediately deserted the sterile nursery with its boiled toys. They went into the big warm kitchen and she gave him baking tins and buttons and clothes pegs to rattle about and play with on the floor. Or they made biscuits together with much floury mess and laughter, and ate them hot and sticky for tea.

Sometimes she took him to the railway station to watch the people and the trains. Sometimes they made an adventure journey to Woolworths to explore the picture books on their shelves and the toy counters. She would buy him something noisy but small enough to hide and keep secret – like a pea shooter or a whistle.

Then one day she made the mistake of succumbing to buying something for herself. A pair of pretty earrings. That day Mrs Livingstone arrived home early and was waiting like a vulture, ready to pounce.

"Earrings with uniform! And where have you been? Where could you buy such cheap-looking atrocities? Where have you had my child?"

"It's all right, Mummy," David piped up. "Woolworths is a very nice place. Alice often takes me there."

"Woolworths?" his mother screeched, her face registering absolute horror. "Oh, the germs! You wicked, ignorant girl! What have you done to my son?"

Mrs Livingstone was in the habit of making regular weekly sorties with David to an expensive restaurant and then to Forsyth's, the most exclusive shop in town. Alice wanted to ask if high-class germs were less potent but didn't dare. She smiled.

"I wish you wouldn't get so upset. I'm sure there's no need."

In a wild flurry of dismissal, Mrs Livingstone waved her hands.

"Get out of my sight! Get out of my house. You're fired!"

Alice felt hurt. But obediently she had packed her case and left for she knew not where.

While she plodded about the city streets, her brain had sought various means of survival. If only she had a home of her own, she kept thinking, and she toyed with desperate plans to make lots of money quickly and achieve this ideal. Bank robbery or prostitution appeared to be the two main ways of getting rich quick. She shrank from the thought of frightening some unsuspecting teller in a bank and perhaps causing him to have a heart attack. Being a prostitute and being generous and loving to men seemed a much better idea. She gazed hopefully around for clients. People thronged and jostled past her. There were hordes of women shoppers but plenty of men on the street too – old men, young men, fat men, thin men. She asked herself curiously, I wonder how one . . . What does one . . . The more she thought about the practicalities of the matter, the more embarrassed and frightened she became. Blushing and lowering her head, she plodded on again.

Eventually she found refuge in the YWCA, then drifted from one job to another until she arrived at Simon's business in answer to an advert for a shop assistant. It had been nearly Christmas – the busiest season – and Simon was desperately short-staffed.

He had never paid much attention to her at first. He was polite but rather distant. She doubted if they ever would have got married had it not been for the incident with the mouse.

She had a problem about mice and rats. Merely catching sight of a humpy body and long tail was enough to send her into hysterics. When she came upon such a sight in Simon's back shop, she screamed and stampeded out to him. Regardless of the proprieties or the customers, she clung shivering around his neck, pleading for protection, nearly suffocating him in the process with her more than ample bosom.

Simon had been taken aback but had seen her as a person for the first time. He had gallantly wasted no time in getting rid of the mouse. Within three months they were married. It had been a very exciting, whirlwind courtship. Simon had been very generous. He had paid for the wedding. It had been a quiet register office affair with a lovely high tea at the Willow Tea Room afterwards.

She felt so lucky. He was so gentle and kind and distinguished-looking. A real gentleman. She was no beauty. She often thought to herself that she had as much femininity and sexual attraction as an elephant. She remembered grabbing his arm at the reception and hugging him with much love and gratitude. She didn't think he would ever be purposely unkind to the Pakistanis, but she wasn't at all sure about their neighbours.

She wished she could explain to Sharif Ali and his family about the other neighbours and their attitude to them. But they seemed blissfully unaware of any hostility in the square and it did not seem either kind or possible to tell them.

The letters she typed for Zaida and telephone calls she made on her behalf bore fruit. An unexpected place in Hilltown became available. Hilltown was a medium-sized place about a hundred miles away.

The whole family shared Zaida's excitement. Her father was so proud and so grateful to Alice, he shouted to Noor Jahan and flung his arms around her in large, extravagant gestures.

"Noor Jahan, give Alice anything she wants – tea, coffee, fruit, rice, curry!"

Over a constantly refilled cup of tea, trying not to feel harassed by everyone eagerly plying her with everything they possessed, Alice attempted to get Zaida organised for the journey. The girl had never once been away from her family overnight in her life. Now she would have to live in digs outside the college.

"Digs? Digs? What's this digs?" her father asked.

Alice tried to explain how it would mean paying money to sleep in a room in another person's house.

Zaida asked worriedly, "How many sheets and blankets shall I take?"

"No, no, you don't need to take sheets and blankets. Only personal belongings."

Alice was amazed at the simple things Zaida did not know that British people took for granted. Yet how could Zaida be expected to know anything about digs, for instance?

The realisation that his daughter would be living away from home dampened Sharif's excitement.

He said, "It's good. Zaida will get the Pharmacy degree. Yet I'm most sad. We'll be alone without her."

"She'll be able to come home during the holidays," Alice soothed. "You're not losing each other for ever."

But he refused to be comforted and his bearded face was crumpling, near to tears, when he left the room. Alice was becoming more and more touched by the strong sense and love of family these people had.

They sorted out what Zaida would need to take with her and Alice thought that was the whole business organised until Zaida said, "I will go to my professor and say, 'Where do I sleep please?' And he will take me to the digs?"

The enormity of Zaida's problem hit Alice like a blow in the solar plexus. Zaida had no experience of being independent and going out and around alone, or of looking after herself. Her whole culture was against such a phenomenon.

"No, dear, I don't think you'd better do that. I think we'd better take things step by step. When you get off the train at Hilltown, take a taxi from the station. Tell the taxi driver the name of the college and he'll see that you get there safely. As soon as you arrive at the college, go inside the building and ask someone to direct you to the Welfare Officer."

"Welfare Officer," Zaida dutifully repeated.

"He or she will be the person who can advise you about digs. They said over the phone that the Hall of Residence was full up so that's why it has to be digs, you see."

"How much money will I need to take for the digs?"

"Oh, well, I'm not really sure. It can vary so much."

They eventually settled on a sum of money that she could take with her and Alice lit up another cigarette and conjured up more problems amid the smoke.

"Now if the train's late or if the college is closed, or something, don't panic. Ask the driver to take you to the nearest YWCA. That's a Christian organisation but they make it their business to look after young girls from overseas. You'll be quite safe there."

Eventually every detail had been chewed over and the whole business settled, and Alice returned next door. She felt drained and exhausted. Worry niggled at her. After all, she wasn't all that clever at looking after and organising herself, never mind somebody else. And she'd never been to college. She was afraid of something going wrong, of something terrible happening to Zaida. It was as if Zaida was her daughter, her own flesh and blood.

Another worry also niggled at the back of her mind. Rasheeda and Russell were seeing too much of each other. She'd come in from the shops the other day to find the two of them in the house. They had been sitting close together on the settee, holding hands. They were in love. Suddenly even she could see that. And she knew it was going to cause much more trouble, and be much more difficult to deal with, than Zaida's problems.

# Twenty-Three

They were waiting for him in Pollokshields Lane – a large group of Pakistani youths in their expensive, well-cut school uniforms. All were the sons of professors and businessmen, doctors and consultants, owners of supermarkets and wholesale warehouses, successful affluent men. Russell was returning home with Rasheeda, Will and Maq. They blocked their path into the square.

One of them said to Rasheeda, Will and Maq, "You three can go on. It's this white bastard we want to talk to."

Russell said, "Get lost!"

And Will put in with, "What's the big idea?"

"The big idea is to warn this fuckin' bastard to keep clear of Pakistani girls in future."

Rasheeda spoke up indignantly.

"I choose whatever friends I like. You lot can mind your own damned business."

Maq joined in with a more pleading, embarrassed tone.

"Come on, guys. Russell's a pal of mine. He's all right."

"You shut up, traitor!" one of the gang said. "Or we'll give you a doing as well. Now, get going and take your big sister with you."

"She's not my sister. She's my aunty."

"Your aunty?" they jeered incredulously. "Well, take your aunty home. We've business to do with this guy."

Maq turned to Rasheeda.

"You go home, Rasheeda. I'll stay with Will and Russell."

"Don't be daft," Rasheeda flung at him. Then, to the tight mob barring the way, "Move! You're a bunch of cowards, the lot of you. You wouldn't dare have a one-to-one fight with Russell. He'd flatten any of you."

Just then two policemen appeared at the end of the lane.

"What's going on here?" one of them enquired as they strolled towards the crowd of youths.

Rasheeda said, "This lot's trying to keep us from getting into the square."

"And why do you want into the square?"

Will said, "We live there. They don't."

One of the crowd said, "We were just having a laugh."

"Well," the policeman told him, "away and have a laugh somewhere else, son. You're blocking the lane."

"Sure, no problem."

They began to swagger off but as they did so, one of them called back to Russell, "See you later."

Once in the square, Maq said, "Maybe you'd better cool it, you two. I know you're just friends and there's no harm done or intended. But it's obviously not a good idea to be seen talking together so much. Others are obviously getting the wrong idea."

"So what?" Rasheeda said. "Who I talk to has nothing to do with anybody."

"They don't understand – you know – that our parents are friends with Russell's and all that."

"Too bad."

"It'll be too bad for Russell, Rasheeda. It's not fair to get him into trouble."

Russell said, "They don't worry me. I don't see why they should tell me who I should talk to and who I shouldn't."

"If you don't, Russell, Rasheeda does. Things aren't that simple and she knows it."

Will joined the conversation then.

"We could get a gang together."

Maq rolled his eyes.

"Oh, brilliant! And what side am I supposed to be on in this race war you want to start?"

"I didn't mean a race war . . ."

"That's how it would end up."

Russell said, "Better to have a square go. I wouldn't mind that. I can handle myself."

"That mob's never going to agree to that." Will stopped at his garden gate. "Anyway, thank goodness tomorrow's Saturday. It'll give us the weekend to think about it and decide what we're going to do."

At the Alis' gate, Maq said to Rasheeda, "Are you coming in?"

"Not yet. I want to talk to Russell for a minute."

Maq rolled his eyes, then left them standing together.

"It's true what Maq said," Rasheeda told Russell. "Things aren't that simple."

"What are we going to do?"

"I'm supposed to be visiting Parveen tonight. I'll see you at the end of the lane at the usual time. OK? We can talk about it then. We'll think of something."

Russell nodded, then watched as Rasheeda swung open the garden gate, walked up the path and entered the bungalow. Only after she had disappeared did he reluctantly move along the few yards to his own house. He felt anxious and apprehensive. He could handle himself. He was confident of that. But he'd need to be Superman to take on a crowd like that. They'd kill him. Probably kick him to death. He felt sick at the thought. He wished he could just run away with Rasheeda. Go somewhere safe where no one would bother about seeing them together. Why should it be such a big deal? He knew perfectly well, of course. It was all to do with religion and two entirely different cultures.

It made him furious. He especially hated all the bloody mumbo-jumbo of religion. Not just the Muslim rules and regulations, but the Christian ones as well. The Catholics with their rituals and their priests with their fancy dresses and their unnatural celibacy vows. Where in the Bible did it say that priests had to be celibate? Then there were all the miserable Protestant sects with all their narrow-minded rules, supposedly coming from God Almighty. And what about the Buddhists with their gods? And the Hindus, to mention but a few religious beliefs?

They couldn't all be right, but each of them believed they were, of course.

Religion had caused more unhappiness, more guilt, more pain, more suffering, more bloody wars, all down through history than anything else.

Why couldn't two people like he and Rasheeda just be allowed to love and cherish each other in peace? They weren't doing anybody any harm.

But people were going to harm them all right.

Especially him. He remembered the gang of Pakistani youths. He saw in his mind's eye the menace of them. He felt their hatred.

And he was afraid.

# Twenty-Four

They had found another secret place in the park and as they walked arm in arm towards it, he revelled in the weight of Rasheeda's head against his shoulder. The delicate perfume of her hair tantalised his nostrils when, every now and again, he kissed the top of her dark head.

Reaching their place, they flopped down on the grass beside some rose bushes and relaxed, fingers delicately entwined. They were silent for a few minutes.

"I love this place," Russell said eventually.

"I love it too," Rasheeda said. "Everything you love, I love."

Each had brought a book of poetry with them. It was something they did regularly now. Russell had never thought much about poetry before and he certainly would have been far too embarrassed to recite it. But he and Rasheeda both knew that no words of their own could adequately express their feelings. Only the poets understood. And so he had introduced Rasheeda to the love poetry of Robert Burns. Now he picked a rose and gave it to her and while she held it to her lips, he read out:

"O my love's like a red, red rose
That's newly sprung in June;
And my love's like a melody
That's sweetly played in tune.
As fair art thou, my bonny lass,
So deep in love am I;
And I will love thee still, my dear,
Till a' the seas gang dry."

"Oh, Russell, that's so beautiful."

Then she enchanted him with lines from a book called *The Prophet* by Kahlil Gibran. She spoke quietly but passionately,

"When you love you shall not say 'God is in my heart', but rather, 'I am in the heart of God'. And think not you can direct the course of love, for love, if it finds you worthy, directs your course."

Gently, tenderly, she touched his face before going on.

"Love hath no other desire but to fulfil itself. But if you love and must needs have desires, let these be your desires: To melt and be like a running brook that sings its melody to the night. To know the pain of too much tenderness."

He knew, and she knew, what the poet meant. They loved each other but it was a strange and painful experience, as well as a joyful one.

"To be wounded by your own understanding of love," Rasheeda continued, "and to bleed willingly and joyfully. To wake at dawn with a winged heart and give thanks for another day of loving; to rest at the noon hour and mediate love's ecstasy; to return home at eventide with gratitude. And then to sleep with a prayer for the beloved in your heart and a song of praise on your lips."

No one had ever spoken to him like this. Nor had he ever spoken to another living soul in such a way. Now poetry – indeed, everything in the whole world, it seemed – had taken on a strange magical quality. He saw things he'd never noticed before – the veins of a leaf, the glisten of a blade of grass, the shape of a cloud.

Reluctantly, they got up again and began walking hand in hand back towards the park gate. At first they were so enchanted with each other and with the new-found beauty of the grass and the trees and the sky and everything in the world that they didn't notice the Pakistani youths. Then he felt Rasheeda's hand tighten round his.

"Just ignore them," she said. "We'll soon be at the gate and out on to the busy street."

"I hate this," Russell said. "Not facing up to things. Running away, mentally as well as physically. Not even talking about our problems."

"I know how you feel," Rasheeda said. "But we've so little time together to be happy. And at the moment, we're just being sensible. You can't face up to a mob. What's the point? Do you want to get killed? Anyway, we're not running. We're walking." She tilted her head up at him. "And I'm walking with calm dignity. I don't feel calm at all but I'm damned if I'm going to let them know how I really feel."

He admired her courage and he tried to emulate it. He forced himself to smile at her as they strolled along with the mob following them.

Secretly, he thanked God that the park was busy. He hadn't noticed before. Families were in the nearby play area, pushing children on swings and watching them clamber up and down climbing frames. White youths were shouting and laughing and kicking a ball about.

He had nursed loving thoughts of how he would always shelter and protect Rasheeda from any danger. But now look at me, he thought bitterly. He had been going to read her another poem by Burns which expressed his feelings beautifully. Actually he had it off by heart, he'd read it to himself so often. He told her that now.

"I was going to tell you another poem but that's spoiled now too."

"No, no," Rasheeda said. "They won't hear you. They're drawing further away. They've given up. Tell it to me, Russell."

He sighed but then began in a low voice:

"Oh, wert thou in the cold blast,
On yonder lea, on yonder lea
My plaidie to the angry airt –
I'd shelter thee, I'd shelter thee:
Or did misfortune's bitter storms
Around thee blow, around thee blow,
Thy shield should be my bosom,
To share it a', to share it a'.

"Or were I in the wildest waste,
So bleak and bare, so bleak and bare;
That desert were a paradise,
If thou went there, if thou went there;
Or were I monarch of the globe,
Wi' thee to reign, wi' thee to reign;
The brightest jewel in my crown
Would be my queen, would be my queen."

Suddenly Rasheeda stopped in her tracks, turned to him, raised herself on tiptoe and kissed him on the mouth.

"I love you, Russell Whitelaw," she said. "And I don't care who knows it. I don't care if the whole world's against us. I love you and I'll always love you."

"And I love you," he said, but his heart was thumping with as much fear as love. The Pakistani youths were quite a distance behind them now but he could sense their indignation and fury like poisoned darts tearing through the air towards him. He imagined he and Rasheeda walking in Pollokshields Lane, the trees hiding them from view and rendering them helpless targets. The only comfort he could find was in the fact that he would be the target, not Rasheeda. Surely they would not touch her. If they did . . . if anyone dared to lay a finger on her . . . He felt a rush of courage that stiffened his back and completely banished all fear.

He'd die for her if necessary. And, as if to prove his new-found courage and defy whatever fate had in store, he put his arm around Rasheeda's waist and kept it there and, as they walked along, her arm encircled his waist too.

The sun was shining again. The streets, the tall tenements with their sparkling windows, the shops, the people, everything became magical once more. He was happy again. Even when Bashir's car suddenly drew up on the road beside them, he wasn't bothered about accepting a lift.

"We're OK to walk," he said, but Rasheeda opened the door of the car.

"No, we may as well, Russell."

And so they got in, and Bashir drove them home.

After he was in the house, however, he felt restless. Their time together had been cut short, first by the menacing youths, and then by the appearance of Bashir. He needed to be in touch with his love again – even if it was just by letter. They had penned notes to each other before and slipped them to one another while walking home, or over the garden fence. Now he locked himself in his bedroom and, hunched over the small table by the window, he poured out his feelings in a letter.

> Rasheeda, my beloved, I feel drunk with happiness. The whole of life is beautiful, because you exist and I've found you. Today was a glorious day, and I believe every day could be like that because we belong to the same world, we live close to the roots of life. We both find the eternal in nature, and the strong and honest relationships of people. Race, colour, religion, tradition – nothing matters but true and honest love.
>
> Even just holding your hand profoundly moves my body and soul. One day, completely belonging to one another, giving ourselves to each other in marriage, we will enter our special paradise. I long for that day. Meantime, my darling Rasheeda, I only want to say – thank you. Thank you for being you. Thank you for being the lovely human being that you are.

He signed it and put the letter in an envelope before going outside and making his way over to the Alis' house. Rasheeda opened the door only seconds after he'd rung the bell, and he knew she had been thinking of him, as he had been thinking of her.

Without saying anything, he handed her the envelope. Without a word, she took it before withdrawing back into the house and gently closing the door. He returned to his own house, dreaming longingly of the day they would never need to part. He closeted himself in his room again and began drawing plans of the house that one day he and Rasheeda would share as man and wife. Bending over the table at the window, he was lost in total and joyful concentration. He was in a beautiful and happy dreamland. He had left the real world far behind.

# Twenty-Five

Constance McFarlane couldn't put it off any longer. Last time Ronnie was home, he had asked her why she hadn't yet invited the Pakistani neighbours in. Then Will started kidding him on, not realising how seriously his words would be taken.

"Mum's just jealous of the gorgeous Pakistani women, Dad. She's trying to keep them away from you."

Ronnie didn't laugh. He just stared at her until Will said worriedly, "I was only joking, Dad."

To Constance's horror, Ronnie said, "Unfortunately, it's no joke. I'm up to here with your mother's insane jealousy."

"No, you're wrong," Constance cried out. "I just haven't had time to organise anything. I'll phone them right now if you like."

"Invite the Whitelaws as well, Mum," Will said. "Maq and Russell are both pals of mine. Russell's mad about Rasheeda."

"Yes, fine," Constance said cheerfully. Anything to cover the fear that she was on the verge of losing Ronnie for good and that it would be her own fault.

"I've been selfish," she managed, and smiled. "I've been selfish trying always to keep you to myself every time you're home. I'm sorry, darling. From now on, we'll enjoy more of a social life. I promise."

Ronnie seemed to relax, but only a little. His eyes were dark and serious. Constance thought he looked even more handsome than usual. The hard, smouldering look in his eyes awakened her sexually. She could have dragged him off to bed right there and then.

"I'll phone the Alis and the Whitelaws. I suppose the Alis will have Mrs Ogilvie's old number. And then I'll go and buy some nice food. Do you want to come with me, darling?" she asked her husband.

He shrugged.

"All right."

"Smashing!" Will said. "Get sausage rolls, Mum, and some of that tinned ham from Marks you got before."

"I don't think Muslims eat ham, do they? Maybe we'd better stick to veggie things."

Ronnie began to look a bit brighter.

"We can get some of each. And we need a few bottles of wine."

"But I didn't think . . ." Constance began.

"Yes, I know," Ronnie interrupted, "Muslims don't drink alcohol but the Whitelaws do and we do. Marks and Sparks have elderberry and ginger wines as well as decent booze. You phone while I get the car out."

He went away whistling and Constance's heart lifted and filled with thankfulness. Once more she vowed to get a grip on herself, to be more trusting and not to allow the canker of jealousy to destroy the very thing that meant so much to her. Ronnie's happy-go-lucky, hail-fellow-well-met character had been what attracted her to him in the first place.

Emma came in while she was on the phone and Will said, "Mum's inviting the Alis and the Whitelaws round."

Emma pulled off her navy uniform coat.

"Super."

Constance put down the phone.

"I feel guilty now about not having them round before. I've always just spoken to them in the square or at the shops. Same with all the neighbours, really."

"You've no need to feel guilty, Mum," Emma assured her. "You work hard all day. You're too tired most nights and weekends to entertain the neighbours, or anybody else."

"Teaching is very draining, right enough. But still, I ought to have been doing something for your dad's sake, if not for my own. I'd better go and see to the shopping. They're all coming at eightish. I'm not sure how many Pakistanis there are. But anyway, it's not for dinner, only drinks and a finger buffet later on."

"Well," said Emma, "I'm glad old Bierce isn't coming."

Constance laughed.

"Yes, I doubt if even your dad could have put up with him."

She glanced anxiously at her reflection in the hall mirror as she passed. She was glad she'd invested in new grey-green eye shadow and black mascara. And her recently conditioned hair had a lively gloss to it. She didn't think she looked fifty-eight. God, she hoped she didn't.

The shopping spree turned out to be quite fun. Ronnie had cheered up at the thought of what he was now calling "the party". She even made him laugh. It was usually Ronnie who mimicked people but on this occasion she gave him an impression of Hilda Malloy. She had been sitting out in the back garden marking some papers, she told him, and she could hear chattering coming from the Malloys' garden but wasn't paying any attention until suddenly Hilda's stiffly coiffured head popped up over the fence. With her affected accent, she'd twittered, "Just a little luncheon party. Two courses and coffee."

Ronnie grinned. "I can just see her face. I would have died laughing if I'd been there."

"I almost did myself. It wasn't just the idiotic expression on her face. It was the way she said it."

Later Ronnie enjoyed himself helping to lay out the bottles and glasses and plates of crisps in the sitting room, while she set the table in the kitchen with different kinds of pâté and biscuits, a selection of cheeses and a few dips. Then a couple of flans, a bowl of salad, a basket of crusty bread. Coffee cups and cream and sugar finished the job.

"All ready?" Ronnie came into the kitchen gleefully rubbing his hands. He had changed into a dark blue velvet jacket, a blue shirt and a paisley silk neckerchief. Constance thought he looked like a big kid looking forward to Christmas. She shook her head at him.

"You're a real party animal, aren't you?"

His expression and the tone of his voice immediately changed.

"I like people. I enjoy company. Is that such a bad thing?"

"Of course not, darling," she hastily assured him. Usually, if he thought she was in one of her jealous moods, he'd try to tease her out of it. She felt frightened. Maybe the time would come when even making passionate love together would cease to make him forgive and forget.

She indicated the table.

"Does everything look all right?"

"Fine." He turned away. "That's the door. Dead on time. I bet it's the Alis."

Constance fought to quell her usual panic attack. She knew it was ridiculous to feel threatened at the mere thought of Ronnie being in the company of other women. It was, she suspected, tied up with her fear of ageing, as well as her insecurity. Often she wished she could go to a doctor and get a cure, or help of some kind. Any kind, from anybody.

Then unexpectedly, a strange thing happened. During the evening she began to view the Pakistani women, and even Alice Whitelaw, in a different way.

Simon hadn't come, a shifty-eyed and miserable Alice explained, because he'd had stocktaking to do. He sent his apologies. Constance suspected she was lying for him. He just hadn't wanted to come. Probably as unsociable as Ronnie was sociable. Poor Alice, Constance thought.

The Pakistani women were beautiful, especially Rasheeda. But it was obvious that Rasheeda had eyes for no one but Russell Whitelaw. It was obvious too that Alice was worried about this – she kept staring anxiously at them – and she wasn't the only one who was concerned. The old father not only cast disapproving looks at Rasheeda, but several times sharply chastised her.

There was anxiety and tension in the air at first as if everyone was trying terribly hard to be on their best behaviour and make a good impression. It was a bit pathetic, Constance thought, the way they all came in clinging to big Alice and trying to keep near to her.

The old man said, "Alice is our best friend. It is because of Alice that Zaida goes next week to college. Alice does many things for us."

Alice shifted uncomfortably in her seat. That big, ungainly body must hide a kind heart.

"Och, I haven't done anything."

At this, the whole Ali family cried out in loud protest and with examples of acts of friendship that Alice had performed.

It made Constance feel ashamed at being so slow in making the effort to make her new neighbours feel welcome. Of course, she'd never gone out of her way to have much – if anything – to do with her white neighbours either.

Very soon it was discovered that Alice had once been a nanny like Emma, and she and Emma enjoyed swapping nanny stories.

Constance, well used to patiently, gently coaxing stubborn, shy or frightened children out of themselves and helping them to feel more confident, concentrated much of her attention on Mrs Ali. She was gratified when she began to be successful in getting the old woman to look more relaxed, even to smile. They spoke about food and Mrs Ali promised to let her have not only the recipe for a Pakistani sweetmeat Constance had never heard of, far less tasted, but also a sample of it.

"I make *badam ki burfi* for you," Mrs Ali said with obvious pride and pleasure.

"Oh, thank you," Constance said. "I'll look forward to that. I really will."

"I will come with it to you."

"Good, good. Then we can have tea and talk together. Just the two of us."

Zaida said, "You are a teacher, Mrs McFarlane? That means you have been to college."

"Yes."

"Tell me about college, please. Our friend Alice does much for me but she has not been to college."

And so Constance described as much as she could about the college experience and how valuable it was. She felt she was slipping into her role as teacher, but didn't mind. They all listened so attentively and with such gratitude to her every word, Constance found it extremely touching. She felt they admired and liked her and now regarded her in much the same way as they did Alice.

They obviously liked Ronnie too. He made them laugh. He entertained them by playing the piano and singing a medley of Scottish songs. Emma joined him in a duet for some of the songs. Everyone clapped with enthusiasm and delight, and Ronnie made theatrical bows as if he were on a stage. Constance could see he was in his element and enjoying himself tremendously.

Will then played some pop music on his guitar. Afterwards he taught Maq and Russell and Rasheeda how to play a few chords. Russell could already play and he strummed away for a few minutes.

Eventually they all crowded through to the kitchen and enjoyed supper and coffee.

Altogether the evening turned out to be a great success and Constance felt glad for her own sake as well as Ronnie's. Friendship and affection still clung around her like a warm comfort blanket long after all the goodnights were said.

In the bedroom later, Ronnie remarked, "I'm sorry for that young couple. Next thing she'll be shipped over to Pakistan for an arranged marriage. What do you bet?"

Constance couldn't help agreeing that such a thing could happen. She knew something of Muslim beliefs and customs and Mr and Mrs Ali were obviously worried about Rasheeda. She sighed.

"They seem so much in love. Poor things."

"Nice family though."

"Yes, I'm glad I asked them in. Alice isn't so bad either."

She joined Ronnie in bed and he put an arm around her and cuddled her against him. She sighed but it was a sigh of happiness. She felt more safe and secure than she'd done for years.

She prayed that she could make it last.

# Twenty-Six

Jenny had invited her daughter, Fiona, and Fiona's new husband, Nigel, to afternoon tea. Fiona, she knew, felt it was her filial duty to keep in touch and that was why she had agreed to come. But Fiona was, and always would be, a daddy's girl.

The first thing she'd asked when they were speaking on the phone was, "Is Daddy coming? Have you asked him?"

"No."

"Why not?"

"Fiona, why should I? We're separated. I want to divorce him, not have afternoon tea with him."

"That's a horrible thing to say."

"But it's true. The trouble is neither you nor Percy are able to face the truth."

"It's you who isn't facing the truth, Mother. You can't divorce Daddy. He's done nothing wrong. It's you who's in the wrong. You've deserted him."

"All right. He's welcome to divorce me. Why doesn't he?"

"Because he's hoping that you'll come to your senses and realise what a mistake you've made. You've a good home with Daddy, Mother, and he's willing to forgive and forget."

"I've a good home here, Fiona. Now are you and Nigel coming for tea or aren't you?"

"Very well," Fiona said stiffly. "You are my mother, after all. It's only right that we should keep in touch."

So it was arranged and despite Fiona's unenthusiastic and unloving tone, Jenny was looking forward to the visit. Fiona was still the baby with the soft downy head who had once suckled enthusiastically at her breast. She was still the fair-haired toddler who had run to her, arms outstretched. She was the same little girl in plaits and hair ribbons who had sat on her knee and been cuddled and comforted after she'd had a fall.

No matter what Fiona did or didn't do now, she was her only child, and Jenny would always love her.

The table was all set and ready for afternoon tea with salmon sandwiches, plain scones and fruit scones, pancakes, fresh butter, cream and strawberry jam. Jenny patted the napkins and set one of the china cups and saucers more in line.

The doorbell buzzed and she hurried to answer it.

"Did you know," Fiona gasped excitedly, triumphantly, "who your new neighbours are in your wonderful square?"

"Yes. Why?"

"They're Pakistani!"

Jenny sighed to herself. She suddenly felt very tired.

"Well?"

"That'll soon change things," Fiona said.

"Fiona, come in and don't talk nonsense. The tea's made. How are you, Nigel?"

"Very well, thank you." He adjusted his glasses – heavy, horn-rimmed things, they were. "I've been doing quite a bit of DIY in the house. Putting in a new kitchen, you know. I've been working up to the last minute before coming here. I feel ready for a cup of tea."

"Well, I'm full of admiration. Putting in a new kitchen can't be an easy job. And don't worry, the tea's all ready on the table."

"My father's very good. He's been helping."

"A nice couple, your parents. I liked them. Do tell them I was asking after them."

Fiona rushed to peer out of the window.

"There's another one. An old man. Good gracious, is that a Corporation lamplighter's uniform? There used to be a man like that come round the streets near Daddy's shop. I can see an old woman now—"

"Fiona," Jenny said sharply, "come away from the window. Sit down and take your tea."

Reluctantly Fiona left the window and joined Nigel and Jenny at the table.

"Now," Jenny said, "tell me all about the new house. Nigel was saying you're having a new kitchen."

"Have you spoken to them yet?" Fiona asked.

"Who?"

"The Pakistanis, of course!"

"Not yet. Why?"

"There's always hordes of them, you know. They all crowd into one house. The place will be overrun with them. You'll see."

"Fiona, will you stop going on about the Pakistanis."

"Well . . ." Fiona enjoyed a few sips of tea and then selected a sandwich. "You'll soon be glad to get away from here now."

Jenny closed her eyes and counted to ten. There was no use getting angry with Fiona. She knew exactly how Percy would be playing on his daughter's sympathies and manipulating her. It wasn't Fiona's fault.

She tried to make the best of the afternoon, encouraging Fiona to talk about her house and what colour schemes they'd decided on and saying wasn't it nice that her mother and father-in-law lived so near.

Eventually Fiona said, "As soon as we're finished, you must come over and see the house, Mother. We'll have a little house-warming party."

"Oh, thank you, dear." Jenny's heart filled with gratitude. "I'll really look forward to it."

Later it occurred to her that probably Percy would be invited too. But she assured herself that she could cope with that and she managed to keep feeling happy and cheerful as she stood at the door waving goodbye to Fiona and Nigel.

It was still quite early and she lingered, breathing in the cool air of the pleasant autumn evening. Her bungalow was nearest to the lane and she'd only been standing a few seconds when her eye caught sight of three or four youths skulking about. Somehow they looked as though they might be up to no good, although they were respectably dressed in the local private school uniform. It was a very expensive school, the one Nigel had once attended.

Probably they were friends of the Whitelaw boy or Will McFarlane, although they seemed to be more interested in old Mrs Ogilvie's bungalow. They were white boys but they could be friends with one of the Pakistani young people. It certainly looked as if Russell Whitelaw was. Satisfied with that, Jenny withdrew into the house after locking up, then went through to the back of the house to catch up on some typing work.

Anjum was very pleased and excited. Not only was her English improving by leaps and bounds, but for the first time she had gone out on her own. Admittedly it was only a couple of houses away to their friend Constance McFarlane's, but it seemed to her a very brave (and very British) act. She had made a dish of *badam ki burfi* for Constance and taken it to her house. She had shyly gone round to the back door which led to Constance's kitchen and had intended just to give her the dish to put straight into her fridge before returning to her own house.

Constance had insisted that she come in to drink tea with her, however. She had been trembling with nervousness and excitement and had hung back at first, but Constance had taken her by the arm and gently led her into the warm, comfortable kitchen. Soon she had lost most of her nervousness and even smiled at some of the stories.

Constance had told her about the pupils she taught. She was a nice woman, Constance, and Anjum was glad she had found a new friend for herself. Alice was a very good friend and she loved her but Alice concentrated more on the young people.

Her friend Constance wanted not only to talk to her but also to listen to her. Constance listened with much concentration and interest and even asked the help of Anjum. Constance had new Pakistani pupils and wanted to learn some Urdu so that she could understand them when they had difficulties and lapsed into their native tongue.

Anjum felt proud. Not only had she helped Constance with a new recipe, now she could help her with language. She felt very proud and very happy. This was her best day in the square, the day when she had found courage to step out alone.

She and Constance said goodbye at the back door after Constance had promised to come to the Ali bungalow the next week for tea. Constance was working as a teacher and had to wait until either weekends or holidays to be free to visit. But she was coming. She'd promised and Anjum was excited at the prospect. Already, as she hurried along the side path of Constance's garden into the square, she was planning what sweetmeats she'd prepare for her friend.

As soon as she reached the pavement, her heart pounded with fear. She could see white boys standing menacingly in front of her house. She clutched her doputta more tightly over her head with violently trembling hands. Even her legs felt weak and could hardly carry her forward. Now she could see a man and woman approaching from the other side. It was "the awful Mr Bierce", as Alice called him. The sight of this man terrified Anjum all the more but, desperate to reach the safety of her house, she kept propelling herself forward, eyes lowered, stumbling, violently shaking all over.

One of the youths bumped against her and said, "Oh sorry, madam." The next giggled and the youth went on, "But you shouldn't be here, you know."

"Aye," Mr Bierce said in passing. "That's right, you tell the Pakis where to go, son."

The youths were blocking Anjum's path and she was standing helplessly trembling and trying to clutch her doputta over her mouth when suddenly Sissy Bierce seemed to go mad. She nearly knocked her husband over as she ran to Anjum and put her own trembling but protective arm around the older woman's shoulders.

"You ought to be ashamed of yourselves, the lot of you," she yelled. "What a bunch of cowardly ignorant bullies, trying to intimidate and frighten an old woman. And that includes you." She glared wildly at her astonished husband. "You're old enough to know better but of course you're worse than any of them. You've been intimidating me for years. You ignorant, stupid, revolting excuse for a man!"

Then she addressed Anjum.

"Come on, I'll see you safely into your house."

After they'd hurried inside the bungalow, they collapsed together on to the nearest sofa in the front room.

"Is that you, Mammy?" a voice called out and Rasheeda entered the room. She stopped in surprise.

"Oh, Mrs Bierce! What . . . I mean . . ."

Her mother spoke up.

"Mrs Bierce has been my friend. She helped me. Please treat her as our honoured guest. Bring tea and biscuits."

"What happened? Are you all right, Mammy?"

"Do as you are told, Rasheeda."

"OK. OK."

Anjum turned to Mrs Bierce.

"Are you all right, Mrs Bierce?"

"Sissy. Just call me Sissy."

"And I am Anjum."

"I'm all right, Anjum. A bit shaken, that's all. I've never spoken up like that before, especially not to my husband. But somehow it was too much. Seeing you so helpless and frightened. I knew how you felt, you see." She dazedly shook her head. "I've never had the nerve to speak up for myself but suddenly I just snapped when I saw him behaving like that to you. He should have stepped in and told those boys how badly they were behaving. He should have chased them off. But oh no! Not him."

Tears began to roll down her cheeks. "Oh Anjum, what am I going to do? He's never struck me or anything like that. But he's intimidated me nevertheless. I've always been afraid of him."

"You help me," Anjum said. "So I help you."

"Thank you . . . but I can't see . . ."

"You come here for safety any time. You come here any time of day or night and feel safe."

Sissy nibbled worriedly at her lip.

"Well, perhaps I . . . Anyway, it's terribly good of you. I really appreciate such a kind thought."

"Not just thought. You understand me?"

Sissy managed a weak smile.

"Yes."

Rasheeda came in, smiling and bearing a tray. Her father was following her looking very pleased and happy.

"Here we are, folks," Rasheeda said. "Tea is served."

"Welcome, Mrs Bierce," Sharif said.

"Sissy," she said faintly.

"Sissy," Sharif dutifully replied.

Then suddenly there was a knock at the door and Sharif cried out in delight, "We've more guests. I'll welcome at the door."

After he'd hurried from the room, Sissy let out a moan. "That'll be my husband."

Anjum put a brown hand over Sissy's white one. She squeezed it and patted it.

They could hear Sharif Ali crying out, "Come in, come in. Welcome to my house."

# Twenty-Seven

"By the way, why have you suddenly started getting a lift home with Bashir, son?" Alice asked.

Russell shrugged. "He was giving Rasheeda a lift and he offered me one."

They were sitting at the table and Russell, changing the subject, said, "This is the house I'm going to live in when I get married, Mum." Eagerly he pushed some drawings in front of her. There was the inside plan of a house and also a painting of the outside with trees, flower garden and all.

"I've designed everything myself! Isn't it the greatest?"

"Married?" Alice bulged her eyes. "You're joking, of course!"

"One day, not now!" he responded impatiently. "How could I build a house like that now? It'll take me years to save up enough money."

"Oh, well . . ."

"Do you notice the Eastern influence? See that roof, and that veranda?"

"Gosh, have you a picture of your future wife as well?"

"As a matter of fact, I have."

He shuffled through his sketches and pulled out a head-and-shoulders drawing of Rasheeda. He had always had a flair for drawing but in this one he was inspired. The girl's beauty had been captured, yet it was wildly alive. She looked poised, courageous, rebellious, ready to escape, ready to wing far away.

"Russell, she's so young, and you hardly know each other. You've plenty of time."

"Oh, for pity's sake,. Mum." His voice loudened to cover his embarrassment. "I know we've plenty of time. I've no intention of dashing off tomorrow to get married. I can't afford to keep a wife yet."

Alice nodded sagely.

"I suppose it would be a bit difficult on the pocket money your dad gives you."

"It's not funny. Mortgages and rates and things like that are a terrible worry for a man. I'm beginning to sympathise with Dad. I know now how he must feel. If it weren't for somebody like Rasheeda, I'd never get married. Already I'm worrying about how much money I'll earn when I leave school to meet all those kinds of expenses."

"I know it's not funny, dear. But you're still in your teens. Surely you shouldn't be giving that sort of thing a thought."

"It's all very well for a woman to talk like that but men have to worry. They have to face responsibilities."

"Not yet, you haven't – thank goodness. Enjoy life while you have the chance."

His eyes anxiously sought hers.

"You're not against Rasheeda, are you?"

"No, I'm not."

He suddenly gave her a hug and a kiss.

"I didn't think you could be, not once you got to know her." He turned to the picture again. "Isn't she beautiful? Amn't I lucky, Mum?"

"Yes, dear. But what does Rasheeda think? What does she say about all this?"

"We don't need to *say* anything. We just know."

Alice felt uneasy. Everything was always so clear cut and simple to the young. It did not seem to have occurred to Russell that he might have more immediate worries than rates and mortgages. The Alis were devout Muslims. She suspected that a prospective white Christian son-in-law would act like a time bomb in their midst.

She attempted to warn him.

"Try not to get too emotionally involved, Russell. There are bound to be complications in a situation like this. Things might not work out as you hope and I can't bear to see you hurt."

"Mum, I'm crazy about that girl."

"Oh Russell . . ."

"I am! I am! You don't understand. You still think of me as a baby. But I'm not a child any more. I've the feelings of a man."

She gazed wistfully at him. It was true. He had the body of a man, the hard muscular neck, the broad shoulders, the flat narrow hips. Only the lantern-jawed face with its wide mouth and slightly bulbous eyes still retained a boyish vulnerability.

She prayed that God would protect him from being wounded. She suspected that the Ali family were in a quandary. They loved her as a friend and they liked Russell. Nevertheless she felt sure they could never accept him as a suitor for Rasheeda.

She had gone into the bungalow to say goodbye to Zaida the morning of the day she left and found both Zaida and her sister trembling with emotion. Zaida could hardly wait to tell her that something was wrong.

"My sister is so upset," she whispered as soon as Noor Jahan had gone through to the kitchen to make coffee. "It is about her husband."

"Oh?" Alice whispered back in the same deadly serious, conspiratorial tone. "What's wrong?"

"Bashir went out to the shop this morning and did not speak to her. She is very worried."

"Oh well, maybe he just didn't feel in a talkative mood."

"Noor Jahan was crying."

"Oh, the poor wee soul."

"She asked him the question. He did not answer. This is most strange. She said, "You are coming with all the family this afternoon to take Zaida to the train?" He went away and did not answer."

"I wonder why," Alice said.

"I am even more upset than my sister. Such a thing has never happened before. If Bashir does not return, what can Noor Jahan do? What will happen to her?"

Alice's expression was suspended between complete blankness and a valiant attempt to understand. She had lost the drift of the conversation.

"Isn't it . . .? I mean . . . Surely it can only be a little tiff at the most. A tiff means . . . eh . . . well, a small misunderstanding."

Zaida bit her lip and wrung her hands and appeared quite distracted. She was joined by a tragic-looking Noor Jahan and a violently rattling tray of coffee cups.

Alice hurriedly rescued the tray and placed it down on the table.

"Now, everything's going to be all right," she soothed. "Just keep calm. I'm sure there's no need to lose our heads."

Noor Jahan's lips trembled.

"No' lose the head. Lose the husband."

Alice had an urge to laugh but immediately smothered it. This was obviously no trivial matter to a Pakistani wife. It suddenly occurred to her that Pakistani women must feel very insecure.

She had come to realise that both the men and the women could be surprisingly emotional in temperament, but she had not known of this insecurity. Now that she gave the matter some thought and tried to put herself in their shoes, she began to understand.

Apparently, a Pakistani husband could divorce his wife by simply repeating three times in public in front of witnesses, "I divorce this woman." If such a thing did happen, it would leave the woman in a precarious and disgraceful position. A husband could seldom be found for someone who was no longer a virgin.

She had read somewhere too that a high proportion of Pakistani women were illiterate and, in Pakistan especially, a woman could not work. She had to fall back on her parents or brothers or sisters or an aunt or uncle to feed and clothe her and give her shelter.

"Oh, but I'm sure everything will turn out all right. Wait and see."

"I am waiting," Noor Jahan assured her. "And I am very worried. Also I am once more pregnant."

"Oh dear!"

Alice had never noticed before but now that she mentioned it, the fact became obvious, although it would have been difficult to guess how far "gone" the girl was. Noor Jahan was so small and neat.

Her beauty was different from Rasheeda's. Her skin was duskier and, although she was older, her face had a childish roundness and there was a gentle naivety about it that Alice found very appealing.

Zaida took off her glasses, rubbed her eyes and then shook her head.

"Such a thing has never happened before."

"I expect it's something to do with you going away. He's been thinking about how he can arrange to be back in time or something. Probably he's just a bit harassed." Alice finished drinking her coffee, then rose with some reluctance. "I'm afraid I have to go now. Russell will soon be in for his lunch."

Both girls came to the door with her.

"Do not worry," Zaida confided, "we will let you know everything that happens."

"Everything," Noor Jahan agreed.

Alice felt a lump swell up in her throat. It seemed to her that they were treating her as one of their family and taking it for granted that she would be concerned and feel entitled to know about such intimate matters. She had an almost uncontrollable urge to reach out and squeeze their hands in hers, to hug them with grateful affection. But instinct told her that this would be a mistake. She had found it to be a mistake with her other friends in the square.

One cigarette after another did little to soothe her. Busying herself with preparing Russell's lunch – Simon took a packed lunch to the shop – and later on, washing up and tidying the house only engaged part of her attention. By afternoon she could not stand the anxiety and suspense any longer. She hurried back to the bungalow praying that Noor Jahan was all right, that Bashir had returned, that they were still married, that Noor Jahan was still respectable, that she still had a father for her children, a protector, a breadwinner.

Poor Noor Jahan, she kept thinking. What she must be suffering.

Noor Jahan opened the door. Her long black plait of hair drooped down the front of one shoulder.

"Zaida, Alice comes again to say to you goodbye."

"Well . . ." Alice followed her into the sitting room. Then Zaida came through looking like a bespectacled doll in a coat with a little shoulder cape and furry hat tied under her chin. Beneath the coat were satin trousers and fur-lined boots.

"I am ready to go to continue my studies. I thank you so much, Alice."

"Yes, but . . ." Alice peered closely at both girls. She lowered her voice. "Is he back, then?"

They stared at her in apparent surprise.

"Who back?"

"Noor Jahan's husband. Is everything all right?"

They gave an airy wave of their hands as if the matter were too trivial to mention.

"Och aye."

Alice was speechless with astonishment as well as perplexed by their change of attitude. In her day-to-day contact with these Pakistani women, however, she was to discover that this childlike resilience was quite common. A terribly dramatic situation would flare up. Emotions flapped free. Stark tragedy appeared imminent and inevitable, only to change like a stormy sky dissolving into a magic rainbow.

She became more and more aware of this fairytale quality. Stories and anecdotes would be told and, in the telling, gathered a momentum of their own, gained flavour and colour, acquired a new dimension. A simple incident like their cousin Arshad coming in through the unlocked back door without knocking was related with saucer eyes and voices that explored the full range of gripping dramatic expression.

"Mammy and Daddy and all the family, we are watching television when suddenly we feel someone else in the room. My daddy he turns round. He is looking. A figure is standing very still and staring at television. I am frightened. What is this? How can this be? Arshad is at the house of his father. 'Oh my God, Daddy,' I cry. Daddy is very worried, very worried indeed. But he says, 'I think it is Arshad.' But I think it is a ghost. I tell my daddy. Then Arshad laughs. He says, 'It is me – Arshad.'"

Alice wondered if their dramatic way of telling a story stemmed from their background in Pakistan where women were much more frequently confined to their houses – especially in the villages – where there would be no television or wireless, and many of them were unable even to read or write to pass the time. The ability to entertain, to stimulate imagination and grip people's interest with ordinary little events and gossip within the family circle would be something not only worth cultivating but necessary in the circumstances.

Their belief in ghosts probably grew from the same fertile soil. Even Zaida, who had Highers in Mathematics, Chemistry and Physics, looked perturbed and anxious at the mention of ghosts, and she too could tell of strange happenings.

Often the same incident would be related by different members of the family and Alice would become confused by what seemed to her contradictions or mistakes in detail. But she could never be sure if it were only the language that was defeating them all, including herself, and causing the perplexities.

Just to make sure, she repeated, "You're all right then, you and Bashir."

"Och aye," Noor Jahan said, with another airy wave of her hand.

# Twenty-Eight

Mr Bierce looked dazed as Sharif Ali hustled him into the sitting room.

"You no' worry," Sharif Ali told him. "We give you Scottish tea." Then to Rasheeda, "You have no' enough cups. Can you no' count?"

Rasheeda rolled her eyes and her father called after her as she left the room, "You're a bad cheeky girl."

He then addressed Mr Bierce. "Sit down, please. My home is your home."

Mr Bierce cast a wide-eyed gaze over at Sissy. Sissy stared back at him. Why, she thought in surprise, he's frightened. He's just a small, frightened excuse for a man. He's a bully only when he thinks he can get away with it. She was still holding Anjum's hand. She gave it a secret squeeze before releasing it. Dignity straightened her back. It was a new and thrilling experience.

She indicated Anjum.

"This is my friend Anjum. Anjum, this is my husband, Timothy Bierce."

Keeping her eyes lowered and holding her doputta modestly over her chin, Anjum murmured, "My husband Sharif and my daughter Rasheeda."

"Hi," said Rasheeda, coming in with more cups and saucers. "Mammy, did you take Constance that almond thing?"

"Yes. She was pleased. We had nice time together. She is coming next week to our house."

Sharif sat down near Mr Bierce.

"It is good that everyone is friendly, eh?"

Mr Bierce looked like a trapped animal seeking some means of escape, but Sharif Ali didn't appear to notice.

"Tea, tea," he cried out. "Pour tea for our friend Timothy."

Sissy could have laughed. She actually felt like laughing and she hadn't felt like that for years.

Rasheeda poured the tea, passed round the cups and offered the biscuits. Sharif was still favouring Mr Bierce with all his attention.

"What is your work, Timothy?"

Mr Bierce cleared his throat and managed, "I don't work now."

"Oh," Sharif said knowledgeably, "so are you retarded?"

Now Sissy did laugh. She laughed until she was sore. Rasheeda joined in with equal hilarity.

"Daddy," she howled. "You mean retired. Retarded means . . ." She pointed to her head. "Not all there. The brain no' working properly."

Sharif looked annoyed.

"You no' so clever. You can't speak Urdu. You say something in Urdu now. Then I laugh at you."

*"Touché."*

"What's this *touché*?"

Rasheeda rolled her eyes. "Och, never mind."

Sharif turned to Mr Bierce. "What to do with cheeky girls? I don't know. She's a big worry to me, that one."

Rasheeda tried to change the subject. "That sounds like Noor Jahan and Bashir."

"Noor Jahan! Bashir!" Sharif called. "Come and meet our visitors, Timothy and Sissy."

Bashir came into the room smiling broadly, followed by Noor Jahan, her eyes lowered and her hand clutching at her doputta.

"Hello there," Bashir greeted Mr and Mrs Bierce. "We've been to the pictures." Then, to his father-in-law, "Do you know what's up with Maq?"

"What do you mean – what's up with Maq?"

"We saw him arguing the toss with some lads. Starting to fight, they were. We stopped the car and rescued Maq. He refused to tell us what it was all about."

"Where is he now?"

"He wanted to go and see Russell. He had to talk to him, he said. He was up to high doh."

"Where is this high doh?"

Rasheeda laughed. "Och Daddy."

"Never mind your och daddys." He turned to Mr Bierce. "Have you girls like this, Timothy? Or are you a lucky man and have only sons?"

Mr Bierce cleared his throat. But it was his wife who spoke up.

"We have no children. It has always been a great sadness to me." She smiled. "Maq is your grandson, is he?"

"Yes. He is a grand boy. A very good boy." He looked anxious. "Now I am worried about him. It is no' like Maq to be fighting with anybody."

Bashir said, "I told him not to be long at Russell's so maybe we'll find out what's up when he comes in."

Sissy's lips were still weakly quivering with laughter but she managed to stiffen them and ask, "What is it you work at, Bashir?"

"At my dad's supermarket in Maryhill." He gave her a happy smile and Sissy marvelled at his dazzling white teeth. "I wasn't clever enough to go to university like my brothers."

Sharif waved his hands about in protest.

"No' true, no' true, Sissy. Bashir is a clever man and a good husband to Noor Jahan."

"Is it true that Pakistani marriages are arranged by the parents?"

"Aye, that's true. And we made a good marriage for Noor Jahan, our eldest daughter. We are all very happy."

Sissy wished the same thing had happened to her. She wished she'd taken her mother's advice and married Tom Gardner, a nice young man who adored her. The only reason she hadn't fancied him was because he had bright red hair. Sissy could hardly believe how stupid she had been. She'd certainly suffered for her stupidity ever since. Well, she'd had enough. More than enough. She just couldn't take any more. To hell with Timothy Bierce. She shivered at the temerity of allowing such a daring thought to enter her mind. But it was a pleasant shiver because her usual fear was now tinged with excitement and pleasure.

Anyway, just look at him, she thought. And she looked at him with new eyes and saw not an evil-tongued ogre, but just a silly wee man. Things were going to be different from now on. It wouldn't be easy. She knew that. But her life was going to change, or she'd die in the attempt.

Bashir suddenly called out, "Maq, is that you?"

Maq came reluctantly into the room. He had a painful-looking black eye.

Sharif cried out, "Maq, what happened? Who has done this to you?"

Maq glared at Rasheeda.

"It's all her fault. She's been far too friendly with Russell. Everybody's talking about it. Now, other white boys are getting involved – just looking for trouble. We've all warned her this would happen. But no, she doesn't care what'll happen to Russell. He's going to end up with more than this." He indicated his swollen eye.

Rasheeda tossed back her hair but her eyes betrayed distress.

"We're not doing any harm. I like Russell."

Sharif shouted, "I like Russell but that's different and you know it, you bad girl. You are always big trouble to our family and now you are big trouble to our friends and neighbours."

Suddenly Rasheeda burst into tears and ran from the room. Bashir turned to Mr and Mrs Bierce.

"Sorry about this, folks."

"Oh yes, yes," Sharif agreed, in some distress himself. "We are neglecting our guests. Sorry, Timothy. I am very sorry indeed. Anjum, give our friends more tea and biscuits."

"No thank you." Sissy rose. "It's time we were going home. Isn't it, Timothy?"

Mr Bierce hastily rose.

"Yes, we'd better be going."

"Thank you for the tea," Sissy said and gave her husband a meaningful look.

"Yes," he echoed, "thank you for the tea."

"You must come and visit us soon." Sissy smiled at Anjum. "Thank you so much for helping me, Anjum."

"No, no," Anjum protested. "You helped *me*, Sissy. I thank you."

After they'd left Anjum said in her own language, "I am very worried. I have seen the way Russell and Rasheeda look at each other."

"Yes, I have too," Sharif agreed. "It is no good. We will have to do something." He pulled thoughtfully at his beard. "I shall write to my friend Umar. He is of an honourable family and he has three sons – good boys. I remember them when they were little. Umar has been looking for wives for them."

Maq said, "Send Rasheeda back to Pakistan, you mean? She won't like that."

Sharif shouted angrily, "It's no' a case of what she likes. Anyway, such things take time and many arrangements to be made and things to settle. But my mind is made up. It is best for Rasheeda. We will make sure we find her a good husband in Pakistan."

Anjum nodded.

"You are right, Sharif. It is time for Rasheeda."

"Aye," Bashir added, "and the quicker the better if you ask me."

# Twenty-Nine

Russell had wandered about like a lost soul looking for Rasheeda. He couldn't concentrate on his lessons. Anxious thoughts about her agonised every corner of his mind. Even Maq seemed to be avoiding him.

"What's up?" He caught a grip of Maq's arm just as he was about to disappear into a classroom at the Academy. "Where's Rasheeda? Has something happened to her?"

"No, it's just she's had to stay in the house for a few days to help her mother."

It wasn't until afterwards that Russell thought – why couldn't Noor Jahan help her mother? He could hardly wait to get back to the square. He went straight to the Alis' bungalow and rang the bell. To his surprise, Sharif Ali answered.

"I was worried about Rasheeda," Russell told the old man. "She wasn't at school."

"You no' to worry, Russell. Rasheeda is OK. But she's been a cheeky, bad girl. She's causing trouble to everyone with being too friendly with white boys. She'll have to stop this. It's no good. We're telling her. From now on Bashir will take her to school and afterwards bring her back and we've instructed her cousin Parveen to keep an eye on her in between times. She must act like a good Muslim girl from now on."

Russell knew of course that it wasn't white boys in the plural Sharif Ali meant. It was one white boy, and it was him. He wasn't sure what to say for the best and, in case he only made matters worse for Rasheeda, he decided – for the moment at least – to say nothing. One way or another, he would talk to Rasheeda first.

With a nod, he silently withdrew and Sharif Ali closed the door.

He couldn't sleep that night. For long dark hours he fought with the bedclothes. Eventually he had to get up and write a note to Rasheeda. He would slip it to her while Parveen wasn't looking. Parveen had been very accommodating up till now but he guessed that after what Sharif Ali had no doubt told her about Rasheeda, Parveen would be afraid to risk being part of any more cover-ups. As it was, Parveen had been a very reluctant and worried ally. If necessary, he would plead with Maq to deliver the note.

He wrote then tore up several notes. He felt on this occasion it was more urgent to speak to Rasheeda, rather than write to her. In the light of this new development, they had much to discuss. In the end, he just scribbled, "Meet me in our close tonight. I'll wait from seven o'clock onwards." He knew that by seven o'clock her father would be at work and Bashir would be working late at the supermarket. It would be easier for her to slip out when the two men weren't there.

"Their close" was in Nithsdale Road. They always called it "their close" and spoke of it in affectionate terms, because it was the secret meeting place they used after the park was closed. It was a clean and respectable entry to the houses in the tenement building, and back closes were quite common places for Glasgow couples to do their courting in. Nevertheless, he felt ashamed of taking Rasheeda there and hiding in the shadows. He longed to be able to meet her openly and honestly.

He'd recently said to her, "I'm ashamed of meeting you here."

"Are you ashamed of our love?" she'd asked and he'd immediately cried out, "Of course not!"

"Well, that's all that matters," she'd said and she'd wound her soft arms round his neck and pulled him against her sweet-scented body.

He longed to make love to her properly and sometimes they went as far as intimate petting until he had to push her away in case he completely succumbed to the waves of passion that kept threatening to engulf him. Sometimes she had to do the same.

"We will have to marry," he'd told her in desperation. "Even if we can't afford it financially, we can't go on like this, Rasheeda. It's more than flesh and blood can bear."

"Oh, if only, if only . . ." she'd sighed.

"I could give up the idea of university," he said. "I could just leave school and get a job."

"No, no, I mustn't spoil your life, Russell. I couldn't bear to do that."

"How would you spoil my life?" he scoffed. "You *are* my life."

He was in the close long before seven and anxiously, eagerly waiting for her. The moment he saw her – so colourful, so beautiful, so different from anyone he'd ever known – he ran to her to enfold her in his arms.

"Oh Rasheeda, I've been so worried about you. What's been happening? Are they trying to stop you seeing me?"

"Don't worry." Her fingers gently traced his features. "No one can ever stop me seeing you. I'll be back at school tomorrow, and soon we'll both be at university."

"It won't be easy to meet if Parveen won't co-operate any more."

"We'll find a way. I found a way tonight, didn't I? And think how much easier it'll be at university, Russell."

"Do you think your father will come round? He does like me, doesn't he? He's always been—"

She put her finger against his mouth, silencing him.

"Don't. Just be happy that we're together now, and we have our dreams."

And so they spoke about how happy they'd be at university, how Russell would one day be an architect and how he would design their dream house. For the hundredth time they planned every inch of it. Rasheeda chose the colours for the curtains and Russell suggested shades for the walls. They happily furnished each room together. They encompassed it all in their shining inward gaze.

Eventually, arms entwined, they made their way back to the square, only separating when they came to Pollokshields Lane. Russell waited in the lane for a few minutes until Rasheeda slipped into her garden and round to the back door of the house. Then he strolled towards his own place.

"I didn't hear you go out, son." His mother met him in the hall carrying a supper tray. He followed her into the sitting room where his father was watching television.

His father said, "You missed the match. I called to tell you when it came on."

"Oh, I forgot. How did it go?"

"A draw, would you believe!"

Alice said, "Fetch another cup for yourself, son. There's plenty of tea in the pot."

"OK." He went whistling through to the kitchen, Rasheeda and the joy of their love still clinging to his senses, lightening his heart, making him thankful.

He settled down beside his parents and listened to his dad telling him all about the match. In the past his dad had taken him to football matches when he was on holiday. Sometimes he risked leaving someone else in charge of the shop if it was a really important game. They still went together occasionally. Russell wasn't as passionate a fan as his dad but didn't let on because he knew his dad didn't like to go on his own. His mum would never dream of accompanying his dad because football matches could turn rough. His mum even worried about him and his dad going. His dad just laughed at her.

"We'll soon fight off all the opposition, won't we, son?"

His dad was kidding, of course. No way would his dad want to get into a fight. Even when he'd been a child and he'd got into a fight with other kids or done something that deserved a walloping, his dad had never hit him. Sometimes he'd wished he *would* hit him, rather than moan and complain about money, for instance. He'd got pretty much immune to all that although, admittedly sometimes he lost his head and shouted at his dad (and indeed sometimes at his mum as well), but that was just out of frustration and temporary impatience. Parents had so little sympathy and the older they got, instead of getting wiser, the less understanding they had.

Sometimes he even felt he hated them. Not long ago he had believed they hated him. According to his dad, his music was crap (and he played it far too loud), the disco dancing he enjoyed was barbaric, his hair was too long, his clothes (when he wasn't in school uniform) were a joke and he hadn't a clue about money. Then, of course, he'd discovered that all parents behaved like that to their teenage offspring. All his pals suffered in much the same way from their parents. So it was just a case of grinning and bearing it as much as possible.

Anyway, they weren't always such pains in the arse. Despite his dad's attitude to decent music, he'd bought him that fab guitar for his last birthday.

He wasn't such a bad old stick. Tonight, such was Russell's happiness, there was so much love in his heart that it overflowed and spilled out to encompass both of his parents as they sat by the fire drinking their tea and crunching at toasted muffins.

# Thirty

Russell was on his way from the last class of the day when suddenly he heard the clatter of feet echoing down the long corridor. His heart drummed painfully against his ribs. Should he speed up or ignore the crowd he suddenly realised was after him? He walked with feigned nonchalance as the group flowed around him.

"See you, you fuckin' creep. We know you're still at it. You obviously can't take a telling. We don't want contaminating by the likes of you."

Angry brown faces closed around him, blurring into an intimidating sameness as panic set in. He was pushed from one to another as the pack mentality took over. He didn't know who hit him first. He felt no pain – just a shock wave, and bright lights flashing as he was struck on the side of the head.

As if this was a signal, the pent-up hatred exploded and, shrieking their rage, the entire crowd started lashing out at him. Buffeted by blows, he sagged on to his knees in the foetal position, arms hugging round his head. He felt numb, sick and helpless as the blows rained in.

Suddenly, it was quiet and still. They had gone. Moaning, saliva stringing from his lips to mingle with the tears of pain and shame, he crawled forward. Eventually he managed to drag himself up the wall to a standing position. Then came the pain, the raw burn of torn skin and the deeper ache of bruised bone. Every step a gasp of pain, he stumbled on his way.

He hardly knew how he reached Bashir's car. Half unconscious, he collapsed against it. The next thing he knew he was in the back seat in Rasheeda's arms and she was stroking his hair and weeping broken-heartedly.

Bashir was saying, "Now do you believe what we've all been telling you? Now do you see that Sharif is doing the right thing?"

"We've never done any harm," Rasheeda sobbed.

"Don't keep saying that," Bashir told her angrily. "You *are* doing harm, that's the truth of it. *Now* how is Alice going to feel? What's she going to think? Russell's her only son. She's going to feel terrible. You know that perfectly well."

"I'm all right," Russell managed. "Have you got a tissue on you, Rasheeda?"

She fished one out of her pocket and he gingerly wiped at his face.

As soon as they reached the square, both Bashir and Rasheeda helped Russell out of the car and, still supporting him, got him to his house. Alice screamed with horror when she saw Russell.

"My God, what happened to him?"

"Some boys at school," Bashir said, helping him into Alice's sitting room and lowering him into a chair.

"I'll be all right, Mum," Russell said. "I'm just bruised and a bit winded, that's all."

"Boys attacked you at school? But why?"

"Och, it was nothing. Don't worry. Once I get a cup of tea, I'll be fine."

"I'll go and make one." She turned to Bashir and Rasheeda in distress. "Thanks for bringing him home."

Rasheeda said, "I'll stay with him."

"No," Bashir said firmly, "you'll come home with me. Now!"

As soon as they went into the Ali bungalow, Bashir related to the rest of the family what had happened. Sharif wrung his hands and smacked his brow.

"It's true what Bashir says. The quicker you're away to Pakistan the better. We've talked enough about it. We've had our family conference. Your uncle and aunty agree. All the cousins agree. Mahmoud and Shereen agree. I must write to my friend Umar without any further delay."

Rasheeda was sobbing, devastated. "But Daddy, I love Russell and he loves me."

"Love! Love! Do you no' know the Arabic saying – Love can

either drive you crazy or kill you? Or the Muslim saying that whenever a man looks at a woman, fitna occurs? Fitna means chaos. Women are the root of all chaos among men. That's why women must be controlled." He pointed an accusing finger at Rasheeda. "And you've no' been controlled enough. That's the big trouble."

"She'd better no' go to school for another few days till all this dies down," Bashir advised.

"Yes, you stay here again and help your mammy in the house. You go nowhere. You just do as your mammy tells you. Now go and say your prayers."

"Poor Alice," Noor Jahan said. "She will be very upset about Russell getting hurt."

Anjum looked very anxious.

"This is terrible. Pakistani boys. White boys. So much bad feeling. I hope Alice is not angry at us. Or Constance. Was her Will hurt too?"

Bashir said, "I don't know. I didnae see him. I'm just hoping Maq wasnae involved."

"Och, he wouldn't hurt his friend Russell, if that's what you mean," Sharif said.

"This is terrible," Anjum repeated. "The mothers of Russell and Will are my friends."

"They will still be your friends," Sharif assured her. "No' to worry."

But he looked worried.

"I'll phone Umar. That'll be better," he announced. "Rasheeda must no' be allowed to see Russell again. I'll take her to Pakistan very soon."

Sissy kept her nerve. At first, Timothy had tried to rally and revert to his usual bitter shouting but she'd just kept shaking her head at him and saying, "Isn't it time you grew up?"

He had been angry. But bewildered too.

"What's got into you?" he asked.

"I've had enough of listening to you rant and rave about everything. You're mad. You should be locked away."

She'd just said the first thing that came into her head but he had visibly paled at this and she'd experienced an unexpected surge of pity. He really was just a frightened little man. It was a temptation to start making him suffer as he'd made her suffer for so many years. Bullying him as he'd bullied her. But she hadn't the heart for it. Nor was it in her nature. She sighed.

"Why do you do it, Timothy? Is it true what Alice said – that you suffered something terrible in your childhood? You've never spoken to me about your childhood or your parents. Except to say that your father worked in India and your mother originally came from up north."

He hadn't answered her. Instead he'd gone into a kind of huff. On a couple of occasions later, when he'd tried to make his usual horrible insulting remarks about the Pakistanis, she'd just laughed at him and told him not to be so silly. She thanked God for guiding her in this direction because it worked. Poor Timothy, he looked hurt and had gone into yet another huff. But she was determined that she'd get him to talk honestly about himself. She'd get to the root of where his sickness came from.

She'd been very daring and gone into town and had her hair cut and set. It did wonders for her self-confidence. That and the new smart suit and blouse she'd treated herself to. She'd always been a thrifty housekeeper and had saved a good few pounds over the years. That was one thing about Timothy: he'd never bothered her about money. He handed over everything to her and let her get on with it. And if they went anywhere – to the pictures or the theatre, or even shopping in town – they went together. At the pictures or the theatre, they shared a box of sweets. He had his good points. He was quite shaken about her going into town on her own. More shaken about that, it seemed, than anything she'd said.

Eventually, she told him she was going to invite the Malloys in for supper so that they could tell Joe and Hilda that they'd met the Alis and got to know them and really and truly there was nothing to worry about. Timothy might have objected but, as well as being shaken by her going out on her own, he was far too taken aback by her new image – a very attractive image, she happily believed.

Joe and Hilda were taken aback as well. After she recovered

from her initial shock at Sissy's transformation, Hilda was generous in her praise. She wasn't really a bad soul, Sissy thought. She was just so terrified that people would find out about her background and the real person underneath. She hadn't the courage to be herself. But who am I to talk about that? Sissy thought.

"You look wonderful, Sissy," Hilda gushed. "I love your suit. From Jaeger, is it?"

"Yes. I saw it in the window and just liked the look of it. I suddenly felt I needed new clothes. A whole new wardrobe, really," she added rashly, getting quite carried away with herself.

"Oh, do let me see what else you've bought," Hilda said.

"Actually, this is all I've got so far."

"Oh, my dear, please allow me to come with you when you go shopping next time. I'd enjoy that so much. I really would. And we could have a coffee or lunch or afternoon tea at Miss Cranston's or the Willow."

Joe accepted the whisky Timothy offered.

"Here, old man. You'd better look out. When women go on a shopping spree, it costs you."

Timothy made a brave attempt at a laugh. Sissy couldn't remember when she'd last seen him laugh. And did she detect a glimmer of pride? Could it be that he was proud of her new self? She warmed towards him. They'd been married for a long time, after all, and he had been a decent husband in many ways. All right, he was a bit of a bully, but really it was just talk. He wasn't a violent man. It was only his talk that was fierce. Indeed, now that she came to think about it, there was definitely a soft bit inside Timothy. They'd once had a dog and they'd both loved it dearly. Timothy had enjoyed taking old Towzer out for walks. They'd walked him together. But Timothy had been the one who always groomed him and fed him. When Towzer died, Timothy had been broken-hearted and refused to replace him with any other animal.

"Well," said Hilda, "that's a date, Sissy. I'll look forward to it."

It wasn't until after supper that they got on to the subject of the Alis. Sissy explained what had happened and how she'd become friendly with Mrs Ali.

"Poor souls," Sissy said, "they are so worried about their youngest daughter, Rasheeda. She and Maq Tanwir go to the Academy like Russell Whitelaw and Will McFarlane. But she's become too friendly with Russell apparently. The Ali family all like Russell but they believe Rasheeda must end up with a good Muslim boy, one of her own kind. It's causing trouble all round. They're thinking of sending her away to Pakistan."

"Goodness!" Hilda gasped. She could never resist any titbit of gossip. "To marry her to someone over there, you mean?"

Timothy said, "That's what they do with their families. Arrange marriages."

Sissy gave him a warning look and he lapsed into silence.

"Fancy!" Hilda said.

"I don't suppose it works out any worse than our way in the end. People get divorced even in this country," Sissy remarked.

Hilda looked fascinated. "When you say they're getting too friendly, do you mean – you know?"

"All I know is poor Rasheeda says she loves Russell and he loves her. It's sad really. They're both such nice young people."

Joe rolled his eyes. "For God's sake, they're both of an age to get legally married in Scotland. What's the big problem?"

"What I've just said. She has to marry a Muslim. Rasheeda realises that herself. They've all very devout and they respect their parents and wouldn't want to hurt them or go against their wishes. Poor Rasheeda's in a terrible predicament. You see, if she chose Russell, she'd be disowned by her whole family. The whole Pakistani community would ostracise her. Feelings can be so strong, and Rasheeda obviously has very strong feelings for Russell."

"Well, anyway," Joe said, "I'd send them all back to Pakistan if it was up to me."

Hilda sighed. She had secretly longed all her life for romance but had been sadly disappointed by Joe's coarseness and complete lack of any romantic gesture or any kind of romance whatsoever. He'd never even given her a bunch of flowers in all the years they'd been married. Marriage, she had come to believe, just meant sex to Joe. And sex just meant a few bumps on top of her before grunting, rolling off and beginning to snore.

"How romantic!" she said. "A tragic love story like in a book."

"Yes," Sissy agreed, and then, trying to be more cheerful, "But it'll all work out. Anjum and Sharif will do the best they can for their daughter, I'm sure. They're a very close and loving family. Both Russell and Rasheeda will get over it. You know what young people are like."

Joe suddenly brightened.

"Once she's off to Pakistan, it'll clear the field for our Kate. She's still keen on the lad."

"I thought I saw her with Will the other day. It looked to me as if . . ."

"No, no," Joe laughed. "I think she was just trying to make Russell jealous."

Hilda shook her head.

"Isn't it ridiculous the daft things you can do when you're young? I did some silly things myself."

"Oh, didn't we all?" Sissy agreed. "Didn't we all?"

# Thirty-One

Alice didn't know what to do. She wanted to protect her son. She wanted to do something, anything, to help him. She had got the doctor to come and minister to him. Now she thought of going to the school and complaining to the headmaster. Violence – or anything else that happened within the bounds of the school – was surely the headmaster's responsibility. And in one of the best schools in Glasgow too! Good gracious, they were paying big enough fees for Russell to attend the place. The least they could expect for the money was that he would be safe.

When she'd mentioned this to Russell, though, and told him about her intention of going to the school, he'd pleaded with her not to do any such thing.

"But Russell—"

"There's nothing that you or the headmaster or anybody can do about it. It's just about me and Rasheeda and it's so unfair. Why doesn't everybody just leave us alone?"

"Oh dear!"

Right from the start, she'd known that there was bound to be trouble over Russell's friendship with Rasheeda.

"I did warn you, Russell."

"That's right," he said bitterly, "gloat! Say I told you so."

"I don't want to gloat. I just want to help you. I can't bear to see you hurt, Russell – either physically or emotionally."

Russell sighed.

"I know. I'm sorry. It's just . . . Oh, I wish things could be different, Mum."

Alice nibbled worriedly at her lip.

"I wonder if I spoke to Rasheeda's father and mother . . . I mean, I know they like you."

Russell's eyes brightened with hope.

"Oh, would you, Mum? Maybe you could persuade them. They think the world of you."

"I'll try, son. I'll try my very best."

"Thanks, Mum."

"Now, you just do what the doctor told you and rest until you're properly healed up."

"When will you speak to them? Will you speak to them now?"

"All right, dear. I'll go right now."

"Thanks, Mum."

Noor Jahan opened the door and greeted Alice with shy eyes and a vulnerable smile.

"Come on in."

Baby Shah Jahan toddled along the hall, flapping his arms like a miniature penguin and making alternate gurgling and loud screeching noises.

"Usually he sleep after two o'clock. But now he is talking and much trouble."

Alice said, "He doesn't look a bit sleepy, does he?"

The baby laughed and clapped his hands. Noor Jahan padded along the hall, past the sitting room. "You come into the kitchen with me? You one of family now."

In the kitchen the first thing that unexpectedly caught her eye was shimmering turquoise satin, winking with many slivers of mirrored glass, draped over a chair.

"I make lenga," Noor Jahan explained, holding up the material and showing it to be a long circular skirt. "You like?"

"It's lovely! It must have taken you ages to put on all those pieces of mirror."

"I wear lenga this colour at my wedding. You see photographs?"

"No."

"You no' see photographs? I show you."

"Actually I came to speak to your mother and father."

"Everyone is out visiting my uncle Mirza."

"Oh dear, will they be long?"

"No, not long."

"All right. I'll wait."

"I go and fetch photographs then."

As Noor Jahan left the kitchen to go and fetch the photographs, Alice saw that she was very pregnant and tired-looking. She was small and dainty and even her swollen abdomen appeared firm and neat as if it were a ball inside her qamiz which she carried with finesse and dignity.

Alice ruefully reflected that she had not looked like that when she was pregnant. She had resembled a mountain draped in a smock and an outsize coat.

She found it interesting that Noor Jahan should be so uninhibited about showing her photographs. Zaida had been evasive and cagey about this. At first she had denied that she possessed any photographs but on a later occasion when Alice remarked, "Is it only Indians who wear saris? I think saris are gorgeous," Zaida had hastily assured her that Pakistani women could wear saris too.

"See, I have photograph to prove to you." She had dived into her bag and produced a photo of herself and her sisters wearing saris and standing in the garden of their home in Pakistan.

The figures of the girls filled the picture. Only a scrap of garden and a tiny piece of wall at the back could be seen. Alice had immediately noticed the wall because it indicated something very different from what she had imagined. It looked as if the bricks were broken and barely held together by mud. But the really fascinating thing was that Zaida immediately realised her attention would be caught by the pinpoint of wall and regretted producing the picture.

"My father was about to have the wall mended and painted," she burst out in agitation. "He was going to have it made perfectly all right."

Zaida had seen through western eyes and felt ashamed. Alice wished she could tell her that there was no need to feel like that. Why should their house in Pakistan be judged by Glasgow standards? Anyway, some Glasgow houses were nothing to boast about.

Noor Jahan seemed to have lost any self-consciousness about her background. She returned with a huge pile of photographs and spilled them proudly on to the kitchen table.

There were many attractive pictures of her wedding. There were also photographs of their house. Alice studied the building with interest. It was completely unlike any she had ever seen before. It was flat and wide and had windows with iron bars and no glass, and there was a veranda held up by pillars.

Noor Jahan beamed with pride. "This is our house where we used to live."

"Fancy!"

"Nice house."

"Yes. But why are there bars on the windows and no glass? Isn't it cold and draughty in the winter?"

"Too hot in summer for glass. In winter we close shutters from inside and light lamps. Bars keep out the thieves and the robbers."

"I see . . . After you have your baby, I must take a photograph of you and your family."

"Yes, you can take. Take now." She pushed some photos towards Alice.

"Oh no, I didn't mean take. I mean . . . I didn't mean take one of yours. I meant I will photograph you with my camera."

Noor Jahan beamed, displaying all her teeth. "I understand."

After all the pictures had been browsed through, Noor Jahan cleared the table and asked, "You like tea or coffee or soup or fruit? Whatever we have is yours."

"Coffee, please. Will I make it? You look tired."

"No, I will make. Thank you very much. My daddy tired too. He is fed up from his duty. Too many stairs so he had a pain in his leg."

"Is Zaida getting on all right?"

"No, we are very worried. She phone every night to tell us she misses us. I know how she feels. I am not happy with my life."

"Oh dear."

"I cook curry and chapattis. Then everybody eat everything. Then everybody goes to their room. Then I clean the house and clean the plates and the cups and everything. Too much work for me. I am very tired. I am in bed at twelve o'clock."

"Gosh!"

"Then I get up at five o'clock. I am too tired to do school work."

"School work?" It was beginning to dawn on Alice that perhaps Noor Jahan was getting mixed up with her tenses.

"I say to Zaida and Rasheeda, 'Look, you do some work!' If everybody do shares, it wasn't troubles. But nobody helped me. My mammy no' help me either."

"Are you meaning before you were married?"

"Yes. Mammy not well for some time. Zaida and Rasheeda were at school. My daddy he say, 'Noor Jahan, you are eldest. You must look after the cooking and the house. Your mammy is too tired to stand near the cooker.' Then I am very worried about my life. I tell my daddy and he say, 'You no worry. I will find you a good husband.'" Noor Jahan sighed. "Now I am tired again but I do not want to make troubles for my daddy. He has enough troubles with Rasheeda."

"That's what I want to talk to them about. Russell's awfully upset, you know. He's terribly fond of Rasheeda. He wouldn't want her to get into any trouble."

Noor Jahan shrugged.

"We all have our dreams. These things pass. Daddy will find her a good husband in Pakistan."

"He's going to send for a man from Pakistan?" Alice echoed incredulously.

"No, no, he will take Rasheeda to Pakistan. Daddy had a good friend there who has sons. At our Uncle Mirza's house, our Uncle Mirza and Bashir and Bashir's father are talking with Daddy and Mammy about money for fare. They will all help get Daddy and Rasheeda to Pakistan."

"Oh dear, poor Rasheeda!"

"No, no, Rasheeda will be all right. Daddy will find a good husband. She will be looked after."

Alice had to light up a cigarette. She knew all the family were non-smokers and she had guessed by now that they didn't like it when she smoked in their house, but were just too polite to say so. As a result, she had taken to resisting having a cigarette when she visited them. At the moment, though, she felt she needed one. She inhaled deeply.

She tried to tell herself that Rasheeda being sent away was for the best. But she failed to convince herself. Russell was certainly not going to like this.

Oh dear, she thought in distress. Oh dear!

# Thirty-Two

He was sitting on the edge of his bed with his back towards her. His head was bent forward and he was clutching the red scarf that Rasheeda had made for him.

Alice could not bear to see him unhappy. She would rather endure a thousand miseries than see him suffer. But she was helpless. She had no idea what to do next.

She said vaguely, "Everyone feels like this at some time in their lives."

He twisted his lantern-jawed face towards her.

"They can't send her away. I can't live without her."

"It's just a part of growing up, Russell. A broken love affair. We all suffer one at some time or another. You'll get over it, darling. You'll meet lots of other girls."

His mouth began to tremble grotesquely and tears overflowed and trickled down his face.

"Oh Russell!" Alice hurried towards him, arms outstretched.

He jerked away.

"Shut up!" he shouted brokenly and crushed the scarf up to his face. "Why don't you just shut up and go away!"

She halted as if he had struck her. Awkwardly lowering her head and hands, she returned downstairs. She had just reached the sitting room when she was shocked into immobility once more by a sudden outburst of sobbing. Never before in her life had she heard such a dreadful, anguished sound. Breathless choking cries lengthened spasmodically into tormented wails.

The sitting room door flew open and Simon shouted in alarm, "What in heaven's name is that?"

He pushed past her and flew upstairs. She followed him with a painful heart.

"Simon, it's Russell. He and Rasheeda . . . They're sending Rasheeda away to Pakistan. That's why he's so upset."

"God knows what she's done to him. Listen to that. This is all your fault, Alice. You encouraged this. You set the whole thing up."

"I didn't," she protested.

But Simon ranted on. She had never seen him so upset. "I knew no good would come of what you've been doing. You've gone too far this time."

He hesitated outside Russell's door, then knocked on it and called out sharply, "Russell, are you all right in there?"

Immediately the sobbing stopped. Then after a minute's silence, a gruff voice said, "Yes, I'm all right, Dad."

Simon turned away.

"Get back downstairs and leave him alone. He doesn't want anyone to see him in that state."

Glad of someone to tell her what to do, she obeyed without question.

After a few minutes in the sitting room, she blurted out, "Surely it's only common sense to try and be friends and live in peace with our neighbours. I don't see what else I could have done."

"In peace?" Simon echoed. "A lot of peace it's meant for that boy upstairs."

She concentrated suddenly on the sound of footsteps. Russell was coming downstairs.

"Is that you, son?" she called anxiously. "Are you all right?"

He came into the room, his face a blank mask.

"I'm going along to Will's."

"The doctor said . . ."

"Don't wait up for me."

Alice turned to Simon. "What are we going to do?"

"Alice, you've done enough. Just leave the boy alone."

"I can't bear to see him suffer like that."

"This is going to put him right off his studies," Simon said. "What with his exams coming up. If he fails his exams, I've as good as flung all that money down the drain!"

"Oh, for God's sake!" Alice shouted at him. "For once, just once in your life, will you stop moaning on about money."

Simon looked taken aback and, before he could recover, Alice went on shouting.

"I don't know whether it's your headaches that cause the moaning or the moaning that causes the headaches, but I'll be getting a migraine or worse myself soon if you don't shut up about bloody money. That's all you think about or care about. You don't care about Russell." She knew she was being ridiculous but was beyond caring.

Simon looked shocked.

"Alice, you don't know what you're saying. You're just upset because of Russell. I'm upset too. He's my son. It's just . . . It's just . . . I'm not good at showing my true feelings, I suppose."

She knew in her heart of hearts that this was right. He expressed his love for Russell not by words but by deeds. She remembered the toys he had made when Russell was a child – the toy fort, the farmyard, the wooden train and carriages.

"It's these headaches I get, Alice. You've no idea what they're like. Let's have a cup of tea and try to calm down. I'll take a couple of my tablets with the tea."

"You keep taking those tablets. Why don't you go to the doctor and get yourself examined? You probably need different medicine altogether."

"All right," Simon said. "I'll go to the doctor. But I *am* upset about Russell, Alice. Just as much as you are."

"That's hard to believe, Simon." She was in such anguish about her son she hardly knew what she was saying any more. "I'm sure Russell doesn't believe it."

"I do care about him. I do. I do. As God's my witness, Alice." Suddenly, to Alice's horror, he burst into tears. "I'm sorry," he sobbed.

She hurried over to put her arms around him.

"Oh Simon, it's me that should be apologising to you. Of course I know you care about him, and don't worry, he'll be all right. He's young. He'll get over this."

She nursed him in her arms and patted his back as she'd once done to Russell when he'd been a baby.

"You really think Russell will get over this, Alice? That was terrible, the way he . . ."

"Ssh, ssh," she soothed. "Everything's going to be all right."

But in her heart of hearts she was even more afraid than he was.

# Thirty-Three

Zaida would have enjoyed her studies had she been at home. As it was, she was far too confused and unhappy to concentrate on them. Frightened too. In the digs, there were white men who came into the house at night, noisy and drunk. There was no lock on her bedroom door. Nearly collapsing with terror every evening, she jammed a chair under the door handle.

She could not eat breakfast because of the bacon and sausages. The landlady was a fat, jolly woman who no doubt was trying to be kind but it was a terrible anxiety and ordeal every morning because she kept trying to force Zaida to eat the sausages and bacon.

"Come on," she'd urge. "A wee skinny thing like you. You need all the good food you can get."

The crowds at the college were also overpowering. So many strangers. Not one familiar face. And no one even speaking with a Glasgow accent. No family to care for her. Then to come back to the digs every day and be alone in her room – it was too terrible. Every night and every morning, she wept for her family.

On the way from college to the digs, she always phoned home. To hear the dear, familiar voices of her mother and father and sisters and brother-in-law and nephews only made her feel worse. Even the sound of little Shah Jahan's voice broke her heart.

The pain of her loneliness and unhappiness was too much to bear. In desperation, she phoned Alice. She had not wept to her family because she did not want to upset them but she wept to Alice. She confessed to Alice the true extent of her misery.

"Oh Alice," she sobbed, "I want to come home but I cannot let my father down and be a disappointment to him."

"Now, try not to worry," Alice said in that calm voice she had.

"I'll think of something. I know! I'll get Constance to help. With Constance being a teacher she'll know better than me what can be done. She went to Glasgow University when she was young. Maybe she still has contacts there. Maybe we'll get you in there yet."

"Oh Alice, you are my best friend."

"I can't promise anything," Alice said, "but rest assured, I'll do my best to get you back to Glasgow. Maybe somebody's dropped out. Maybe there'll be a place available at Glasgow University now. We'll see."

Zaida's spirits rose. She trusted Alice, and Constance McFarlane too. Constance was a good friend to her mother. And maybe with Constance being a teacher, she would have influence and know even better than Alice what to do.

She said many prayers in the strange bedroom with its high bed recessed into the wall. It was dark with shadows and rows of pictures of strange white men and women stared down at her from the walls. She dreaded needing to go to the toilet because it meant hurrying fearfully down a long corridor past other bedroom doors behind which she could hear men's voices and raucous laughter.

During the day, she pattered through the crowded streets, a tiny figure in her turquoise salwar qamiz and chiffon doputta, reciting prayers to herself. There were no prayer rooms available in the college or in the digs. She felt as if she was a piece of flotsam buffeted about in a dangerous sea.

She phoned Alice again.

"Have you spoken to Constance, Alice?"

"Yes, and we both went to the university to put your case. I'm sorry, Zaida, but it's not possible for you to be accepted for this term. The advice is to get some work experience in Glasgow and then apply early for next year."

Zaida burst into tears.

"Now, don't worry," Alice soothed. "I'll explain to your father. He loves you and I'm sure he'll understand. He won't want you to be unhappy. The advice is for you to try for a job in a chemist's shop here in Glasgow just now. That way you won't be wasting your time. You'll be getting good experience. Then if you apply early enough, you can start at Glasgow next year. They were very sympathetic and optimistic about your chances. I'm sure it'll be all right next time."

Zaida said timidly, "I would like to get work experience in chemist's shop, Alice. But I am worried about my father."

"I told you, I'll speak to him. It'll be all right."

"I too should speak. You are too kind."

"I'll explain tonight. And then you phone and speak to him tomorrow."

"Oh, Alice, it will be so good if I can return to Glasgow. That is where I belong."

Alice laughed.

"There's a song about that – 'I belong to Glasgow'."

"You must teach it to me."

"I will. I will."

They said their goodbyes and Zaida's heavy heart lifted with hope. She prayed for time to pass quickly until the next day when she could phone her father.

"Daddy," she managed, before bursting into tears. "I'm sorry. I disappoint you."

"Zaida, you work in chemist shop and get good experience like Alice and Constance say. Next time you get into Glasgow University and all the time you live at home. We are not happy without you. We need you here with us."

"Oh Daddy, thank you."

She didn't even try to sleep that last night in the digs. She jammed the chair under the door handle as usual. Then, trying not to listen to the terrifying sound of the voices and the thumping of footsteps outside the door, she packed her case. Once everything was ready, she brushed and plaited her hair, draped her doputta over it and then sat rigidly upright and fully clothed on the edge of the bed, waiting for the long night to pass.

# Thirty-Four

At first Constance didn't recognise Sissy Bierce. She looked so different.

"Hello," Sissy greeted her. "I must do something with our garden. You put my husband and me to shame. There you are out working all day, yet still able to tend to your garden."

"Oh, I got away early today," Constance said, but couldn't help staring. "What on earth have you been doing to yourself, Sissy?"

"Oh, I just had a hairdo and bought one new outfit at first. Then Hilda persuaded me to go the whole hog – change from my flatties to these court shoes, and get a facial and buy some make-up and more new clothes. I said to her, 'Not make-up, Hilda, at my age,' but she was determined. She's not so bad really when you get to know her. She's actually been very helpful and kind to me. Getting me all organised, you know."

"My word, she's done a marvellous job," Constance said and meant it. "You look great, Sissy. I bet your husband has fallen in love with you all over again."

"Well . . ." Sissy blushed with pleasure. "I must admit, we've been getting on much better lately. We've been talking more. He had a really ghastly childhood, you know. A dreadful mother and father. They used to leave him in the house all day and sometimes all night with an awful Indian couple. Sometimes the couple would lock him in the house and go out without his parents knowing it. At other times they'd take him to some shocking places that frightened the life out of him. And they used to threaten him that he'd have his fingers cut off like some of the beggars if he told his parents what was going on. He still has nightmares about them and the things they did to terrorise him. But you know his parents were just as bad, if not worse, in my opinion. I feel I'm getting to know Timothy for the first time. I mean really get to know him." She laughed. "That must sound silly. After all, we've been married for years. But, believe it or not, it's true. We've never been so close."

"It doesn't sound silly at all. I'm very happy for you, Sissy." Constance sighed and lowered her voice. "I only wish that everyone's problems were working out so well."

"How do you mean?" Sissy asked in an equally conspiratorial tone.

Constance gave a quick meaningful look in the direction of the Whitelaws' and the Alis' bungalows.

"Poor Russell and Rasheeda. Apparently they're very much in love. You know how terribly extreme teenage emotions can be. There's been a lot of trouble – Russell's been attacked. Maq's been attacked. Now Rasheeda is going to be packed off to Pakistan for an arranged marriage. Russell is broken-hearted. So, it seems, is Rasheeda."

"Oh, poor things," Sissy said. "And I can just imagine how Anjum and Sharif feel. Especially Anjum. Have you met Rasheeda's parents?"

"Yes, we had them in for supper one night. Next time you must come too, Sissy. I don't see enough of the neighbours with me working full time, but I should get myself organised better. For my husband's sake, especially. He loves company."

"I'd like to come but I've never had you to my place." Sissy flushed with her own reckless courage, but with the pleasure it gave her as well. "I must arrange a party for all the neighbours."

Constance laughed.

"Even the Malloys?"

"Yes, even the Malloys."

"Make sure it's when my Ronnie's at home. He adores a party. And rest assured, he'll be the life and soul of it."

"Right," Sissy said eagerly. "How about popping in to my house for coffee tomorrow? We can arrange a suitable date for the party. It's Saturday so you won't be working, will you?"

"Fine. I'll look forward to that. I'll phone Ronnie to see how he's placed and I'll let you know tomorrow. I could make a contribution to the party. Bake a cake or something."

"Lovely."

They parted, each with a smile on their face and their mind filled with happy thoughts.

Constance was feeling more settled in herself than she'd done for years. For the first time, she'd really thought things through. All right, she was jealous. But, as she'd often told other people, there is nothing wrong with emotion. Emotion is perfectly natural. The important thing is how we control our emotions. She had been allowing her emotions to get out of control, that was her problem. All right, she was ten years older than her husband and one day he might decide to leave her. But there was no point in hurrying him, pushing him towards making that decision sooner than he might otherwise have done. Surely it made more sense to be thankful for, enjoy and make the most of each day they had together. Make each day especially happy and enjoyable for him. Live in the present, live for each day that she was given, and let the future take care of itself. She had felt so much better, calmer, and more content after she'd made this commitment.

The more she thought about employing a private detective to watch Ronnie, the more ashamed she felt. What on earth had she been thinking of? It should have been a psychiatrist she'd gone to for help – and for herself. There was nothing wrong with Ronnie. She could hardly credit that she'd sunk so low. What had Ronnie ever done to deserve such treatment? She looked back at all her snide questioning of him, the way she kept taking the joy out of his life, spoiling their time together, and she despised herself.

Her of all people! How often had she sat with the problem parents of problem children at school, dishing out advice like a marriage counsellor?

Talk about "physician heal thyself"! Well, at least she was trying to do that now. After she had spoken to Sissy, she went into the house, found her address book and picked up the phone.

A woman answered. "Wylie and Baines. Mr Baines's secretary speaking. How can I help you?"

"This is Mrs McFarlane. It was Mr Wylie I saw when I called at your office."

"Mr Wylie isn't available at the moment. Can I take a message?"

"Yes, will you tell him I've changed my mind. I want to terminate our arrangement. Could he just send me his bill?"

"Very well."

"Thank you."

Constance replaced the receiver and relaxed back into her chair with relief. She'd made a start. She wouldn't just change overnight. She knew that. But at least she was now able to face the truth. From now on, she'd nip any suspicions in the bud. She'd tell herself, This isn't about Ronnie. It's about me. And she'd swallow down any questions she might be tempted to ask Ronnie about where he'd been, who he had been with, and what he had been doing. She'd keep her mouth shut.

Already she'd begun to be more outward than inward. Take the Alis, for instance. Will had been putting her in the picture about what was happening with them and she had become really concerned about Rasheeda. All right, they were a very nice family and she was sure Sharif Ali loved Rasheeda and wanted to do the best he could for her. But did he really know what was best for Rasheeda? Could he really foresee what would happen to such a free spirit once she was forced into a loveless marriage and sent to live so far away in what to Rasheeda would be a strange and foreign land?

She hoped and prayed that the young couple would be given courage and strength to weather this storm in their young lives.

She picked up the phone again and dialled the last contact number Ronnie had given her. A woman answered and Constance was immediately plunged into a morass of fear and suspicion. Like a drowning woman, she desperately struggled to surface from it.

The voice repeated, "Hello, Mrs Bannerman speaking."

Ronnie was staying at a B&B, he'd told her. He'd even mentioned the landlady's name.

"Oh yes, hello Mrs Bannerman. This is Mrs McFarlane."

"Oh, Ronnie's wife? He's not in at the moment. Do you want me to give him a message?"

"No, it's all right."

She put her address book back into her handbag. Her hands were trembling. She took some deep breaths. This isn't about Ronnie, she told herself. This is about me. Why shouldn't Mrs Bannerman call Ronnie by his first name? He always stayed in B&Bs. He'd probably had the same regular stop-overs for years, and Ronnie being the friendly type that he was would immediately get himself on first name terms with everybody.

There was absolutely no need for her to feel so frightened and insecure. Lurking in the back of her mind, though, was a tiny niggle of regret that she'd cut her ties with the detective agency. They could have checked just to make sure. Firmly she banished the regret. She had done the right thing. And she was glad next day when the bill arrived. She wrote a cheque right away, put it in an envelope with the bill, addressed it and stamped it. She'd post it in the nearest box after she'd been to Sissy's.

Emma was on duty all day this Saturday as a favour to her new employers who were off to a wedding in Edinburgh and couldn't take their little daughter with them. Will was away for the day as well – also to Edinburgh, as it happened. There was some important rugby match on there. She'd be glad of Sissy's company.

Still struggling for calmness and self-confidence, she went through to the bedroom to fetch her raincoat from the cupboard. The cupboard was a handy walk-in place in which Ronnie had fixed a brass rail for coats and a shelf above for hats and shoe boxes. He was so good-natured and never complained about doing any jobs needed in the house when he came home, instead of having a well-earned rest. He must get exhausted at times with travelling around so much and keeping on talking and persuading buyers to give him orders, Constance thought. She felt guilty at her own behaviour. A lot of help and support she'd ever been to him when he was at home.

The door bell rang as she was struggling into her coat and crossing the hall on her way back to the sitting room.

It was two Jehovah's Witnesses. Damnation, Constance thought, harassed now. They were so persistent, these people. She never liked to be rude to them because they seemed so earnest. As a result, she always had a terrible job to get rid of them.

"I'm very sorry," she told them, grabbing her keys from the hook behind the door. "I'm just on my way out."

To prove it she stepped outside and shut the door behind her. "Sorry," she repeated. "Must rush."

She hastened away towards Sissy's bungalow. Rain was gusting round the square making the rose bushes shiver and the trees sway about. Yet it was still a cosy place, a pretty backwater near the city's bustle and yet completely shut off from it.

Sissy welcomed her with open arms. It really cheered Constance to see her so well. Her happiness was shining from her plain, homely face. Despite the discreet little touches of make-up Hilda had persuaded her to wear and the fashionable clothes, Sissy was still dumpy little Sissy. Constance gave her an affectionate hug.

It was then that she noticed Mr Bierce, or Timothy as Sissy now said he was to be called, hovering uncertainly in the background. Oh well, she thought, in for a penny, in for a pound. She gave Timothy a hug too.

Sissy laughed and Timothy laughed as well. Happiness was like sunshine in the house. Constance basked in it. She thought, My God, if Sissy can make such a difference in the horrible Timothy Bierce, anything is possible. She could surely do something with her suspicious, jealous self.

After coffee, Sissy persuaded her to stay to lunch.

"Oh, I couldn't put you to that trouble."

"It's no trouble, is it, Timothy?"

"No trouble at all," Timothy agreed.

"And you've said you're on your own all day today, so it'll save you cooking just for yourself."

"Oh well, thank you," Constance said. "It's very kind of you. To be honest, I hate it when everybody's away and I'm left on my own. The children are at that independent stage now. They've their own lives to lead. And of course I miss Ronnie terribly. You're so fortunate, the pair of you, to have each other and be together all the time."

"We know, don't we, Timothy?"

"Oh yes, we do," Timothy agreed.

It was a pleasant meal and afterwards they decided on the date and all the details of the party to be held at Sissy and Timothy's. It was to be a cold buffet and Constance volunteered to provide a couple of bowls of salad.

Then she said, "For goodness' sake, would you look at the time? I'd better go. I want to have a hot meal ready for Emma and Will tonight."

They hugged again as they said their goodbyes and then she made a dash through the rain to her own place. As soon as she got into the house, she realised she hadn't posted the letter. In her rush to get out, she'd left it in the sitting room. She went through to pick it up and immediately saw the other envelope propped up next to it. She recognised Ronnie's writing. Feeling sick with fear, she collapsed into a chair and ripped open the envelope.

The letter inside told her that he didn't need to ask why she was corresponding with a detective agency and he didn't want to know how long this spying on him had been going on. It didn't matter any more. He'd had enough. This was just the last straw. He had packed an extra bag and this time, he wouldn't be back.

She was faint with shock. She didn't know how long she sat holding the letter. It was only the cheerful voice of Will calling out, "It's me, Mum. What's to eat? I'm starving," that jerked her into action. She stuffed Ronnie's letter and the envelope to the agency into the pocket of her coat and got to her feet.

Will came into the room and made straight for the television. He switched it on and barely glancing round at her, said, "Been out?"

"Just over at Sissy's," she managed. "Pie and beans all right?"

"Smashing."

She was in the kitchen automatically putting the pie in the oven when Emma popped her head round the door.

"Nothing for me, Mum. I'm meeting somebody for a meal in town and then we're going dancing. I forgot to tell you – sorry."

"That's all right, dear."

"I've just time to get changed and rush out again."

In a few minutes there was a shout. "Bye!"

Then there was silence except for the television in the other room. She took a tray through to Will.

"Aren't you having anything, Mum?"

"I ate at Sissy's. A cup of tea will do me just now."

As Will dived into his plate of pie and beans, he told her – with one eye still on the television – that Russell had asked him to arrange a secret meeting between him and Rasheeda the next day. Will could get into the Ali house on the pretext of seeing Maq. He was to pass a note to Rasheeda telling her to slip out and meet Russell in the Whitelaw kitchen. If she went out of her back door, across the back garden and in through the Whitelaws' back door, the chances were no one would see her.

Will said Russell felt they just had to talk. She understood how they must feel. They couldn't just be torn apart, never see each other again, without even saying goodbye.

They were to meet the next afternoon, on Sunday, because Sharif and Bashir would be making arrangements for the journey to Pakistan. Anjum had to go to see Rasheeda's aunt, Shafiga. Only Maq and Noor Jahan would be in the Ali house and Russell's mother and father had been invited for afternoon tea at the Malloys'. So everything was working out to at least give Russell and Rasheeda a last chance to see each other and to say their goodbyes.

The word goodbye echoed and re-echoed down the dark tunnel of her mind. She gulped at her tea, struggling not to faint.

Goodbye had been the last abrupt word in Ronnie's letter. He hadn't even signed his name.

She didn't know what to do. She wished she could go back and be with Sissy. She needed to talk to somebody. But she hadn't the energy right now.

"I think I'll have an early night," she said to Will. She went to bed after taking two sleeping tablets to knock her out. She didn't wake until Sunday afternoon and, still in a daze, wandered over to ask Sissy what she should do.

# Thirty-Five

Jenny Saunders was feeling happy. A quiet confidence and sense of security had taken root and was growing inside her. First of all, she was continuing to enjoy her freedom and her lovely home. She enjoyed her job. She felt lucky that she could work in her nice cosy kitchen and didn't need to suffer the hassle of commuting into town and getting snarled up with traffic jams in rush hours. She felt lucky that she had acquired a new client. He was an attractive widower who was writing his family history. It was a most interesting story and she was really enjoying it. He insisted in delivering each batch of chapters to the bungalow, rather than having her go to his place to collect them, although she had gone on the first occasion, and been most impressed with his handsome villa in Newlands. She had liked him the moment she saw him. She liked his eyes. They were sometimes serious, sometimes glimmering with laughter, but always kindly. She also liked his strong cleft chin. John Maitland was his name. He was a tall, well-built man. She liked tall, well-built men. Poor old Percy was a bit shrunken and skinny, probably because of his experiences as a prisoner of war. Although, in fact, Percy had always been lean and wiry. He had often boasted that that was why he'd survived his imprisonment.

Maybe her feelings of familiarity with John stemmed, to some degree, from what she was learning of his family history. She certainly felt comfortable with him – as if she'd known him for years. He always stayed for a drink or a coffee every time he came to deliver work or called for completed chapters, and they enjoyed a chat and a good laugh. Some of the anecdotes in his book were hilarious. His late grandfather, a High Court judge, had been quite a character.

She felt John was like a rock, solid and strong. His voice had something to do with it. It had such confidence and authority. He made her feel safe as well as happy. She told him about the trouble that she'd heard was brewing in the square, but she found herself worrying more about the poor young lovers, Russell and Rasheeda than about how any trouble in the square could affect her personally. It didn't matter in the slightest to her now what Percy or Fiona would think of what had happened, or was happening, or might happen in the square. She'd already told the pair of them to mind their own business.

"You're like a couple of old women," she'd said. "Either that or a couple of vultures hovering over my head."

John told her about his late wife and their happy marriage. She told him how her marriage, unfortunately, had not worked out and that she wished she could get a divorce. John was a barrister and he said that if she wished, he could put her in touch with a good firm of solicitors who would help and advise her.

The thought of him being a barrister thrilled her. She visualised him in exciting, dramatic situations in court. She was looking forward to seeing him in action one of these days. Her life, indeed, had become full of promise and exciting plans.

That made her think of the young lovers again. What kind of future could they look forward to?

It was awful of Rasheeda's family to interfere and spoil things for her. She'd said to John how different things could be for the young couple. They could get married to each other and be happy, if their parents helped them instead of hindering them. They could set up home in old Mrs Bell's bungalow. She had already moved out to join Mrs Ogilvie in the Pollokshields Private Nursing Home, and the bungalow was up for sale. But oh no, everyone else in the family thought they knew what was best for Rasheeda. Just like Percy and Fiona thought they knew what was best for her.

John said, "You're a romantic at heart, aren't you?"

"I suppose I am," she agreed.

Soon after that, a beautiful bunch of red roses was delivered to her door. She waltzed about the house with them, happily, dreamily, holding them close to her face. There was a card with them saying he'd call on Sunday after lunch and next day, by early afternoon, she was at the sitting-room window straining to see through the trees to catch the first glimpse of John's car driving down the lane.

Russell was waiting anxiously at the kitchen door and as soon as he saw Rasheeda approaching, he held it wide and allowed her to enter. The moment he closed the door behind her, she fell into his arms. They clung to each other, both struggling not to break down and cry.

"My mother and father probably won't be long," Russell managed. "We've maybe only got a few minutes."

He could feel her slim body trembling against his.

"Russell, I can't bear it. They're going to take me away and give me to a stranger over in Pakistan. I just want to be with you. I feel . . . I feel we're one heart, one mind, one flesh."

"I feel that way too. Can't you refuse to go? Can't you tell them you want to be with me and that we're going to get married as soon as we can? We're of age in Scotland."

"Oh my love," Rasheeda said brokenly, "it's all a dream."

"No, no," Russell cried out desperately. "We could run away, right now."

Tears had begun to overflow from Rasheeda's dark eyes.

"In my flimsy salwar qamiz? And without any money? We haven't even our bus fare into town, have we?"

"I could phone Will. Maybe he has some cash. He'll help us."

Rasheeda gazed at him. "Will has no money. He's the same as us. He's dependent on his parents."

"I could have taken a job. I wanted to, so did Will, but no one would hear of it until after the exams."

"It's the same with Maq. Exams are important to parents. They want us to do well."

"Why don't they want us to be happy?"

Rasheeda lovingly smoothed back his hair.

"They do. They do. They just don't understand."

"Oh, Rasheeda." He suddenly didn't care if it wasn't manly to cry. Tears gushed out and sobs racked his body. "I can't let you go. I can't let them do this to you. To us. I can't."

Rasheeda began to sob too, to sob and wail in tragic despair. "There's nothing we can do."

"Stay here." He clutched her closer. "Stay here with me now."

"They'll come for me. Your mother and father can't prevent them. They'll not want to. Our parents are good friends. And my mammy and daddy mean well. They believe they're doing the proper thing. It's our custom and tradition, our religion."

"I don't care about any of that. All I care about is you."

"Oh Russell, love of my heart and soul, I've thought and thought about it and it's impossible for us to live together." Her head tipped up in the defiant, courageous way she had. At the same time, her gaze melted tragically into his. "We can't live together, but we can die together."

Russell held her gaze. He prayed that she wouldn't see his fear. He didn't want to die. He'd so many plans for the future but it was a future that always included her. He prayed to God to help him, help them both. He couldn't remember ever having prayed before. At least not since he was a very young child. He'd forgotten about that until now.

His mother had read to him from a book about Jesus and together they'd recited:

"Gentle Jesus, meek and mild
Look upon a little child
Pity my simplicity
Suffer me to come to thee
Fain I would to thee be brought
Dearest Lord, forbid it not.
In the kingdom of thy grace,
Give a little child a place . . ."

Rasheeda sobbed broken-heartedly.

"I don't want to leave you. I can't give myself to another man. I'll kill myself. I'll die alone rather than do that."

Oh, he was afraid. But he loved her. Truly loved her.

"No," he said. "You'll not die alone. We'll be together, Rasheeda. If this is the only way, then that's how it has to be."

He was remembering prayers again and vague pictures of Jesus. It was all he had to cling to, to give him strength.

"Dad's car's in the garage. I know what to do."

Still clutching her close to him, they left the house and went in through the back door of the garage.

He took a piece of hose and put one end in the exhaust pipe. Then he put the other end inside the car and he and Rasheeda got in and shut the doors. He turned on the engine. They held each other close.

"We'll just go to sleep now," he told her. "And be together for all eternity." He felt himself relax. It was so good to hold her in his arms.

"I love you," he said, and she echoed his words. He kissed the top of her dark head. He tried to remember other prayers but all he could think of was Dear God, forgive us our sins. Please Jesus, let us stay together. And she was thinking, In the name of Allah, the Beneficent, the Merciful, Owner of the Day of Judgement, Thee we worship, Thee we ask for help. Forgive us our sins. Please Allah, let us stay together.

As soon as Hilda and Joe opened the door of the villa to see Alice and Simon out, they saw an agitated Sharif Ali standing with Anjum in the square outside their bungalow.

"Simon, Alice," the old man called. "Have you seen Rasheeda? She has gone from our house."

"No," Alice said. "Unless she's with Russell. He was in the house when we left."

They all hurried into the Whitelaw bungalow but there was no sign of either of the young people. In increasing agitation, they hurried outside again. At that moment, Sissy came to her door, arm in arm with Constance.

"What on earth's wrong over there?" she said.

All the Ali family were now crowding about loudly discussing the problem and wondering aloud what could be done next. Alice and Simon looked equally upset.

Sissy hurried over to see what was wrong, dragging Constance along with her. The urgent aura of distress also brought Hilda and Joe Malloy hurrying outside. Jenny too ran from her house.

Alice told everyone anxiously, "We're wondering if they've run away together."

"They couldn't have got far," Simon said. "I'll take the car out . . . They can't have got far," he repeated and hurried to swing open the front door of the garage.

"Oh God! Oh my God! Oh no! Oh Russell!"

They all crowded forward and a terrible tide of weeping filled the square. Simon and Alice clutched at each other. Alice was making strangled, choking screams.

Hilda and Joe Malloy took charge. Hilda shepherded everyone back. In a few moments, she bleakly informed her neighbours, "They're dead."

The Ali family began to wail like lost souls.

"Joe," Hilda said, "phone the police." He had already pulled out the hose and turned off the engine. "And everybody, keep back."

"Oh my God!" Sissy and Jenny were white-faced and trembling with shock. "Oh my God!"

Constance began to weep at the tragedy of lost love when love was so precious.

All was chaos and confusion.

Hilda called out to her husband as soon as he returned from phoning, "Joe, you wait here until the police arrive. I'll look after everybody. I'll take them all into our place."

Joe nodded in agreement.

"Terrible business," he muttered. "Poor devils!"

And so the sorrowing tide washed into the big villa and in the air echoed the last thoughts of Rasheeda and Russell.

For the love of Allah — For Jesus' sake

Amen